PRAISE FOR WINTER RENSHAW

"Winter Renshaw crafts the best romances! She always delivers it all—angst, emotion, and humor. Her books are a true delight."
—Adriana Locke, *USA Today* bestselling author

"Passion. Drama. Angst. Renshaw nails the romance trifecta with her perfectly paced office love affair."
—Deanna Roy, *USA Today* bestselling romance author of the Forever Series

"If you're looking for stories that are thought provoking, wildly sexy, and unputdownable, you'll never be disappointed with Winter Renshaw!"
—Jenika Snow, *USA Today* bestselling author

"The queen of contemporary angst knows how to curl toes while breaking hearts! A perfect romance for two imperfect lovers!"
—Sosie Frost, *Wall Street Journal* bestselling author

fake
-ish

OTHER TITLES BY WINTER RENSHAW

THE NEVER SERIES

Never Kiss a Stranger

Never Is a Promise

Never Say Never

Bitter Rivals

THE ARROGANT SERIES

Arrogant Bastard

Arrogant Master

Arrogant Playboy

THE RIXTON FALLS SERIES

Royal

Bachelor

Filthy

THE *AMATO BROTHERS SERIES*

Heartless

Reckless

Priceless (a Rixton Falls crossover)

THE *P.S. SERIES*

P.S. I Hate You

P.S. I Miss You

P.S. I Dare You

THE *MONTGOMERY BROTHERS DUET*

Dark Paradise

Dark Promises

THE *PAPER CUTS SERIES*

Hate Mail

Yours Cruelly

Dear Stranger

STAND-ALONES

Single Dad Next Door

Cold Hearted

The Perfect Illusion

Country Nights

Absinthe

The Rebound

Love and Other Lies

The Executive

Pricked

For Lila, Forever

The Marriage Pact

Hate the Game

The Cruelest Stranger

The Best Man

Trillion

Enemy Dearest

The Match

Whiskey Moon

The Dirty Truth

fake
-ish

winter renshaw

 Montlake

Published by Montlake, Seattle

www.apub.com

Amazon, the Amazon logo, and Montlake are trademarks of Amazon.com, Inc., or its affiliates.

ISBN-13: 9781662513428 (paperback)
ISBN-13: 9781662513411 (digital)

Cover design by Hang Le
Cover photography by Wander Aguiar Photography
Cover image: © icemanphotos / Shutterstock

Printed in the United States of America

For Maxine—just 'cause.

CHAPTER ONE

BRIAR

One Year Ago

"You can't tell me all of these people are having fun." A turquoise-eyed stranger sporting a five o'clock shadow and messy chocolate-brown hair takes the barstool beside mine. He swirls the amber-hued liquid in his lowball tumbler before pointing around the bar. "They're all pretending. They have to be."

Stealing a better glimpse of my new neighbor, I recognize him as the man who mostly kept to himself in the back of the party bus, even when one of the bride's college friends shamelessly tried twerking in his face. The way he looked through her, she might as well have been invisible. As soon as we stepped inside this place, he ordered two fingers of whiskey and disappeared—until now.

"I don't know." I scan the dark and neon space that surrounds us. He and I are the only ones not singing, dancing, or falling over drunk. "Hate to say it, but I think *we're* the wet blankets."

"There's a reason we're an hour into this thing and these people are already trashed. It's the only way you can have fun at a joint bachelor-bachelorette party."

A Lil Jon song comes on, and behind me, the sash-and-tiara-wearing bride-to-be begins whoo-hooing and grinding against her fiancé, who is so hammered he can't stand upright without stumbling backward. His near fall is broken by one of his big-muscled buddies, who swoops in to catch him. A few seconds later, the groom is back with his beloved, pretending to slap her ass to the rhythm of a song about sweat dripping down someone's balls.

"Glad to see romance isn't dead," I say.

The night is young, and these people remind me of sheltered church-camp kids sampling freedom and adulthood for the first time.

"Twenty bucks says at least one person in our group will be throwing up before midnight," I say.

"I've never understood the whole joint-bachelor-bachelorette-party thing," the guy beside me continues, turning away from the spectacle behind us. "They said it's more cost effective and the more the merrier, but you know damn well the bride and groom don't trust each other, and that's the real reason." He takes a generous drink before sliding his empty glass toward the bartender and giving a nod. "How can you marry someone you can't trust?"

I don't disagree with any of what he's saying—I would just never say those things out loud . . . to a fellow partygoer . . . at the actual party. Everyone here knows about Vivi and Benson's colorful relationship saga, which is peppered with unproven cheating allegations and more break-ups than any of us can count on our fingers.

"Even toxic love is love," I say. "Just be happy for them. That's all we have to do."

"Hard to do that when odds are they won't make it to their fifth wedding anniversary. It's like watching a train wreck about to happen and doing nothing to stop it."

"It's not our train wreck to stop. And you never know, maybe they'll beat the odds?" I say this knowing damn well those odds against them couldn't be stacked higher. "I'm sorry, I don't think I caught your name."

"Dorian."

"Briar," I say. "How do you know the groom?"

"We were college roommates a lifetime ago. Syracuse. How do you know the bride?"

"Vivi's my cousin." I sip my blackberry mojito, catching a lime seed in the straw. I swallow it like the bitter little pill it is, trying not to make a face.

"So you're here out of familial obligation."

"I mean, I'm also in her wedding," I say. "Just here to show my support like everyone else."

The bartender tops off Dorian's whiskey, using a bottle he grabs off the highest shelf.

How this painfully attractive grouch of a man can be drinking expensive liquor at a flashy club in the Caribbean is beyond me. He should be tossing them back, hitting on beautiful women, and living his best life—god-awful music be damned.

"What would you be doing right now?" I ask. "If you weren't here?"

He exhales, contemplating his response. "Probably catching some shitty sleep in a tour bus, making sure the bassist doesn't try to quit again."

"You're in a band?"

"No," he says. "I manage one."

"So you'd rather be working right now?"

"They do better when I'm there to keep them in line," he says.

"What band is it?" I ask.

"Phantom Symphony."

"Stop." I smack my palm against the bar top. "You manage *Phantom Symphony*? Are you serious? I have their entire album *and* their new EP in my iTunes. I was just listening to them on the flight this morning. I must've had that new song . . . 'Moon Drop Envy' on repeat for a solid hour earlier. When I tell you I'm ob-*sessed* . . ."

Fishing into my clutch, I pull out my phone to show him, but he waves me off like he doesn't need proof.

"You and everyone else," he says.

Last year, Phantom Symphony exploded onto the music scene after they released a track called "Starlight Serenade" and it went viral as a sound on every social media platform under the sun. It wasn't long before they were performing on *SNL* and, shortly thereafter, at the Grammys. Now they're one of the top ten most streamed bands on the planet. Their upcoming tour was sold out less than a minute after ticket sales went live.

They're not just some band . . .

"So you're worried one of the biggest music acts in the entire world is going to throw their career away because you're not there to micro-manage it for a single weekend?"

He cracks a semblance of a smile for the first time tonight.

"When you put it that way . . . ," he says.

"Right?" I place my hand on his stiff shoulder for a second before releasing it. I'm a hugger, a touchy-feely type, and sometimes I forget not everyone is like that. "Anyway, we're here. We should be having fun."

It'd be easy to sit and stew, to bristle at the outdated pop music and spotty cell phone service, or to resent the fact that Vivi and Benson made thirty of their closest friends fly to an ungodly expensive all-inclusive resort in the Dominican Republic just to take a party bus to a bunch of bars off property.

It'd also be easy to get hung up on all the other traveling this wed-ding has required thus far: a joint bridal shower in Chicago, a joint engagement party in Breckenridge, and next month, a weeklong wed-ding in the Poconos. When it's all said and done, I'll have dropped over ten grand on this whole thing, and she'll never have to do the same for me because I'm never getting married.

But what good would come from being upset about it?

Plus I've never been one to keep score.

"How come you're not having fun, then?" he asks.

"Who said I wasn't?" I give him some side-eye and a raised shoulder. He says nothing, though I can tell he's rethinking his assumption. "No one forced you to come here, you know."

"I didn't go to anything else. I'm just making an appearance because it's the right thing to do. We've been touring, so I've missed everything."

"I'm sure you could've gotten away with just going to the wedding."

My handsome associate shakes his head.

"These two, with all their planning, didn't send out their save-the-dates early enough. I'll be in Scotland that week, kicking off our European tour. It's not too late for you, though," he says, though I suspect he's teasing. "There's still time to tell them you won't be joining them in the Poconos for seven days and nights of luxury wilderness celebrations."

"My thousand-dollar bridesmaid dress begs to differ." I take a sip of my drink. "Plus Vivi would never forgive me."

"Really?" He cocks his head. "I find that hard to believe, given the number of times she's forgiven Benji."

I snort. I've never heard anyone call Benson *Benji*, and it makes me think of that scruffy little dog from the movies. Now that I think about it, Benson kind of resembles a scruffy little dog, with his sandy hair and his dark shiny eyes and his golden retriever level of excitement when it comes to anything sports related.

It's kind of perfect.

"Look, we're here for two more days," I say. Behind us, the rest of our group dances and laughs and throws their inhibitions in the air via contorted, drunken moves. "If we can't beat them, maybe we should join them."

"You first."

"Okay, not to be annoying, but I have to ask: What's Connor Dowd like in real life?" I couldn't have wiped the childlike grin off my face if I'd tried. I still can't get over that the man sitting beside me knows Phantom Symphony personally, and someday I might regret not asking this question when I had the chance.

"If I told you, you wouldn't be smiling like that anymore." He takes a sip. "Hell of a musician, though."

My grin fades just as he predicted.

I don't ask him to elaborate.

Connor is famous for pulling a fan onstage every night and kissing them in the middle of the instrumental bridge of their song "Cosmic Echoes." The fantasy of someday being that fan getting pulled up onstage has comforted me on many a sleepless night, however unrealistic it may be. I'm also pretty sure he has a girlfriend or fiancée or something, so even if he did pull me onstage in real life, my conscience would get the best of me, and I wouldn't be able to go through with the kiss—even if it was purely for entertainment.

"Are you always this negative?" I ask.

"You call it negative. I call it authenticity."

"Semantics." I brush my hair from my face. "Regardless, here you are, this good-looking man in his prime, sitting at a tropical bar, drinking expensive alcohol, talking about how you manage one of the most popular bands in the entire world, and all you can do is act like you'd rather be anywhere but here. I mean, I'd get it if you were secretly in love with the bride or something but . . . *wait*." I lean in, tucking my chin. "*Are* you secretly in love with Vivi?"

He chokes on his response. "God, no. Not even close."

I study his face, searching for a sign that he's lying, but there isn't a drop of sweat on his forehead, and he isn't blinking or licking his lips or avoiding eye contact or looking suspiciously to the left.

"Then what's your deal?" I ask.

"I don't have a *deal*," he says. "There's just nothing I hate more than weddings and wasted time."

"Okay, so then you *do* have a deal: you hate weddings and wasted time."

"Guess so."

"It's just . . . you don't hate nuclear bombs or animal testing or career politicians? You hate . . . weddings? *That's* what you hate the most? Out of *everything*?"

"It's not that deep." Dorian swallows a mouthful of whiskey, appearing lost in thought for a second. I can't help but wonder if he's thinking about something—or perhaps some*one*. Maybe he's not so much loathing the fact that he's here as he is loathing the fact that a certain someone else isn't here with him.

"Do you have a girlfriend back home?" I ask before quickly tacking on, "or boyfriend? Partner? Person?"

"Nope. No girlfriend."

"Have you ever been engaged?" I ask.

"Never." He doesn't hesitate. "What's that have to do with anything?"

"Have you ever been in love?" I ignore his question, asking another as I try to piece together a picture of why this guy hates weddings more than world hunger.

"Ish," he says, face wincing.

"Ish?" I arch a brow. "What does that mean?"

"I've been in relationships that felt a lot like love," he says. "I was in love . . . ish."

"I'm sorry to hear that," I say. He can't be much older than thirty if he went to college at the same time as Benson. That's a long time to live without experiencing love.

"Don't be."

"Who ended it, you or her?" I ask.

"She did."

"Recently?"

"Time is relative." He presses his thumb against his tumbler, leaving a fingerprint-shaped smudge on the pristine glass. "What about you? What's your story? Ever been engaged or any of that bullshit?"

I shake my head. "Not the marrying type."

His eyes light up as if I'm finally speaking his language.

While I have nothing personal against marriage or those who choose to get married, I find it a slightly antiquated concept—one that holds zero appeal for me.

Doesn't stop me from celebrating others, though.

"If I want to be with someone, I will. I don't need to legally bind myself to them or take their last name to prove my love or commitment," I say.

He lifts his glass. "I'll drink to that."

"I hope I don't sound like a pick-me girl," I say.

"I don't even know what that is."

"It's when a woman acts like she's not like other women. She wants to seem different. Special."

"Isn't that a good thing?" he asks. "Who'd want to be with someone who was like everyone else?"

"Pick-me girls advertise that they're not like everyone else, but deep down they are—they just act like they're not because they think it makes them more attractive to men."

The song changes to the new Katy Perry number, and a dance circle has formed around the still-grinding couple who are now full-on making out like it's their junior prom and someone passed around a flask of vodka in the limo before they all got out for pictures.

I'm shocked the DJ hasn't played a Phantom Symphony song yet, though the majority of their music is better suited for stormy Sundays, self-reflection, rainy walks in Central Park, and wistful daydreams of relationships past.

The next time I catch the bartender's eye, I order two ice waters and slide one of them to Dorian. Tomorrow's supposed to be a day at the resort's private beach, but I have a feeling half of these people are going to be too hungover to enjoy it.

"You're giving me a hard time about not having fun and now you're ordering water?" he asks with a huff.

"It's called pacing myself. Tomorrow's beach day, and I love beaches more than anything in the world. I'll be damned if I miss it." Pointing to his water, I say, "Drink up."

"Who said I was going to the beach?"

"You're just going to sit in your room, feeling sorry for yourself? Thinking about the girl who broke your heart in the relatively near or distant past?"

He fights a smirk and rolls his eyes. "Do you always say the first thing that comes to your mind?"

"Pretty much."

"How does that usually go for you? Not having a filter?"

"Most people are more open than you think." I sip my icy water. "Sometimes all you have to do is ask the right question or say something that catches them off guard, and they open up like a flower." I tighten my hand into a fist before unfurling my fingers to illustrate my point. "I mean, look at the dialogue we're having right now. This isn't exactly small talk."

"Never been compared to a flower before," he says. "That's a first."

"Would you rather be compared to a can of beans?" I learned a long time ago that the majority of people enjoy talking about themselves, even if they don't think they do. That, and almost everyone has something they need to get off their chest.

Curiosity is a good thing.

It sparks questions that ignite the kinds of conversations that make connections.

More people should be curious.

"Nope," he says.

"That's what I thought. See, I'm already getting a read on you, and I barely know you. All I had to do was ask the right questions."

He half smiles, soaking me in with his Caribbean-hued gaze. I can't tell if he's entertained by me or annoyed or something in between, but he hasn't budged from his seat, so that has to count for something.

"You say you're not *not* having a good time." Dorian breaks his studious observation of me. "But you're drinking ice water and sitting here with some random guy who clearly woke up on the wrong side of the bed."

"I'm absorbing the fun just being in the room, like osmosis." I keep a straight face, hoping to get him to laugh, but he only seems confused by my lame attempt at a joke. "No, seriously, this is great. There's no place I'd rather be right now than here with my cousin and her fiancé, thirty of their closest friends, and the grumpiest guy in the entire Republic . . . of . . . the Dominican."

I'll spare him the saga of losing my job, my boyfriend, and my best friend all in the same week. It's neither here nor there, it's ruined the last month of my life, and I refuse to let it ruin this expensive trip.

Besides, it's hard to be angry when there are so many palm trees and an abundance of sunshine and contented, suntanned vacationers wearing brightly colored clothing everywhere you turn.

If Lexapro were a country, it'd be the Dominican Republic.

Truthfully, I'd be on the dance floor with everyone else if it weren't for the blister forming on the back of my heel—a little detail I've no intention of sharing with this striking curmudgeon. It's my fault for wearing brand-new sneakers to the airport today instead of my trusty broken-in baby-blue New Balances. The heels I'm wearing tonight aren't helping anything, but they're the only things I packed that go with this dress.

"Could've fooled me." Dorian slides his water closer. "Why'd you order me this?"

"Because it's going to be a long night, and if you hate being here now, you're really going to hate being hungover on the beach tomorrow. And you *are* going to the beach. Drink up."

I lift my glass to his, urging him to toast me, but he refuses.

"It's bad luck to toast with water," he says.

"That's the dumbest thing I've ever heard." I clink mine against his.

He watches while I take a sip of bad luck, and I silently pray he's wrong—because more misfortune is the last thing I need.

CHAPTER TWO

BRIAR

Present Day

"We're almost there. Do you have any more questions before we . . . ?" My boss, Burke, checks the time on his phone, his words trailing into silence when he finds himself distracted by yet another work email.

"No." I twist the flawless five-carat solitaire on my finger, watching how it dazzles in the midday sun and throws flecks of light against the black interior of our chauffeured Escalade.

The ring was originally purchased for Burke's ex-girlfriend Audrina earlier this year—before they were exes. I'm told he planned an elaborate marriage proposal involving some wait-listed rooftop restaurant, her closest friends and family, and a private acoustic performance from one of her favorite singers . . . only the drop-dead gorgeous society girl dumped him for some up-and-coming Broadway actor a week before any of it could happen.

They say one woman's trash is another woman's treasure, but calling Burke a treasure would be giving him too much credit.

Treasures are rare and priceless.

Burke's just another workaholic New Yorker in an overpriced designer suit.

He's also successful, wealthy, and classically attractive—but that's beside the point since his personality cancels all that out.

"Did you study the pdf?" he asks, referring to the password-protected autobiography he sent me, one that included everything from his birth story (he almost died) to his favorite color (jet black) to his preferred cuisine (French), as well as his education history (bachelor's degree in finance from Columbia, master's in business administration from Yale), his favorite places to travel (Morocco and Thailand, in that order), his political and religious affiliations, and an assortment of stances on several modern-day table topics.

"Of course," I say. For the next eight weeks, my only job is to convince his father that we are undeniably in love and moving full speed ahead with planning our nuptials. All he's told me is that his father is getting "up there" in age. Since this could be their last summer together, he wants his father to see him happy and not heartbroken. He's assured me we won't actually have to marry. "Did you study mine?"

Our driver, Lenny, glances into the rearview.

I have no idea what Lenny knows or doesn't know, so any words I've spoken during this excursion I've tried to choose carefully, though maybe I shouldn't have asked that last question.

"You're ruining your manicure," Burke says without looking up from his phone. "And yes."

Checking my hands, I discover he's right. I've been picking at my nails this entire car ride—an old nervous habit. While the nude-pink paint is still glossy and unchipped, several of my cuticles are noticeably irritated.

"Unfortunately, there are no nail salons on Driftway," he says, referring to his family's sixty-five-acre private island off the coast of North Dune, Massachusetts.

I press my palms together and tuck them between my thighs, opting not to tell him I did my nails myself and can easily fix them when we get there. Cuticles aside, I've gotten pretty good at this. With my money tighter than it's ever been, learning how to do a spa-worthy mani-pedi was more of a necessity than a choice, but all that will change two months from now (pending the successful completion of this summer mission).

If his father believes we're in love after eight weeks, I get a cool million dollars.

If this entire thing explodes in our faces, I get twenty grand for my time and a ride back to the city, where I'll return to my desk job in the online marketing department of Burke's global investment firm.

"You're clearing your throat a lot," he says, his gaze still locked on his shiny phone screen as he taps out a quick email. "Makes you seem nervous."

I hadn't noticed. "Sorry."

And I *am* nervous.

As hell.

I'd have to be a sociopath to not care about putting on this kind of charade.

I don't take what we're doing lightly, but Burke assures me this is nothing but a way to put his father's old mind at ease.

I uncap the room temperature bottle of Evian he brought for me and attempt to swallow the lump in my throat—along with any ounce of self-doubt about pulling this whole thing off. I've been prepping for a month now, and I've probably read his pdf no fewer than twenty-five times. He could quiz me on it at this point, and I'd pass with flying colors.

Up ahead, through lush trees and charming coastal houses, I can already see the rolling blue-gray waves of the Atlantic.

My stomach knots with every traffic light we pass, but I try to focus on the fact that it feels like we're cruising straight into a storybook town.

A few minutes from now, we'll be dropped off at a private dock; Lenny will load all our luggage into a waiting boat, and Burke and I will be on our way to spend the next eight weeks on Driftway Island with his family.

I adjust my posture, anxious to get out of this suffocating SUV so I can stretch my legs and breathe air that doesn't smell like new-car leather and posh cologne. Over the years, I've traveled from New York to Massachusetts a couple of times—mostly to catch some Red Sox home games—but today's trip feels like it'll never end, like we've been driving to another planet light-years away.

Burke puts his phone away for the first time in hours once Lenny pulls into a small parking lot marked with signs that say **PRIVATE— ROTHWELL FAMILY ONLY** and **PERMIT REQUIRED— VIOLATORS WILL BE TOWED**. There are a handful of vehicles parked here already, though I've no clue if they belong to family members or Driftway staff members.

By the time I step outside, my legs are as unsteady as Jell-O, and my heart is beating so hard the pulses in my ear almost drown out the ruckus a few yards away from a group of seagulls fighting over a sandwich wrapper.

I've never been one to let my nerves get the best of me, but I've also never done anything like this before. There's no way to know how this will go, and that's the thing that's been stressing me out the most lately.

That, and I hate lying.

Burke said to think of it as acting, not lying.

When I asked him why he didn't just hire some out-of-work actress, he said, *This is real life, Briar, not some cheesy TV movie. I want authenticity. That, and you look like my type.*

I wasn't sure what he meant by the last part.

Audrina comes from money and travels the world with a glam squad and a personal photographer, so she never has a shortage of content for all her social media channels.

I live in a shoebox apartment on the Lower East Side with an NYC-born-and-bred roommate named Maeve, who has never left the continental United States in her twenty-eight years.

Our differences also spill over to the looks department.

Audrina is a platinum blonde with perky C cups, eyes the color of a South Pacific lagoon, and legs up to her neck. I'm five feet four on a good day, average in the cleavage department, and I can only afford to balayage my dishwater-blonde hair twice a year.

Not to mention, my wardrobe is a little less . . . *exciting* . . . than Audrina's.

While I definitely have style, I tend to play it safe, buying classic, timeless pieces I can wear for years over trendy fast fashion. Let's just say no one has ever stopped me on the street to interview me for their New York street-wear vlog.

A young man in jeans and a T-shirt waves from the dock, and Burke heads his way, leaving me in the proverbial parking lot dust.

Slinging my Lands' End canvas tote over my shoulder, I head to the back of the Escalade to help Lenny with bags.

"Oh, you don't have to do that, ma'am," he says. "I've got it."

There are seven large suitcases here, three of which are mine, and it's a decent trek from here to the dock. He shouldn't have to do that multiple times when Burke and I have perfectly functioning arms and legs.

"No, it's fine," I say. "I want to help."

Lenny shoots me a quizzical look before glancing Burke's way, almost as if he's worried he'll get in trouble for letting me assist. I take it as a sign not to press it any further.

"Why don't you wait by the dock?" He offers a humble smile, but his rigid stance implies he's not taking no for an answer. "I'll have these moved in a couple of minutes, and then you two will be on your way."

I trail toward Burke and the guy in jeans, breathing in the briny ocean air and basking in the sunshine that warms the top of my head.

There are worse ways to spend my summer than on some private island with a butler, daily housekeepers, a world-class chef, and a beach. Burke mentioned in his pdf that Driftway had been in the Rothwell family for generations, that the main house was built in the late 1800s, and as it was passed down, other family members added things like guest cottages, a horse stable and riding ring, an Olympic-size pool, a solarium, a lighthouse, and a jogging path that encompasses the entire perimeter. The way he described the island made it sound like something out of a classic-lit novel from the Gilded Age.

He assured me I wouldn't be bored here, not for a second, not even if I tried.

When we're loaded onto the boat and about to disembark from the dock, Burke takes the seat across from the young captain and immediately digs into his pocket for his phone.

I wave, trying to catch his attention from where I'm sitting in the back of the boat. It takes a minute or so, but when he finally notices, I pat the beige vinyl cushion beside me and motion for him to come over.

"You're going to need to be a little more engaged with me," I say when he sits down.

"What are you talking about? You have a ring." He glances at the rock on my finger. "We *are* engaged."

Maybe he misheard me . . .

The motor is noisy back here, and the wind in our faces isn't helping.

"No, I mean, interact with me. You're always on your phone. And you talk to me without looking at me." If this is how he treated Audrina, it's no wonder she left him for someone else. No one wants to play second fiddle to the latest iPhone model. "I'm just saying, if you want to sell this, you're going to have to actually act like you like me. You'll have to stop acting like you're at work and start acting like you're in the company of a woman you want to spend the rest of your life with."

Burke looks me in the eyes for the first time all day, though he doesn't respond. I can only hope he's chewing on my words and giving them the consideration they deserve.

If this mission fails, it'll be because of him, not me—at least that's what I've decided.

I'm giving this 200 percent.

Go big or go home.

I've already made a list of all the things I'm going to do with that million dollars, too, starting with paying off my mom's mortgage back in Nebraska.

Not only that, but I'd like to pay off the mountain of physical therapy debt she's accrued since being rear-ended by an uninsured driver a few years ago. The woman deserves to finally retire comfortably after raising me solo and putting in forty faithful years with the public school system.

I'll probably buy her a Toyota as well—something safe and reliable that'll last until the end of time so she'll never have another car payment ever again.

I'm also going to make some donations to a few of my favorite charities, finally pay off my student loans, and look into that MBA program I've been hemming and hawing about for the past few years.

My father, on the other hand, has more money than he knows what to do with since my grandparents passed and left their entire farming estate to him, though I wouldn't mind doing something special for him too. He's always wanted to go storm chasing, but he's never had anyone willing to go with him . . . maybe I'll plan a storm-chasing trip for us. That kind of memory could be priceless.

I'd love to take some time off work and travel the world too.

A year of aimless wandering sounds divine.

And of course, a good chunk will go straight into an investment account because if there's anything I've learned from working at Burke's firm, it's that compound interest is the eighth wonder of the world.

This money might be a drop in the bucket for people like the Rothwells, but for me? It'll be life changing.

It could completely alter the trajectory of my future.

Not to mention, it'll be a funny story I can tell people someday.

A million years from now, I can look back at this time in my life and laugh about the crazy boss I had who paid me a million bucks to pretend to be his fiancée for eight weeks—and I didn't even have to sleep with him.

The stories in life that are stranger than fiction are always the best ones.

Pinching the bridge of his nose, Burke exhales.

"Just trying to tie up any loose ends with the merger." He slips his arm onto the seat cushion behind me—a step in the right direction—though nothing about it feels natural.

Yet.

"You left everything in good hands. Jonathan will hold the fort," I tell him, though I don't know if that's true. I've only worked for the company for eight months. While Jonathan seems like an intelligent, capable person who knows what he's doing, I've never actually spoken to the man. Not sure I've ever even spoken to his assistant either. "There's Wi-Fi on the island, right?"

"Sort of." Burke's lips turn flat. "It's satellite internet, so it's spotty and unreliable. And the data is limited. It's mostly for emergencies."

Damn.

Maybe this is why he had a whole page in his document dedicated to all the things I could do for fun on the island . . .

I've always talked about taking a technology break, but I never thought one would be forced on me without notice.

"Besides, my father has this rule about us not working when we're here," he adds. "He's kind of . . . old school like that."

I can't wrap my head around the concept of someone telling Burke what he can and can't do and Burke accepting it without an ounce of pushback.

Burke is a dictator, not a dictatee.

I've seen him make interns cry and watched him fire people on the spot in meetings.

"I'm sure he'd let you take a phone call or send an email if you had to, right?" I ask. I hope for my sake he says yes because Maeve is going to freak out if she can't reach me for eight weeks. But also . . . same. She's more than my roommate; Maeve is my person. And because she was around the day he proposed this insane scheme, she's the only other human I can talk to about it. The nondisclosure agreement Burke had me sign strictly prohibits me from breathing a word about this to anyone else.

He made Maeve sign one as well.

As far as I'm concerned, she's in this with me.

"I bet he'd make an exception if you asked," I say with misplaced confidence.

"You don't know my father."

I'm about to ask what he means by that when our boat slows, and a tree-lined island comes into view. An expansive shake-sided house peeks out from behind the leafy foliage, looking too perfect to be real—like a scene from a movie or a photo from a coffee-table book.

"Is that Driftway?" I ask.

"It is."

My heartbeat quickens once again, my anxiety ice cold in my veins, as the reality of all this becomes more tangible by the second.

Without giving it another thought, I slide my hand into his.

"What are you doing?" he asks.

"Practicing." I interlace our fingers. His hand is limp and unreceptive. We should've been doing this the whole drive here. "Hold mine back."

He gives me a squeeze, though I might as well be holding hands with my brother.

There's nothing here, not even the tiniest spark—not that I wanted there to be. It just means we might have to overcompensate for our lack of chemistry.

The contract he gave me had a section on public displays of affection, stating I would be "expected and required to reciprocate any displays of affection, including but not limited to hand holding, hugging, and tongueless kissing, strictly for show and only when in the company of others."

A few days ago, I spent three hours on YouTube, watching videos on how actors handle love scenes and kissing. Ironically, the most overstated advice was to *not* practice; that way, it seems authentic when it happens.

I may or may not have practiced on my hand—a fact I'd never tell a soul.

Not even Maeve.

The last person I kissed was this incredible guy I met last summer at Vivi's bachelorette party—which in many ways feels like yesterday and forever ago at the same time.

The taut and tanned boat captain adjusts his gold-rimmed aviator sunglasses before glancing back at us.

I smile at him and lean my head against Burke's tense shoulder.

As soon as the spotlight is off us, I lean back, though our hands are still unnaturally intertwined.

"Your pdf only had one little section on your family," I tell him, though it was more of a single paragraph than an entire section. He had written two full pages dedicated to his favorite places to travel, but he only managed to write seven measly sentences about the people we're about to spend the next eight weeks with. "I know your dad will be here . . . and then you have a brother and a sister. They'll be here too?"

The lone paragraph mentioned nothing about his mother.

Not a sentence, not a word, not even a name.

I'm afraid to ask.

No one unintentionally leaves their mother out of a family write-up.

"Yes." Zero emotion of any kind registers in his voice.

"What are their names? How old are they?" I wanted to ask these questions on the six-hour drive here, but I didn't want to let the cat out of the bag in case Lenny was in the dark about our arrangement. "What are they like?"

The boat coasts up to a long dock, and the captain kills the engine—effectively killing our ability to have this conversation in front of him.

"You'll meet them soon enough," Burke says. "I don't like to tarnish first impressions with my subjective narratives."

Reading between the lines, I get the sense that he isn't close with any of them—or perhaps there's some bad blood.

At least he's classy about it. Some guys I've known in the past would shrug and say "My brother's a dick" or "My sister's a raging narcissist" and then launch into a long-winded story about some family drama from years ago.

Whatever happened between them couldn't have been that bad if they're willing to spend eight weeks together on an island, though I suppose with sixty-five acres and a multitude of houses, there's plenty of room to avoid one another.

The captain ties the boat to the dock, and Burke climbs out first, turning to offer me his hand.

In the distance, a grinning white-haired man stands at the top of a makeshift stairway carved into a rocky patch of land, with wooden beams for steps. He's leaning on a cane, which leads me to believe he's going to wait for us to get to him—not the other way around. His physique is thin and almost crooked, and the deep lines on his face are clear even from a distance.

"Is that your father?" I ask.

Up until now, Redmond Rothwell has been nothing but a name on a pdf I've spent the last weeks memorizing.

I tried to google their family, assuming that anyone wealthy enough to afford a sixty-five-acre island home would at least have a Wikipedia page or some website articles.

Only there was nothing.

It was like everything had been intentionally scrubbed from the internet.

I suppose when you can afford an island, you can afford online privacy too.

"Redmond Rothwell the third," Burke says under his breath as he follows my gaze, "in the flesh."

I'd almost forgotten Burke's first name is also Redmond—making him technically Redmond Burke Rothwell IV. With his chiseled features and penetrating perma-stare, my boss doesn't strike me as a Redmond *or* a Burke.

I don't suppose things like that matter when you're passing down a family name.

The captain unloads the last of the seven suitcases onto the dock, and a couple of staff in resort-style uniforms show up out of nowhere to help transport them to a waiting all-terrain vehicle at the end of the dock. We haven't even made it to the physical island itself, and already I feel like I'm staying at an ocean-side Ritz-Carlton.

"Mr. Rothwell," one of the guys says as he grabs a suitcase. "Welcome home. Great to see you, as always."

Burke thanks him before giving his father a wave followed by a smile more obligatory than sincere, though I doubt his dad can tell the difference from where he's standing.

"Should we hold hands again?" I keep my voice low.

Without a word, he interlaces our fingers and leads me up the wooden staircase to his waiting father.

"Dad, this is Briar," he says, "my fiancée. Briar, meet my father, Redmond."

With a death grip on his cane, Redmond extends his wrinkled right hand to me. "Lovely to meet you, my dear. I can't say I've heard all that much about you yet, but I'm excited to learn how you managed to sweep this one off his feet."

I offer a gracious smile. "It's more like the other way around."

Redmond's eyes fill with light. "Is that so? I know my son can be quite the charmer. Can't, for the life of me, seem to figure out where that came from."

We share a chuckle, and I decide I adore Redmond already, though I'd hardly call Burke a charmer.

Burke's father looks much older than I anticipated, with his clothes hanging off his gaunt frame and his paper-thin skin covered with deep lines and age spots. If I had to guess, he must be the same age as my grandparents, who are approaching their eighties, suggesting he started his family much later in life since Burke is pushing his midthirties.

On top of that, he seems warm and friendly—a contented-grandfather type—which is far from what I was picturing when Burke mentioned he wouldn't be allowed to send an email. I imagined some ruthless *Succession*-esque patriarch, but Redmond reminds me more of the jovial grandfather from *Jurassic Park*.

"Well, I for one am a sucker for a good love story. Come on, now. Let's head to the house. Dinner's almost ready, and you two can fill me in on everything." Redmond climbs behind the wheel of an idling golf cart and waves for us to hop on the back. After being in the car for so long, I wouldn't mind walking from here to the main house, but of course I don't want to be rude.

Taking in the sights along the way, I point at an adorable white cottage with a swing on the front porch and bushes upon bushes of blue and purple flowers in full bloom. Pretty sure I could retire in that house and die happy.

"Caretaker's cottage," Burke says. "His name is Maurice. His wife, Yvette, is the house manager. You'll see them both quite a bit."

Next, we sputter past a horse stable, where two palomino mares and a miniature painted pony graze on a rolled-out bale of hay. In the distance is another house—this one larger than the cottage—with more windows and an ornate roofline. It must be one of the four guesthouses on site, though in my hometown of Prairie Grove, Nebraska, a place like that would qualify as a mansion.

When we arrive at the sprawling coastal estate house a few minutes later, Redmond steers us up the circular drive, past a bubbling marble fountain with clear blue water, before parking mere meters from the weathered oak double front door.

A silver-haired woman in khaki shorts and a crisp white button-down waits to greet us with curious, observant eyes and a cautious smile directed toward me. She folds her hands in front of her hips and stands as still as a statue.

"That's Yvette," Burke tells me, though I'd guessed as much if only because she exudes an air of quiet authority, like someone who runs a tight ship.

Cane in hand, Redmond descends from the cart with a jubilant expression. It's clear that having his son around puts a pep in his step—a bittersweet detail when juxtaposed against Burke's lack of enthusiasm.

"Let me be the first to officially welcome you to Driftway, Briar," Redmond says as he extends a bent elbow and leads me inside. "For the next eight weeks, our house is *your* home."

One step past the front door, I'm met with the heavenly scent of salted air, sunshine, and line-dried linens. Yvette waits for the men with the bags, directing them to a bedroom upstairs, before disappearing into some pocket of the house.

A gentle breeze floats through the open foyer, wrapping me in a warm, welcoming hug. Turning my attention to a wooden console against the wall, I find it covered in so many photographs I can hardly see the tabletop beneath them.

"May I?" I point to the frames.

Redmond's eyes glow with pride. "Absolutely, my dear."

Scanning the pictures, I note that most of them are older candid shots—some grainier than others. There are a handful of sepia-toned images as well as some black-and-white shots peppered in.

A girl in riding gear on a chestnut-colored horse.

Two shirtless boys fishing off a dock.

Three suntanned kids building sandcastles.

I can't locate a single recent-looking image in the mix, but it isn't hard to identify Burke with his hair the color of a midnight sky and his perma-frown. An image of him with a tall, skinny girl and a cocoa-haired boy half his size takes center stage in a large gold frame. They're standing on a beach, their arms linked around each other, as the sun sets behind them. To the right is a wedding photo—a younger Redmond feeding cake to a beautiful, laughing blonde. The bride reminds me of Carolyn Bessette-Kennedy, with her elegant, striking features and classic white off-shoulder dress.

To the right of that, however, is another image—an even younger Redmond holding hands with a little girl sporting gingerbread tresses all the way down to her waist. Behind them is a woman with matching curls and a baby on her hip. It's the only photo like it among all the others.

I'm tempted to ask about it until a woman's voice steals my attention.

"There you are, Dad. I've been looking all over for you," she says. "It's time for your afternoon medications."

The tall, lithe brunette in a coral-striped sundress carries a glass of still water and offers her outstretched palm to Redmond.

"Thank you, Nicola." Redmond tosses the pills back with a shaky hand and chases them with two generous gulps of water before wiping a drip that trails down his chin. "Whatever would I do without you?"

Her steeled facade softens with his words but only for a second.

Everything about this woman is straight as an arrow and perfectly manicured, from her posture and her glossy tresses to her starched dress and her immaculate sun-kissed complexion.

"Nicola, this is Briar," Burke says. "Briar, meet my sister, Nicola. She and her husband are staying with us this summer."

Nicola's shiny green gaze flicks to my ring for a fraction of a second before she extends her hand to mine.

"Pleasure to meet you, Briar," she says, though there's no warmth in her tone. It may as well be ice cold. "Forgive my brother for failing to mention that his niece and nephew are here as well. Sometimes I think he forgets he's an uncle except at Christmas and birthdays. Even then, I suspect he has an assistant who helps him remember."

"Nicola, your passive aggression is as unparalleled as ever," Burke says to her before turning to me. "But yes, I have a niece and nephew. What are their names again?"

Nicola shoots him a death glare.

Burke fights a smirk, as if getting under her skin brings him pure joy.

I can't tell if they're enjoying this or if my hunch about there being bad blood between them was dead on.

Only time will tell.

"Dinner's almost ready," Nicola says. "Dashiell's cleaning up the kids, but they'll be down shortly. Dorian's around here somewhere . . ."

Dorian . . . ?

My stomach does the tiniest of somersaults as my breath catches.

It's a name a person doesn't hear every day—a name I haven't heard in over a year.

I remind myself there are other Dorians in this world besides the one I met last summer.

The odds of *that* Dorian being *this* Dorian are slim to none.

Laughably impossible.

On a planet of eight billion people, it would take divine intervention for the two of us to wind up on the same island for a summer, and

27

I've never been a believer in fate or destiny or anything that suggests our future isn't in our own hands.

The sensation of Burke's stiff hand on the small of my back steals me from my runaway thoughts, and I follow Redmond and Nicola to a dining room down the hall, where walls of open windows usher in an evening sea breeze that complements the savory scents wafting from the kitchen.

Burke pulls out my chair before situating himself between me and his father.

Nicola settles Redmond at the head of the table, then hurries to the spot directly across from me—a move I can't help but feel is intentional based on the scrutinizing glances she continues to throw my way when she thinks I'm not paying attention.

My stomach rumbles as staff place baskets of warm bread on the table and begin pouring ice water into glasses much too extravagant for such a simple beverage.

A girl could get used to this . . .

"There they are." Nicola wears a genuine smile for the first time as her husband ushers in a boy and a girl who can't be more than eight or nine.

The young girl is the spitting image of her mother—long and lithe with stick-straight dark hair that drips down to the middle of her back. She wears a wide sky-blue velvet bow on the back of her head and a gauzy empire-waist cotton dress the color of snow. The son, identical to his father from their shared sandy-blond hair to their matching aquiline noses, scans the room, his curious gaze landing on me.

"Take a seat, my loves. I'm sure you're famished," she says with a sweetness in her tone that could rival a kindergarten teacher's lilt any day of the week.

The children don't fight over who sits where; they simply take two chairs at the far end of the table—a few spots down from where the adults are sitting.

"Augustine, Remy," she says to the kids. "Meet your uncle's . . . *fiancée* . . . Briar."

She says the word "fiancée" as if it leaves a sour taste on her tongue, but I don't take it personally. Maybe if we were truly engaged and I was madly in love with her brother, her coolness toward me would sting, but for now, I'm emotionally bulletproof, so it ricochets off me.

And to be honest, if I had a wealthy brother who showed up engaged to some random woman after ending a three-year relationship, I'd be skeptical too.

Besides, with this beautiful scenery, this five-star meal we're about to enjoy, and another eight weeks to go, I'd be wasting my time getting worked up over something so trivial in the grand scheme of things.

I'm here to do a job.

Everything else is inconsequential.

"Where are your manners, my darlings?" Nicola clucks her tongue. "Say hello to Miss Briar."

"Hi," they say in unison before they reach for the bread basket someone has just placed in front of them.

"We're still working on fine-tuning our etiquette." Nicola drapes a white linen napkin over her lap. "But we're making progress."

"I think they're doing a fine job," her husband says when he sits next to her. "Speaking of good manners, I'm Dashiell, since no one has bothered to introduce us yet."

Nicola swats at him, rolling her eyes. "I was getting to that."

"Wonderful to meet you, Dashiell," I say, deciding now would be a terrible time to mention my childhood dog's name was Cash, but somewhere along the line, we gave him the nickname Dash because he was always dashing off.

Something tells me these people wouldn't find the humor in that.

Before I left, Maeve told me that out here, you can always tell if someone comes from old money because they have names better suited for dogs or horses: Busy, Birdie, Dolly, Kitty, Topper, Darby, Duke . . .

Maeve went to school with a lot of people like them and filled my head with scandalous tales of marital affairs, family quarrels, and white-collar crimes.

Things are never what they seem with these people, she told me last night. *They're skilled at putting on a good front, like everything's perfect— it's practically embedded in their DNA. In Nebraska, maybe your mom would teach you how to bake a blue-ribbon pie for the county fair. Out here, a mother might teach her daughter how to look the other way when her husband knocks up the tennis instructor at the country club.*

"Margaret, could you please fetch Yvette and have her send Dorian down for dinner?" Redmond asks one of the staff. He reaches for a slice of bread and slides a white ceramic butter dish closer. "Tell him if he's not here in two minutes, we're starting without him."

"No need," a man's voice says from behind me.

The chair beside me slides out, and a man in ripped jeans and a gray V-neck T-shirt takes a seat; however, I can't bring myself to look at his face—not yet.

"Unfashionably late as always," Nicola says under her breath, though loud enough for the whole table to hear her.

"It's not my fault the airline lost my luggage," he says in a voice that's vaguely familiar, but I could be imagining it.

It's been a long day.

I'm starving.

Physically and mentally exhausted.

And my nerves are frazzled.

"Oh?" Nicola's brows lift. "So you're saying you *wouldn't* be dressed like a roadie if your suitcase were here?"

Roadie?

The Dorian I met last year was the manager of Phantom Symphony. At least, that's what he told me. I tried googling him when I got home— despite both of us agreeing not to contact each other. But all I could find was that the band was managed by something called Beacon Music

Management LLC. The business was registered in Delaware, so any further investigating was fruitless since most people who register in that state do it for privacy and anonymity.

"Wishful thinking on your part," the man beside me counters, swiping bread from the basket in front of us. His arm brushes mine in the process, and my skin is on fire for an entire two seconds. "I'll have you know, this T-shirt wasn't cheap."

"That flimsy fabric screams otherwise," Nicola bites back.

Burke sighs, reaching for his water. Once again, I get the sense he'd rather be anywhere than here.

"All right, all right," Redmond interrupts them. "*Enough.*" He directs his gaze at me, offering an apologetic wince. "Apologies, Briar. My kids spend so much time apart throughout the year that they forget how to behave like civilized people when they get together. Anyway, Dorian, now that you've joined us, I'd like you to meet Briar—your brother's fiancée."

My stomach is knotted, and my neck is so tense that I can't bring myself to turn to look at the man sitting beside me.

I don't want it to be him.

And yet I do.

I'd be lying if I said thoughts of him hadn't haunted me at least once a day since the night we met. The connection I shared with that man was one I'd never experienced with anyone else before. It was brief and intense, and I've lived off that high—and the promise we made to one another—ever since.

Gathering a short breath, I turn to the stranger beside me, ready to shake his hand. Only the second our gazes catch, I freeze, my body turning to solid stone.

It isn't a stranger.

It's him.

Dorian.

Recognition colors his teal-green irises, and his lips begin to move, but before he can say a single word, I manage a quick "It's wonderful to meet you, Dorian."

He slides his hand into mine, sending a shiver of goose bumps throughout me the moment our palms touch.

"Likewise," he says with a cruel, knowing squint. His perceptive stare falls to my left hand, where my glimmering five-carat diamond can't be missed. "Couldn't possibly imagine what you see in my brother, but I guess we'll find out soon enough, won't we?"

"*Dorian*," Redmond says with a huff that turns into a coughing fit. He reaches for his water, choking down the last drop before the natural color returns to his face. When he's finished, he staggers to a standing position and thumps a trembling fist against the table. The silverware bounces and the children gasp. "There'll be no more of . . . *this*."

His angry sneer moves from Nicola to Burke to Dorian. Gone is the cheerful-grandfather type who carted us from the dock to the door with pleasantries and enthusiasm and the winds of joy in his sails.

"We're going to enjoy these next eight weeks. Do you understand me?" There's a crazy look in his shaky eyes, one that sucks all the air from the room.

His question is met with palpable silence.

"*Do you understand me?*" he asks, louder this time, enunciating each syllable. "Have I made myself crystal clear?"

"Yes," the three of them say with averted eyes like scolded schoolchildren.

I'm beginning to understand why Burke said there'd be no exceptions to his father's no-working-while-on-the-island rule. He doesn't seem like the kind of man who takes no for an answer.

Focusing on my glass of water and the empty wine goblet beside it, I'm acutely aware of the weight of Dashiell's stare from the other side of the table. Perhaps he's gauging my reaction to see if I have what it takes to marry into a family like this one.

Fortunately, none of us will ever know.

A parade of servers with plates covered in stainless steel cloches enters the room in a single file, breaking up the tense silence with their accidentally perfect timing.

Another staffer, wielding a crystal pitcher, refills Redmond's water glass before uncorking two bottles of wine and making her way around the adult part of the table.

"Welcome to the family." Dorian leans close, his voice so low it tickles my eardrum. I think he's being sarcastic, but I don't dare laugh.

Burke takes my hand on the other side, giving it a reassuring squeeze.

I swallow my doubts with a mouthful of wine and pray we make it through these next two months.

An hour ago, I was certain it'd be a piece of cake.

Now I'm not so sure.

CHAPTER THREE

BRIAR

One Year Ago

Dorian drinks his water as the song changes to the Bruno Mars number about doing something dumb tonight and getting married.

"Vivi definitely requested this," I say as the wedding-bells echo plays. "She's loved this song since middle school."

"It sounds exactly like something a middle schooler would love."

"Whatever. It's catchy. Admit it. If you were in a better mood, you'd be cutting a rug right now."

"Cutting a rug?" He cracks another semblance of a half smile—second one of the night. "Who says that?"

"I think you secretly love this song." I razz him again to get him to loosen up a little more. "I can see it in your eyes. They're practically twinkling."

"Is that right?" He sips his bad-luck water, keeping his hypnotic gaze focused on me. "Sorry to say, but you're wrong. I hate it."

"Hate's a strong word," I say. "Maybe your feelings are more hate-ish?"

"No, it is pure hatred."

"How do you know?"

"When you know, you know."

While the rest of our group is dancing and singing along with the obnoxious-yet-fitting tune, I make the fatal error of accidentally catching Vivi's eyes. She motions for me to join her, but I'm a couple of shots away from being dance floor drunk, and my feet are still on fire, so I shake my head no. Fortunately, she moves on, linking arms with two of her girlfriends. That's the thing about my cousin; she's not going to waste a single second of her favorite song.

"You sure you don't want to join in on that?" Dorian asks. "I can save your seat."

"I'll go if you go," I say, but I don't mean it. Blisters and sobriety aside, I was born with two left feet. Not literally. But I can't dance to save my life, and it's not from a lack of trying. My mom stuck me in every dance class under the sun until I was twelve, hoping one day it would eventually stick. All those recitals, all those costumes, all those hours practicing, all that money . . . it was all for nothing. "I bet you've got some moves."

"You're right." Dorian downs the rest of his bad-luck water, grabs my hand, and pulls me out to the dance floor before I have a chance to object. "I do."

Oh, shit.

Thinking fast, I step out of my heels and kick them to the side. The floor is sticky against my bare feet, but I'm too distracted by his hands circling my waist to give it more thought. My heart hammers as he pulls me in. I'm pressed against him for a fleeting moment, barely long enough to inhale the intoxicating spice of his faded cologne and to learn that my head fits perfectly beneath his chin.

Dorian towers over me, reeling me in and sending me out, never once taking his eyes off mine, which is a relief because the last thing I need him focusing on is my lack of coordination.

It's rare to meet a man who can actually dance, but this man has rhythm. Most guys flap their arms like chicken wings or lift their drinks in the air while nodding their heads to whatever song is playing and call it dancing.

But not Dorian.

It all seems to come naturally to him, and there's nothing *cringe* about it.

Since he manages a band, I can only assume he comes from a musical background.

"Hey, I think we're leaving after this song," Vivi yells when she trots over to us. Her eyes are glassy, and her face is flushed, and she's having the time of her life. "Get back on the bus after this, okay?"

I nod, and Dorian pulls me against him once more, his arm pressed against my lower back. For a sliver of a second, a euphoric warmth flashes through me, followed by an electric flicker that radiates to my fingertips. Everything's happening too fast for me to process what it means or if I'm imagining it. It can't be the mojito—I'm a lightweight when it comes to drinking but not *that* lightweight.

The three-minute song ends after what feels like thirty breathless seconds.

"You ready to go, Pick-Me Girl?" he asks with a teasing glimmer in his eye.

A second later, his eyes turn glassy. He blinks as if he's blinking away tears.

I'm confused . . .

I thought we were having a good time.

Rubbing his eyes, he sniffs.

"Are you okay?" I place my hand on his forearm.

"Think I got something in my eye," he says.

I resist the urge to reply with a sarcastic "Yeah, mm-hmm, okay" when I realize that his hands are covered in glitter—from my dress.

He must have somehow touched his left eye, which is now growing redder and more irritated by the second.

"Oh my god—I think you got glitter in your eye from my dress," I say. "You have to flush it out so you don't scratch your cornea."

Without another word, I take him by the hand and lead him to the single-stall ladies' room, locking the door behind us so no one barges in. Twisting the cold-faucet handle, I point to the sink.

"Tip your head and get your eye under that stream," I say, guiding him with my hand on his back as the scent of cheap air freshener and women's perfume floods the space.

He rises, blinking and taking a break from the steady stream of H_2O. His eye is still watering like crazy, making his nose run in the process, and to top it off, he's yet to say a single word.

Dorian dunks his head under the faucet again.

"I'm so sorry," I say, watching and wishing there was more I could do. "This stupid dress—I found it on a clearance rack and thought it would be perfect for tonight . . ."

Dorian finishes rinsing a minute later. I yank a few paper towels from the dispenser and hand them over.

"I'm sure we can stop for eye drops before the next bar," I say as he dabs the wetness away.

"I'll be fine." He straightens his posture, sniffing, before tossing the crumpled paper towels into the overflowing trash can in the corner.

It's then that I catch my reflection in the mirror; my sparkling ice-blue dress looks garish under the unflattering fluorescent light. I should've worn the flowy skirt and white crop top I'd originally picked out. Lord knows they would've been more comfortable.

"Hey, hurry it up in there." Someone pounds on the restroom door.

"You ready?" he asks, his hand on the lock.

The woman on the other side of the door gives us a dirty look when we emerge. Dorian doesn't seem to notice, or if he does, he doesn't care. She shoves past us, shoulder checking me.

This time Dorian notices.

He turns back to say something to her, but she slams the door in his face.

"It's okay," I tell him, resting my hand on his arm.

We need to get going anyway.

"I need to find my heels," I yell over the Dr. Dre and Snoop Dogg song blaring from the speakers as we return to the main area. The dance floor is emptier than it was a few minutes ago, making them easier to locate despite the fact that one appears to have been kicked a few yards away from its mate.

Once we get to the parking lot, it's as bare as the dance floor.

"Where's the party bus?" I ask the obvious.

"Good question." He rakes his palm across his sharp, shadowed jawline.

That repurposed school bus was painted neon green and lit from within by flickering LED lights and a disco ball—there's no way it's hiding in plain sight.

"Did they . . . did they leave without us?" I stand on the sidewalk in disbelief, my dirty feet shoved into uncomfortable heels and my ears still ringing from the dance music. When I look at Dorian, he's already on his phone.

"No signal." He exhales, shoving the useless device into his pocket. "Did they say where they were going next?"

"Nope." I check my phone as well.

No bars.

Even if we knew where they were going, we wouldn't be able to order a cab to meet them there.

"Guess it's us against the world tonight," I say. "Not to use a line from a Phantom Symphony song . . ."

Raking his hand against his angled jaw, he looks me up and down.

I'd give a million pennies for his thoughts.

CHAPTER FOUR

DORIAN

Present Day

"Maybe you should slow down on those." Dashiell points to the row of empty Stella Artois bottles lined up in front of me.

"Nicola tell you to say that?" I fire back before uncapping another one. The more my lips are glued to the rim of a glass bottle, the less likely I am to say something I might regret, and my mind is teeming with all kinds of opinions.

"Of course not," Dashiell lies. Nicola clipped his balls and hid them somewhere the day they got married. It's been ten years, and legend says he still hasn't found them. "It's just the first night. Got to pace yourself. We've got an entire summer ahead of us."

I take a generous drink.

"I'm training for a marathon if you want to jog with me in the mornings?" he asks. "I get up around six, drink my peptide electrolytes, and—"

"Pass." I take another sip. It's not that I don't like running, but it's just that in all the time I've known Dashiell, he's never once run an actual marathon, despite constantly "training" for one, and there's nothing I loathe more than wasted time, weddings, and liars.

After a dinner of freshly caught seafood and suffocating small talk, my father insisted we come outside for after-dinner drinks.

The second the sun went down, the groundskeeper lit a bonfire, and the kids managed to talk my sister into making s'mores.

Nic didn't appreciate it when I told her, "It's okay to be fun sometimes." But someone's got to make her lighten up, or it'll be another never-ending summer on this godforsaken island.

Briar and Burke stroll hand in hand in the distance, barefoot in the sand.

It's like a car crash—I don't want to watch, but I can't stop looking.

I down a gluttonous swig of Stella.

"What do you think of her so far?" Dashiell asks, motioning toward the "happy" couple.

"Who?" I play dumb, pretending like she isn't the one and only thing plaguing my every waking thought since the moment I laid eyes on her all over again.

Then again, I've never stopped thinking about her since last year.

Not for one minute.

"Briar . . ."

"She's all right, I guess." I shrug and take another gulp.

Two hours ago at dinner, she shook my hand and told me it was nice to meet me—never mind that a year ago, I was *inside* her.

And don't get me started on the fact that the night we met, she swore up, down, and sideways that she was antimarriage, that she didn't need a piece of paper or someone's last name in order to be with them.

Funny how all that changed when she met my wealthy asshole brother.

Next thing you know, she's going to be some Upper West Side housewife with a robust social schedule, a face full of filler, and a couple of nanny-raised children.

"She seems nice," Dash says. "Almost too nice for Burke."

I sniff an amused laugh.

In our younger days, I called my brother Burke the Jerk. It wasn't exactly an inventive nickname, but it was fitting. As we grew older, the moniker suited him even more.

There isn't a nice bone in his body.

Never has been.

Never will be.

He's the second coming of our father in every way possible. The only difference is our father has become nice-ish in his old age—but that tends to happen when a man wakes up one day and discovers time is no longer on his side and health is a luxury he can no longer afford even with his overflowing bank accounts.

"I think she's going to be good for him," Dashiell says as he watches the lovebirds dip their feet in the water.

Briar laughs, trotting away from the cold ocean spray. Burke chases after her.

I look away so I don't throw up in my mouth.

"You're awfully optimistic given the fact that you've known her all of three hours," I tell him.

"I don't know. You could be right. I just have a good feeling about her. Maybe she could humble him, you know? Ground him a bit. Bring him down to earth. She said she's from some small town in Nebraska. She went to school in the Midwest. She's not like us," Dash says. "She's like . . . Kate Middleton."

I almost choke on my beer. "She's *nothing* like Kate Middleton."

"I don't mean literally. I mean, she's an outsider. She might be the breath of fresh air this family needs."

Breath of fresh air . . .

Liar . . .

Opportunist . . .

Gold digger . . .

It all remains to be seen.

Nicola passes through the sliding glass door to the patio, arms full of bagged marshmallows and Hershey bars. The kids trot behind her, Augustine carrying a box of graham crackers and her brother carefully hauling the roasting sticks with the sharp ends pointed down.

"Dad's tired. He's staying in for the night," Nic says when she places all the items on the table. "Must've had too much excitement for one day." Following our gazes, she asks, "What are you two gossiping about?"

"Your husband thinks Briar is the next Kate Middleton," I say.

Nicola frowns, and Dash lifts his hands in protest before explaining himself.

"Really, Dash? You've always had a thing for Kate Middleton," she says when he's done, clearly not caring about his analogy. Now she's going to worry about Dash's wandering eye for the next eight weeks.

Nicola and the kids head off to the firepit.

"Sorry," I tell him.

"You just had to say something, didn't you?" Dashiell sinks back in his chair, sulking like the man-child he is.

"Oh, come on." I peel the label off my bottle. "This is our last summer together. We should shake things up a bit and stop trying to be so perfect all the time. And you two need to stop taking every little thing so seriously. Sometimes being around you two is exhausting."

Dash says nothing.

Then again, there's nothing to say.

He knows I'm right.

Three months ago, my father was given two to six months to live. The fact that we're here at all right now is a miracle, and every day is borrowed from the next. The day we have to put him in the ground will likely be the last time my brother, sister, and I are in the same place at the same time—and it's for the best.

We bring out the worst in each other.

Besides, there's no law saying you have to be friends with your siblings after childhood—especially a childhood like the one we shared.

"All I'm saying is it couldn't hurt to not take ourselves so seriously all the time," I say. All day today, when Nicola wasn't parading around like mother of the year or looking like she was about to bite someone's head off, she was on the verge of tears. And Burke has been so much more stoic and devoid of emotion than ever that I'm convinced he's part robot. My father's moods are swinging like a pendulum. While Yvette claims it's a side effect of his newest medications, I know better. It's nothing more than a side effect of being a Rothwell. "You remember what that's like, right?"

It didn't always use to be this . . . intense.

Once upon a time, we were a saccharine and happy bunch—back when Mom was still around. I can easily draw a line in the sand dividing the time before and after her death, and it would perfectly demarcate the good memories from the bad.

Dashiell rolls his eyes and angles himself away from me. "Forgive me for not feeling overly celebratory this summer."

He's always had a particular fondness for my father, but I chalk it up to the fact that Dash's dad died when he was a kid, and his mother never remarried. It was one of the things he and Nicola bonded over since our mom died when we were young, and our father never moved on.

"It's not like he hasn't lived a good life," I say. At eighty-one, my father has lived a longer, better life than most people. Sure, there've been tragedies along the way. No one's immune to that sort of thing. But the way I look at it, he's lived a long life on his terms, and there's not much more a man could ask for. Dash heads to the firepit, abandoning our conversation the same way he abandoned my sister at Dartmouth when he knocked her up their junior year. They lost the baby early on, only it strangely made them closer than ever. She may have forgiven him for the way he behaved in her time of need, but I haven't forgotten.

Once a douche, always a douche.

I'm peeling the label off another bottle when Briar and Burke return to the table, flushed and smiling, their fingers intertwined, and their hair windswept. The more this night goes on, the more touchy-feely these two get. At first, they would hardly look at each other. If a person didn't know better, they'd think the two of them were hardly more than strangers at dinner.

Now there're moonbeams in their eyes.

It's like I'm watching them fall in love in real time.

"How was the water?" I ask but only to break the dead weight of silence that has settled between the three of us.

"Freezing," Briar says, turning to Burke. How she can stand here and pretend we're nothing more than strangers kills me. *Kills* me. "Thought it'd be warmer."

Burke takes her hand in his. "Wait until the sun is out tomorrow. Midafternoon, you'll be in heaven."

"Beach day tomorrow?" she asks.

I flinch on the inside, remembering how fond she was of beaches last summer, how she said they were her "favorite thing in the whole world."

He chuckles. "Every day's a beach day up here."

I roll my eyes, but neither of them notices.

They're too busy making googly eyes at each other.

Burke takes her hand, leaning in to whisper something in her ear that makes her blush.

If only she knew the truth: he doesn't love her.

He's only after his portion of the Rothwell inheritance—which requires him to be married or engaged to be married. I bet she hasn't got a clue that she's nothing more than a pawn in Burke's game. The second my father dies—which will be sooner rather than later according to his recent diagnosis—Burke will leave Briar high and dry.

But if she was willing to throw her antimarriage convictions—and her promise to me—out the window all because Mr. Tall, Dark, and Wealthy charmed his way into her life, then that's on her.

I don't wish heartbreak on anyone, but some people are just asking for it.

I toss back the last of my Stella and head upstairs to bed.

CHAPTER FIVE

BRIAR

One Year Ago

Kicking off my heels, I point behind me. "I think the hotel's back that way a couple of miles."

There are worse things in this world than being stranded in a foreign country with a teal-eyed stranger.

"You're going to walk barefoot?" he asks.

"Unless you want to trade me shoes?"

He doesn't offer. I don't push it. Not that I would.

"Give those to me." He motions to my heels.

"I was kidding . . ."

"I know." With my heels in his hands, he trots toward a group of women half a block down. I hadn't noticed them until now. He says something, though I can't make out the conversation from here.

After a few seconds, he reaches into his pocket and takes out his wallet. When he returns, my high heels are gone, and he's carrying a pair of black flip-flops in their place. But not just any kind—the super soft ones with the yoga-mat soles.

"Did you really just trade my stilettos for flip-flops?" I ask.

"Are you mad?" He angles a single brow.

"Not at all. I'm impressed." I take the rubber sandals and slide my aching, dirty dance floor feet into them. The second we get back to the resort, I'm taking a shower and scrubbing the hell out of them, but for now, I'm beyond grateful for Dorian's swift thinking. "How much did these bad boys run you?"

"A hundred."

My jaw falls. "You realize these are thirty bucks back in the States, right?"

"I was paying for her kindness. And for your convenience." He slides his hands into his pockets and treks in the direction of the resort. I follow, jogging a few steps to catch up.

"Thank you," I say. I hope I didn't come off as ungrateful, as I'm quite the opposite. I'm just . . . in awe. Half an hour ago, I never would've thought the jerk bitching about being in some tropical paradise would ask me to dance and then shell out a crisp Benjamin so I could walk home in comfort.

"No problem."

"And thanks for the dance," I add. "How's your eye?"

"I can still see out of it, so . . ."

"They probably sell eye drops at the resort gift shop." They sell everything at those places: Dramamine, Claritin, Tylenol, swimsuits, beach towels, key chains, candy bars, mini bottles of wine . . .

"I'll be fine."

We're stopped at an intersection, waiting to cross, when I steal a glimpse of him in my periphery, only now it feels like I'm seeing him in a completely different light. In silence, I curse my glittery dress for ruining what this night could have been.

Who knows what would've happened next? Would we have danced again? Would he have shed another layer of his intricate facade? As we walk home in silence, I conjure up various scenarios—one involving more drinking and making fun of bad music, another involving him pulling out his phone and putting Connor Dowd on to talk to me. There's even one where his hands are tangled in my hair and his lips are pressed hard against mine.

I'm not a romantic person.

I generally don't get ahead of myself, especially when it comes to men.

But for a fraction of a second, there was an actual *spark* between us. I felt it on the dance floor.

"Oh, shoot," I say when the brightly lit resort comes into view less than an hour later. "My room key is in my purse . . . which is on the bus . . . which is who knows where . . ."

There's no way the resort's going to give me a spare key when I have no ID or way to prove I'm even staying there. Even if I had all that, I'm splitting the room with my other cousin, Tiffin, and everything's under her name. I check the time—it's not even ten. It'll probably be another four or five hours before everyone gets back, and that's if they don't stop for food somewhere on the way. We have free twenty-four-hour room service here, but knowing Vivi and the gang, they'll spot a food truck or an all-night restaurant, and they'll be drunks on a mission.

"You can hang out in my room," he offers.

"I don't want to put you out. I'll probably just hang out in the lobby." We're strolling down a palm tree–lined street, getting closer to the main entrance with every step.

"That sounds like something a pick-me girl would say," he says.

"What?" I scrunch my nose. "No. That's not what that means . . ."

He chuckles, marking the third time for the night I've seen him smile, giving me the impression that he forgives me for the glitter incident.

"I'm just giving you shit," he says, giving me a stone-faced wink. "But seriously, don't be a martyr. You're not hanging out in the lobby for the rest of the night."

My stomach somersaults with his words.

It's impossible to know if he's offering out of the kindness of his heart or because he, too, felt that same jolt of electricity on the dance floor and isn't ready for the night to be over.

Despite the past two hours being chock full of surprises, something tells me I haven't seen the last of them.

We're strolling through the lobby, en route to the elevator, when my phone vibrates—my phone that didn't have a signal an hour ago.

"It's Vivi," I say as her name shows up on the FaceTime call. My phone must have connected to the resort's Wi-Fi when we walked in. I tap the accept button and bring the phone in front of my face.

"I'm so glad you answered," she says, breathless. I can hardly see her from all the flickering lights behind her, and the music on the bus almost drowns out her voice. "We just realized we left without you two—I'm so, so, so sorry. We're leaving the second bar now and we're going to swing back to the hotel and pick you guys up."

I glance at Dorian, who doesn't remotely try to hide the disappointment on his face, though it's anyone's guess as to whether his disappointment stems from being forced back into the party or losing our one-on-one time.

"We'll be waiting out front," I tell her.

I came here for Vivi, not to sneak off with one of her fiancé's friends the second he pays me a little attention. I may be heartbroken, but I'm not desperate.

"It's the right thing to do," I say to Dorian after I end the call, though by saying those words out loud, I feel like I'm trying to justify it to myself more than anything.

I was actually looking forward to going up to his room. I wanted to tease him and peel back his layers and rouse some more half smiles from his handsome, frowning face. I wanted to flirt and be flirted with. I wanted to feel the rush of wanting someone and wanting them to want me back. I wanted to bottle this—whatever it is—and drink every last drop until the sun comes up, all in the name of innocent fun.

We head out front to wait for our ride, his arm brushing against mine as we walk.

Outside, a balmy breeze tousles my hair and kisses my face. I brush a loose curl off my shoulder and gaze up at the starry sky. Back in Manhattan, it's rare to see the stars this clearly, if at all. It's easy to forget they even exist sometimes. Out of sight, out of mind. But they're always there, day or night, even when you can't see them.

Glancing at Dorian, I can't help but notice the rampant misery wafting off him along with his fading cologne—almost worse than when I first laid eyes on him earlier tonight. He looks like he's waiting for a prison bus rather than a party bus. And he hasn't said more than two words since Vivi called—in fact, I don't think he's said a single one.

In the distance, a flashy green bus pulls into the palm tree–lined circular drive.

"This is your fault, you know." He finally breaks his silence.

"What do you mean?"

"The water toast." His expression is deadpan serious, but there's a playfulness in his tone. "I told you those are bad luck."

The rumble of the bus grows louder as it approaches, and the scent of diesel exhaust fills the air, overpowering both Dorian's cologne and his misery.

When we climb on, the only two remaining seats are so far apart they might as well be on different continents.

Vivi squeezes between me and another partygoer once the bus gets moving.

"Someone said they saw you and Dorian go into the bathroom together at the first bar . . . ," she says, cupping her hand and speaking into my ear so I can hear her over the Prince song blaring overhead.

I clap my hand over my mouth. "Viv, it wasn't like that. I swear. We were just—"

She doesn't give me a chance to explain. She simply takes my hands in hers, tucks her chin, looks me dead in the eyes, and says, "Oh, thank God. Because believe me when I say that one will break your heart into a million pieces."

CHAPTER SIX

BRIAR

Present Day

"How do you think it went?" I pull back the covers on my half of the king-size four-poster bed we're sharing. "So far, so good?"

I spent the last ten minutes washing up for bed, changing into a set of matching satin pajamas in an en suite bathroom easily the size of my Lower East Side apartment. As I washed the day off my face, I eyed the claw-foot bathtub in the mirror's reflection. I never realized how much I missed taking actual baths until I moved into a place with a shower the size of a coffin and water that only stays hot in unpredictable three-minute increments. I have every intention of taking as many bubble baths as humanly possible during these next eight weeks.

Burke unfastens his watch, placing it on a leather tray on his nightstand, next to his charging phone—which may as well be a decorative object at this point, much like the bowls of seashells, branches of dried driftwood, and coastal New England–themed coffee-table books that adorn this palace.

"You did well," he says, speaking like a boss would to his assistant. "The whole frolicking-on-the-beach thing was a nice touch. Good call."

I got the sense at dinner that we were under more scrutiny than I'd anticipated, and the energy between us felt stiff and stifled. We had to do something, and a nighttime stroll on the beach seemed innocent enough.

Besides, I also needed a break from Dorian. Being in the same room as him was stressful; he sent my stomach sinking to the floor every time his heated gaze steered in my direction.

I can only imagine what he thinks . . .

I nestle myself under the covers, sliding one of the jumbo pillows between us.

"I hope you don't mind . . . I just don't want to accidentally spoon you or something in the middle of the night." I chuckle. He doesn't. "I'm a touchy-feely person."

"I've gathered as much." He climbs in beside me, the bed shifting with his weight, and then he switches off the lamp.

The room abruptly darkens.

There's no TV in here for some ambient light or sound to fall asleep to, though the open window to my left offers the gentle, lulling sound of the ocean.

Turning to my side, I slide my hand under my cheek. "I don't think your sister likes me."

"Nicola doesn't like anyone," he says. "And besides, she doesn't have to like you. She just has to believe you."

"She obviously likes her kids. Seems like a good mom."

"Sure." His tone is indifferent.

Burke's silhouette tosses and turns in the dark, and he rubs his eyes a few times before yawning. A second later, he sits up, punches his pillow to make it fluffier, then tries to get comfortable all over again. After a few more attempts, he throws the covers off his legs, tromps to the bathroom for a glass of water, and returns.

If this is his nightly routine, it's going to be a long summer . . .

That, and I didn't pack nearly enough Ambien. Without it, I'm a tragically light sleeper. Every little sound or movement rouses me from the deepest of sleeps. I tried to refill it before we left, but the pharmacy said it was too soon.

"Are you always this high maintenance at bedtime?" I ask, half teasingly.

He shoots me a look in the dark as if he doesn't understand my question at first.

"Can I ask you something?" I clear my throat and change the subject.

"Mm-hmm."

"Is your dad . . . is he sick?" I ask one of the numerous questions that have been on my mind all evening. Between Nicola giving Redmond a handful of pills, his coughing fits at dinner, and the fact that he retired for the evening by eight o'clock, I have my suspicions. Then again, he's no spring chicken. He could simply be . . . aging.

He doesn't answer right away. "Yes."

"Why didn't you mention that before?"

"Because it has nothing to do with you." He rolls to his side, his back to me. "It is what it is."

"I hate that expression."

He's quiet—as per usual. Getting Burke to say more than a handful of words at a time is a laborious chore, unlike his grouch of a brother.

A year ago, Dorian and I stayed up all night talking about anything and everything until the sun came up—literally. From the beach outside our hotel, we watched it rise, still lost in a conversation that hadn't ceased since the second he sat down next to me at the first bar of the night.

"Burke?" My voice is whisper soft in case he's asleep. If we're going to foster something remotely genuine, he's going to need to open up to me a little more and let me in.

We can start with pillow talk.

Several seconds pass before he responds. "Yeah?"

"If you don't mind me asking, what happened to your mom?" Earlier tonight, I found yet another table covered in family photos. From those, I was able to deduce that the beautiful Carolyn Bessette-Kennedy blonde was their mother, but based on the pictures, it seemed like she never made it past her late thirties. "You didn't mention her in your pdf . . ."

Silent tension settles between us, and I realize I'm holding my breath when my chest begins to ache.

Maybe I shouldn't have asked so soon.

Maybe it would've come out eventually in some fireside conversation on some sleepy summer night, but the more I'm around these people, the more I'm curious about their history and their intricate dynamics.

I've never seen so much loyalty and resentment all at once.

In fact, I'm not even sure if these siblings know how they feel about each other half the time. One minute they're trading barbs, and the next, they're coming to one another's defense over something that happened years ago.

After another never-ending pause, he says, "She passed away a long time ago."

I wait for him to elaborate, foolishly forgetting that Burke never expands on anything, ever.

My lips are parted, ready to fire off my next question, but I think better of it. If he doesn't want to talk about it, I'm not going to pry it out of him at the end of a long day.

I'm curious by nature, not cruel.

"I'm so sorry," I tell him. And I am. My parents divorced before I made it to elementary school, but my father simply moved across town. I still grew up with both of my parents in my life. They might have been cheering me on from opposite sides of the stand during my volleyball games, but they were always there. I can't fathom the immeasurable pain of not having one of them around for every milestone, big and small.

I imagine that's the kind of thing no amount of time heals.

Burke doesn't respond.

His breath steadies.

I don't know him well enough to determine if he's pretending to be asleep to get out of this conversation or if he's one of those rare unicorns who can magically fall asleep the second their head hits the pillow—like Maeve.

What I wouldn't give for a head emptied of its thoughts at the end of the day.

Rolling to my back, I stare at the ceiling, replaying the events of the day in my mind's eye.

None of it feels real.

And the fact that Dorian and I are back in each other's lives *here*?

Under *these* circumstances?

I'm still processing it.

How I wish I could pull him aside, whisper in his ear, and tell him this is all for show—that I still mean every word I said to him on the beach that morning—but that would be a direct violation of my non-disclosure agreement.

In fact, the way it was written, I'm never allowed to speak of this arrangement to anyone except Maeve for the rest of my natural life.

Had I known this deal would cost me Dorian, I *never* would have said yes.

And now that I'm here, now that I've been introduced as Burke's fiancée, and now that I know his father is sick, what kind of person would I be if I told Dorian this was all pretend? What kind of person would I be if I made this about me and my guilt and my feelings?

NDA or no, I didn't come here to make a mess of things, nor do I want to come between Dorian and his brother during an emotionally tenuous time in their lives.

The last thing I'd ever dream of doing is causing Dorian more pain.

I drift off, my mind heavy from the weight of all the things I can't tell him.

CHAPTER SEVEN

DORIAN

One Year Ago

"Can I ask you something?" Briar splays her hand across her chest before I can respond, leaning so close to me I can smell the sweet scent of her hair. "And you have to be honest."

"Okay." I shove my hands in my pockets as we follow our group from the bus into some new bar pumping with techno music and filled with a crowd so thick that people are dancing shoulder to shoulder.

"Vivi told me you were a heartbreaker," she yells over the music. "What'd she mean by that?"

I sniff a laugh. Vivi says all kinds of crap. It doesn't make it true.

"Who the hell knows," I yell back, scanning the space for somewhere to sit down, but it's so busy here all the seats are taken, and there's a line at the bar. I suspect it's the two-for-one tequila shots. "She was always trying to hook me up with her friends back at Syracuse. Whenever it didn't work out, it was always my fault."

"Did it ever work out?" she asks, leaning closer as we push our way through throngs of drunks.

From what I can tell, this place is somewhere between a bona fide dive and a dump. The brass placard outside proudly states it's the oldest bar on the island, though I suspect it's the buy-one-get-one shots that are luring people in like flies to shit.

Once again, this could have been avoided had we stayed put at the all-inclusive resort we paid out the ass for.

"Nope," I tell her.

There's a spark of curiosity in her eyes like she wants to continue this conversation. I'd rather not as I don't like wasting time wallowing in the past, but I'd give anything to get out of this claustrophobic shithole that smells like cheap cologne, body odor, and beer farts.

I check the bar one more time before determining it's going to be a lost cause trying to get a drink in this place. The line isn't moving, and there are only two poor saps making drinks, both of them dripping with sweat as they mix and pour as quickly as they can. "I'll be outside," I tell her. Her brows knit as she studies me like she's waiting for a hand-written invitation. "You coming?"

She nods and places her hands on my back as we weave and squeeze our way to the exit.

"That's got to be, like, a fire code violation or something, right?" she asks once we're outside. "Nothing about that seems safe."

"Or remotely enjoyable."

Next door is a quiet sports bar with a flickering neon sign proclaiming that they have LIVE AMERICAN SPORTS. Through the window, I spot the Yankees–Red Sox game playing on one of the TVs.

"You like baseball?" I ask. "Yankees are on."

"Actually . . ." She follows my gaze. "I love baseball. And I'm more of a Red Sox fan."

I wince and take a step back, feigning disgust.

"I'm sorry," I tease. "Huge red flag."

"Good thing we're not on a date," she zings back before heading for the door.

I trot ahead and open it for her.

While she's right—we're not on a date—I can't help but feel like we are anyway. It's a strange, unfamiliar sensation, like a pull in my middle and a lightness in my chest at the same time.

I don't know what to think about it, to be honest.

If I could, I'd gladly blame it on the whiskey I had earlier, but I'm as close to sober now as a guy can get. I could walk a straight line and recite the alphabet backward if I had to.

"So tell me more about your failed college relationships," she says ten minutes later.

We've snagged a high-top table for two next to the Yankees game, and she made sure to order two large waters with our drinks when the server came by.

"I wouldn't call them relationships," I say. "They were more like awkward double dates. She always wanted one of her friends to date one of Benson's friends."

Briar laughs. "Sounds like Vivi. She was always trying to set me up with her boyfriend's friends in high school. She thinks she's some kind of matchmaker, but she's actually pretty terrible at it."

"Right?" I'm glad I'm not the only one who sees it. "For a while, I thought there was something wrong with me, that I was the problem. Turns out she's just terrible at determining compatibility."

"How many friends did she set you up with?"

Our server delivers our drinks and waters, and I glance up at the TV to check the score. Yankees are up, which instantly elevates my mood.

I blow a breath past my lips. "Oh god. I don't even know. Too many to count."

Some of them are actually here tonight, though we all might as well be ships passing in the night.

Briar sips her chocolate martini, running her tongue gently against the sugared rim—a move that sends an unexpected stiffening to my cock.

There's no denying she's a gorgeous woman and, so far, the best thing about this whole trip, but I've got to keep my head on straight. Hooking up with—hell, hitting it off with—someone is the last thing I need right now. "There was one friend of hers, though," I add. "We dated maybe four months. My longest college relationship ever. After a while, it fizzled out, ran its course. I broke it off, and Vivi took that very personally. She wouldn't speak to me for weeks. Meanwhile, her friend moved on pretty much the next day. I don't even think those two are friends anymore. But Vivi's going to hold that against me until the day I die. She told me herself."

Briar rolls her sapphire blues. "She's so dramatic sometimes, but that's kind of the best thing about her. Never a dull moment. And she means well."

"Of course." I sip my beer.

I have nothing against Vivi despite her antics.

If I did, I wouldn't be here.

I also wouldn't have helped Benson arrange his elaborate proposal back in Syracuse. I managed to persuade our lead guitarist to come with me and surprise her with a song in their hotel suite. There were candles everywhere. Dozens of red roses. Cristal champagne on ice. And friends waiting outside on the balcony to congratulate them when it was over. It was a scene out of a cheesy romance movie, but I was happy for them.

I still am—even if they've been acting like they're the first people to ever get engaged in the history of the world.

"Do you date now?" Briar asks, blinking at me with her mile-long lashes. "I mean, are you actively dating? Are you on any apps or anything?"

"God, no." I cringe. "I don't have time for that. And even if I did . . . I'd rather be single than do any of that. It's unnatural. People don't realize how important it is to have that genuine connection. It's lost completely on our generation."

"I was reading this article the other day about how people spend more time swiping on those apps than actually going on dates or messaging people. They just browse and browse and browse," she says. "And it's the same for a lot of streaming platforms. People will surf for shows for hours, refusing to settle on one, because they're worried they're going to miss out on something better, convinced that if they scroll long enough, they'll eventually find the perfect show. It's like that with dating apps. Exact same phenomenon. People are worried they'll choose wrong, so they don't choose at all."

"It's a waste of time."

"Maybe not for everyone. I'm sure some people find love on those apps," she says. "Just because they're not for us doesn't mean they're not for other people."

"You're not on them either?"

Her full lips press together, and she takes a deep breath like she's about to delve into some long-winded story.

Then she stops herself.

"You have someone back home?" I ask. I shouldn't have assumed she's single. She's been nothing but cordial and ladylike all evening, though I imagine if she had a man, she wouldn't have been dancing on me like she was earlier.

Briar shakes her head. "Newly single."

I swallow a mouthful of beer and then utter the words "His loss" before I can stop myself.

She sits straighter, head cocked and eyes almost squinting, as if she's questioning if she heard me right.

"Who broke up with whom?" I ask.

"I broke up with him," she says, adding, "after I found out he was sleeping with my best friend."

"Let me guess . . . you met him on a dating app?"

Her lips crack into a half smile. "Wish I could say I didn't."

"The thing about cheaters," I say, "is that, deep down, they know they're not worthy of the person they're with, so they self-sabotage. That, and they're too chickenshit to end a relationship. They're cowards with extremely low self-esteem."

"Is that true, or are you just trying to make me feel better?"

"Both." I take another drink, scan the room, and check the score. But the heaviness of her gaze is sending a flush beneath my skin, like the room is ten degrees hotter than it was a minute ago. "But something tells me you don't need me to do that—to make you feel better."

"You're not wrong." Glancing at the game, she winces. "Ugh, why the hell did they put Devers on first? Who's coaching this game?"

There's something about a girl in a sparkly dress in a sports bar getting angry about a losing team that's sexy as hell—and I'm here for it.

She tosses back the rest of her martini in one angry, impressive gulp.

"They're going to blow this game if they don't put him back on third," she says, throwing her hands in the air. "That's where he belongs, for crying out loud."

"The game's already blown."

She shoots me a look. "It's only the bottom of the fourth. What are you talking about?"

"It was blown the second the Yanks stepped foot in front of the Green Monster."

She leans over to swat my arm. "Whatever. Talk to me five innings from now."

Briar moves to her water next.

"Thanks for not making us toast with that this time," I say. "Not about to walk two miles back to the hotel, only for you to make us get back on that godforsaken party bus all over again."

"Just for that . . ." She mimes like she's going to clink her glass against mine, but I scoot mine away.

"Speaking of the party bus . . ." I rise from the table and walk toward the wall of windows, scanning the parking lot across the street for that neon monstrosity—which is no longer there. Returning, I drag my hand along my jaw. "Hate to tell you this, but I think they left us."

"Shut up." Popping up, she darts off to see for herself, going so far as to step outside and peer up and down both ends of the street. She returns with her mouth agape and her flip-flops scuffing the floor with each slow, staggered shuffle she takes. "What the hell? We've only been here fifteen, twenty minutes. They left already?"

I'm guessing the place next door was too crowded for them to enjoy it.

That, or they got their two-for-one shots and went on their way, too blitzed to realize we weren't with them—again.

"At least I have my bag this time." She holds up a small silver pouch just as glittery as her dress. "Not that my phone works here, but at least I have my room key." Pulling out her iPhone, she fires off a text. "This probably won't go through, but I'm sending it anyway, just in case."

"Please tell me you're not telling them to turn the party bus around." I finish the last of my beer, wondering if I should order another. If it were just Briar and I the rest of the night, said night would feel young. The prospect of continuing this barhopping escapade makes me feel like I'm ninety-two and it's past my bedtime.

"I'm letting her know we got separated again." She places her phone down and folds her hands, releasing a sigh. "I just feel bad."

"*They* didn't notice *we* weren't with them, and *you* feel bad?" I cock my head. "Should be the other way around."

"We're the ones who left the bar. We technically ditched them."

"What choice did we have? The air was thin, and it smelled like something died in there. Plus they were blasting techno like it was 1997. There aren't enough two-for-one tequila shots in the world to make that remotely enjoyable."

She rolls her eyes. "You must be really fun at parties."

"I'm not. At all. Actually. It's never been my scene."

"So what *is* your scene?"

Our server comes by, pointing at our empty drinks.

The two of us exchange looks.

And then we order another round.

The night, as it turns out, is still young.

"I don't have a scene," I tell her when our server leaves. "I'm more of a quiet-night-in kind of guy. Give me some Macallan 18, my vinyl collection, and a good cigar, and I'm golden. Maybe a handful of close friends if I'm feeling social. Otherwise, I prefer my own company."

Resting her chin against the top of her hand, she juts her lower lip out.

"I've never heard anyone admit that before," she says.

"Is that a good thing or a bad thing?"

"It's the best thing." Briar sits straighter. "Do you know how many people lack that self-awareness? How many people our age are still trying to figure out who they are? And you already know. And you're not afraid to say exactly who you are. There should be more people like you."

"If you're impressed with that, wait until I tell you that I've never had a social media account in my life." Of course, I used to run the band's socials, but I was only on their accounts long enough to post tour updates and a handful of behind-the-scenes pictures. After that, I couldn't log off fast enough. These days, we have an intern to handle that—thank God.

"No way."

"Way." I give her a wink. "It's never been something that makes sense to me. All these people posting these cringey statuses and pictures, trying desperately to look like they're having the time of their life. It's one big circle jerk of everyone pretending to be happier than they really are. That, or it's people fighting with each other over stupid shit instead of spending time on things that matter. I'm convinced it's going to lead to the demise of our society—if it hasn't already."

"You sure know a lot about what goes on on those apps for someone who's never had one . . ."

"There are documentaries on this topic. News articles. You know, *actual* media," I say. "Plus I have friends who use those, so I get a bird's-eye view of that stupid shit."

"You're like a grumpy philosopher. A modern Nietzsche. Okay, wait. No. You're a grumpy-*ish* modern philosopher." She flashes a megawatt smile, the kind that belongs to a woman who has no idea how damn gorgeous she is. "I feel like you're starting to shed that bad mood you had earlier."

Our server delivers round two just as we're heading into the fifth inning. The Red Sox are closing in on the Yanks, but even if they steal this win, the night won't be a complete bust because I'm enjoying myself more than I thought I would.

And it's all because of her.

CHAPTER EIGHT

DORIAN

Present Day

"Good morning, Briar," my father says from behind his newspaper at breakfast the next morning. He folds it closed and rests it beside his steaming black coffee, a glass of water, and a small mountain of pills. "I trust you slept well?"

"Like a dream," she says with a breathless smile. Stealing a glance her way, I can't help but notice how bright eyed and bushy tailed she's looking this morning. Before I can fight it, an image of my brother railing her from behind floods my thoughts, her lush lips forming an O shape, his fist tangled in her sandy-blonde hair.

Bile rises up the back of my throat.

"And where's my son? He sent you down here all by yourself?" my father asks.

Briar presses her full pink lips flat before saying "He isn't feeling well."

Dad's brows knit. "What's the matter?"

"I . . . I'm not sure. I think he ate something last night that didn't agree with him," she answers, choosing her words carefully. "He was up all night, poor thing. I told him I'd bring him some food."

For someone who supposedly doesn't believe in marriage, she's stepping into the dutiful-wife role like it's a second skin, which invites the question: Was she acting last year? Or is she acting now?

Which version is the real Briar?

And why the hell do I care so damn much?

"Here you are, Dorian." One of the kitchen staff places before me a generous platter of scrambled eggs, buttered toast, crispy bacon, and an assortment of local jams. I wish I knew her name since she knows mine, but she appears to be new since last summer. "Enjoy."

The intrusive mental image of Briar and Burke from a second ago combines with the savory breakfast smells wafting off my plate, nauseating me, but I swallow it down with a mouthful of orange juice.

I don't usually eat breakfast. Most of the time, I'm on the road with the band, and I'm lucky to be up before noon, but given that my father's days are numbered, I set my alarm for this morning and made sure I was the first one down—ensuring I'd beat Burke the Kiss Ass and Nicola the Darling Daughter.

I've never been the favorite child, and I don't need to be.

But this isn't about that.

It's about proving a point to my siblings—that I'm here because I want to be and not because I'm worried he's going to write me out of his will.

That's already been done.

My father made it crystal clear years ago that none of us would inherit a single red cent if we weren't married or engaged to be married at the time of his passing. His ridiculous decree was the same one his father inflicted on him and the same one his grandfather inflicted on his son as well.

I'm positive he'd have broken that chain if it weren't for the loss of my mother.

It changed him and not for the better.

He's adamant that no one should go through life alone, that "all the money in the world can't buy you a true companion with whom to weather life's hardships."

His dying wish is to ensure that each of his children is loved and that they have someone to comfort them as they transition into their next phase of life as adult orphans. At least that's what he says. I suspect there's another angle to it—in his old-fashioned mind, all married couples should have children, and he wants as many grandchildren as possible to carry on the Rothwell legacy.

Dangling dollar bills might work for Burke, who has made an entire career of investing other people's money and who'd do just about anything to grow his own coffers.

It also might work on Nicola, who married into money and spends her time helicopter parenting her twins because she has no genuine identity or real hobbies in life. While I don't believe she married Dashiell because of my father's stipulation, I'm certain the stipulation is what's keeping them together.

Mark my words: the day Nicola receives her cut of the Rothwell estate is the day she files for divorce from Dash's fake-marathon-training, Proust-quoting, pretentious ass.

"Ugh, sorry we're late," Nicola says when she and her brood shuffle into the breakfast room. "I'll spare you the details of Dashiell's iPhone-alarm debacle. I thought those things were supposed to improve with each new model, not get glitchier."

"Human error." Dash lifts his palms, forever the apologist when she's around. I doubt he'll miss this someday. "Forgive me. It'll never happen again."

The kids settle into their spots at the end of the table. Why my sister insists that they eat separately from us is beyond me, but I don't have the energy to give a damn about her weird parenting rules because I slept like shit last night, and it's taking every ounce of strength I have just to keep my eyelids open at this point.

I'd only been in my room for a few minutes when I realized I was staying next to Burke and Briar. Their muffled voices coming through the wall were enough to make me spring out of my bed like the mattress was on fire. I relocated to the last guest room at the end of the hall, though despite the change in proximity, I couldn't stop thinking about what those two were doing behind their closed door.

In fact, I thought about it all night long.

"What's on the docket for today?" my father asks, slicing into his fried egg. The yolk oozes onto his white plate, stopping when it reaches a triangle of buttered toast. This man has eaten the same thing for breakfast for decades. How he hasn't grown tired of it is beyond any of us. "A little fishing? A little hiking? Horseback riding? What sounds like a good time?"

My father can barely make it to the caretaker's cottage without stopping for multiple breaks to catch his breath or rest his knees, but I applaud his ambition.

"Oh, we're doing group activities?" Nicola asks. It's a valid question. Normally when we summer here, we come together for meals and conversation, then go our separate ways the rest of the time.

We're together—but also apart.

Exactly the way we like it.

Dad chuffs as if Nicola should have read his mind. A flash of his old temper lights his eyes before dissipating completely, replaced with a calm and relaxed smile.

"I think we should," he says to her. "Don't you?"

My father is allergic to two things and two things only: cats and any talk of death or dying.

This is our *last* summer together.

But we can't talk about that . . .

We can allude to it.

We can imply it.

But we don't dare breathe a word of it.

"Briar, what sounds like fun to you today?" my father asks the newest soon-to-be member of our family.

Her brows rise as she's midbite, like he caught her off guard.

"I'm up for anything," she answers after she swallows. "Was hoping to catch some sun today. Burke said the water might be warmer this afternoon."

"Perfect weather for a beach day—or the pool, if that's more your speed," Dad says with an amused twinkle in his gray eyes as if he finds everything that comes out of Briar's mouth endearing. "Calling for a high in the upper eighties and not a cloud in the sky, so plenty of sunshine. Hope you brought your sunscreen. Nothing worse than starting off the summer with a sunburn."

My father's efforts to make Briar the guest of honor are nothing more than a desperate attempt to ensure that she feels like one of us, that she's making the right choice by marrying into our family, and more importantly, that she remembers him with fondness when he's gone.

He was the same way with Audrina, but as we all learned, no amount of hospitality, generosity, or kindness can force someone to stick around.

When she's finished eating, Briar says, "If you'll excuse me, I'm going to grab a tray for Burke and take it upstairs."

"No need, dear. Let Yvette take care of that." My father wags his finger. "That's what she's here for—to make all of our lives easier."

"I don't mind," Briar says, getting up before he has a chance to shoot her down again. "I'm headed that way anyway."

Before anyone can say another word, she carries her dirty dishes to the kitchen.

I don't know if she's the breath of fresh air this family needs, but I do know one thing: she's going to make a terrible Rothwell.

Dashiell wasn't wrong last night when he said she wasn't one of us.

Once upon a time, it was the best thing about her.

Turns out, she's nothing but a liar with dollar signs where her eyes should be.

Maybe she'll fit in after all.

CHAPTER NINE

BRIAR

One Year Ago

"What about you? Are you on any socials?" Dorian asks as we start our second round of drinks at this hole-in-the-wall American sports bar.

Given how late it is, they've got to be playing this game from a recording. That, or it was delayed. To quell my anxiety, I'm tempted to google the final score—until I remember my phone is a useless brick at the moment.

"Uh, yeah," I say. "Unfortunately. I'm not as active as I used to be, but I still have all of my accounts. I can't bring myself to delete them yet."

"What's stopping you?"

"It's fun to look back sometimes."

Dorian makes a face. "Spending time in the past is the biggest waste."

"You have an unhealthy obsession with time, you know that?" I reach for my martini before remembering I already finished it. "I bet quality time is your love language. Then again, you probably don't even know what your love language is since you've never been in love . . . supposedly."

"It's not *supposedly* when it's a fact."

"Guess I'll have to take your word for it, then."

"As you should." He anchors his turquoise gaze on mine, and I'm powerless to look away.

"I hope you get to experience it someday." I break his hold on me and check the score. "It's not that bad. When it's real, I mean. It's actually pretty magical."

"As magical as a Cohiba Behike and some Coltrane on a Friday night?" He flattens his lips in staunch disagreement with my statement. "I doubt it."

"What's a co . . . hi . . . ba . . ."

"The most magical Cuban cigar money can buy."

The Yankees score another point, and a handful of guys at a nearby table erupt into cheers and celebratory backslapping. One even runs around the room fist-bumping strangers while his buddies look on and laugh.

It's a good night to be a Yankee.

Dorian shoots me a look, shrugs, and offers a smirking "Sorry."

Smart-ass.

"We can still do this," I say, though I'm not sure if I'm talking to myself, Dorian, or the baseball gods. "They put Devers on third, where he belongs, so we're back in the game."

"The coach must have heard you from all the way down here."

Usually when I'm watching the Sox, I tend to get vocal and animated. It brings out something in me that doesn't always live on the surface. He's lucky I'm reining it in tonight because it's taking all the strength I have to sit here and not yell a string of profanities at my favorite team in the world.

The Yankees get another runner home.

I shield my eyes and take a deep breath.

I can't watch this.

"Okay, not going to lie," Dorian says. "But you getting stressed out is making me stressed out. You need something stronger?"

He points to my martini.

Another drink is the last thing I need, and yet, it just may be the one thing that's going to calm my frazzled nerves for the foreseeable future.

Without a word, he flags down our server and orders two shots of mango vodka.

"Why mango?" I ask when she leaves.

His brows furrow. "Why *not* mango?"

"It's just random."

"Vodka's the easiest shot to shoot, and mango is the least disgusting of all the flavored vodkas. Everyone knows that."

"Huh. Just like everyone knows it's bad luck to toast with water."

"Exactly."

The server returns with our mango-vodka shots.

"Now is probably a terrible time to tell you that I hate vodka," I say. I won't go into detail with him, but it involves an ill-fated Friday night in college and a bottle of Hawkeye vodka, and to this day, I can't stomach the idea of doing vodka shots without the burn of bile inching up the back of my throat.

"Why didn't you say something before?"

I toss my hands up. "I don't know, I was too distracted by the fact that this broody, sexy guy is ordering mango freaking vodka to think about the fact that I hate vodka."

His eyes flicker and squint, and I realize I just said the quiet part out loud . . .

"You think I'm sexy?" he asks, one brow raised.

"Doesn't everyone?" I attempt to play off my admission. "I'd have to be blind not to notice. And you're too self-aware to not know."

He brushes his messy chocolate hair from his forehead and offers the cockiest grin I've ever seen, one dazzlingly white and flanked by dimples.

It lights his entire face.

Hell, it lights the whole room.

"Thanks . . . I think." He flags down our server again. When she returns, he points to me. "What shot would you like this time?"

"I don't need a shot," I tell him, nodding to the screen. "The Yankees just had their third out, and we're at the top of our batting lineup. It's going to be a good inning."

"Do you like rum?" He ignores my baseball hype.

"I'm good. I don't want anything."

"Liquid cocaine, please," he tells her. "Double."

"Liquid cocaine? Are we in college?"

"You were taking too long to tell me what you wanted, and it was the first shot that came to mind that doesn't have vodka."

Placing my hand over my heart, I gift him an apologetic grimace. "Oh, no. Was I wasting your time again?"

Arroyo hits the first pitch and makes it to first.

"All right." I rub my hands together. Devers is next and then Yoshida. We should have bases loaded soon enough.

I still can't believe I told him he's sexy . . .

It just rolled off my tongue as if it were any other thing, like I was talking about the weather or stating a fact such as the sky is blue.

Our server drops off my double liquid cocaine just in time for Devers to strike out.

"No!" I yell.

Screw it.

I toss the shooter back and slam the shot glass on the table, wiping my mouth with the back of my hand when I'm done.

Dorian watches, almost in awe.

That, or he's disgusted by me.

Hard to tell with him.

Liquescent heat glides through me from head to toe, though I can't be certain if it's stemming from the alcohol or the intense way he's staring.

"Feel better?" he asks.

"I will soon." I nudge the two shots of mango vodka closer to him. "Your turn."

Dorian tosses back both shots without so much as a wince.

I push his water closer to him.

"You're serious about that beach day, aren't you?" he asks before taking a sip.

"As a heart attack." I reach for my glass. "I don't think you understand how much I love beaches."

"Clearly, I don't."

"I grew up in Nebraska. We didn't have beaches—we had lakes and ponds with this thick brown clay for sand. And leeches. So many leeches. Anytime my mom would take me to Florida to visit my grandparents, I would basically live on the beach the entire time. Building sandcastles. Finding seashells. Getting tan. That teal water and soft white sand was heaven on earth. Now that I'm older, I associate beaches with a simpler time in my life."

"I see."

"Where'd you grow up?"

"New York, mostly."

Two couples at the table across from us are all nose deep in their phones. One takes a picture of their drinks before nudging her partner to take a selfie with her. The flash lights up the entire bar, sending a painful zing to my eyes. After that, she insists on taking another selfie with the other woman before politely pleading with a nearby stranger to take a group photo.

As soon as the photo shoot is over, all four of them are back on their phones.

"How do they have service and we don't?" I ask. "I even added an international plan before I left."

"How much do you want to bet they're not going to remember anything from this trip," he says. "All they'll have are some shitty selfies."

"I hate how right you are." I watch the foursome for another few beats, waiting and hoping that he's wrong. "I used to be just like that."

"What, taking a million selfies and drink pics everywhere you go?"

"No," I say. "Romanticizing my life online. It's sad when I think about it. If I look back at my old posts, I don't remember half of those moments as vividly as I should. I was never present."

"If only there were more people like you."

"Ew. A bunch of me's walking around? No thank you," I say.

He bristles. "That's a horrible thing to say about yourself."

"As opposed to thinking I'm the most amazing thing that's ever walked the face of the earth, and everyone should be like me? C'mon," I say. "Plus if everyone was like me, no one would get married, and bachelor-bachelorette parties would cease to exist, and I can't do that to people. I can't take away their party buses and inclusive resorts and penis straws."

Dorian almost chokes on his water. "Fair enough."

I'm word vomiting, which means the two martinis and double shot are kicking in.

I work on finishing my water and try not to think about the fact that I called him sexy a few minutes ago—or the fact that the Red Sox are still losing and it's not looking good.

We're in the bottom of the ninth. Down by three. Two outs.

"You want to get out of here?" he asks.

"You don't want to stick around and watch your team win?"

"Nah," he says, studying me. "I told you—we had that game in the bag the second we stepped out. Anyway, I'm craving a change of scenery. You?"

His words are neutral at surface level. Innocent enough. But the thrill running down my spine as I think about what lies ahead tonight sends me reeling.

"It's not so bad being here, is it?" I ask later when we're meandering down some palm tree–lined sidewalk, passing row after row of late-night hot spots. "Don't you love being a world away from all your problems?"

"Sure. My problems aren't much different from anyone else's, and I tend not to let them take up real estate in my head if I can help it."

"Where are we headed, by the way?" Our arms brush as we walk, and his cologne mixes with the humid night breeze that encircles us. "I feel like we're just walking aimlessly."

"Ever seen the ocean at midnight?"

"No, but that sounds exactly like something you'd be into." I chuckle, elbowing him in the rib as an excuse to touch him once more. "I can picture you under a moonless sky, the ocean roaring in the distance as you enjoy your own company, lost in your thoughts, not another soul in sight . . ."

"Someone's got jokes . . ."

"Am I wrong, though?"

A slow smile slips up the side of his mouth. "Not at all."

CHAPTER TEN

BRIAR

Present Day

"Burke?" I poke my head into our suite after breakfast only to find him passed out, phone in hand. An hour ago, he was awake, rattling off his meal request—which was a little too ambitious given the stomach situation that developed overnight.

When I was thinking we needed to foster a deeper connection last night, I didn't know that would come in the form of Burke getting a horrible gastrointestinal bug at one o'clock in the morning.

Be careful what you wish for . . .

Naturally, Burke didn't want me to help him, but I insisted—it's not like I could sleep with all that going on anyway. I stayed out of the bathroom, of course, but for hours, I refreshed and replaced cool washcloths on his forehead and tiptoed downstairs for ginger ale and crackers.

"Burke?" I whisper again. Maybe I should let him sleep, but he can't have been out for that long because his phone screen is still lit with a selfie of Audrina and himself in happier times. His arm is around her. They're both grinning, their teeth blindingly white and their skin bronzed by the sun. There's some white villa with a blue roof behind them and the ocean in the distance.

If only Audrina were here to see the state he's in . . .

Then again, maybe he isn't heartbroken.

Maybe he's simply feeling sorry for himself.

It sucks being sick *and* rejected.

I place the breakfast tray on his nightstand and remove the phone from his loose grasp to keep it from getting lost in the covers, only as soon as I do, his fingers curl around nothingness, and he stirs awake.

"I put it back on the charger for you," I say, knowing exactly what he's feeling around for. "Brought you something to eat. How's your stomach?"

Clearing his throat, Burke sits up and rakes his hand through his messy hair.

"I know you wanted sausage and eggs, but the chef thought you should stick to toast, bananas, applesauce, Jell-O . . . you know, bland food," I say. "He assured, though, that this bread was made at four o'clock this morning, so it's fresh and tasty, even without butter. And the banana's perfect—not too green, not too ripe."

I situate his pillows behind his back as he sits up; then I place the food tray over his lap.

"What the hell did I eat last night?" he asks.

"We all ate the same thing, and you're the only one who got sick. Must be a bug. Hopefully, you'll be as good as new this time tomorrow."

I take a seat on my side of the bed as he picks around at his food. I'll admit, it's not half as appetizing as the feast the rest of us enjoyed, but it looks a hell of a lot better than most hospital food.

"What was she like?" I ask before tacking on, "Audrina, I mean. Couldn't help but notice you had a photo pulled up on your phone."

He chews a bite of dry toast, staring straight ahead.

Hard to tell if he's ignoring me or contemplating his answer. "I've only ever seen pictures of her on social media," I add. "And you know how that is . . . curated and everything . . ."

There's another pause or hesitation, or maybe he's still ignoring me. The silence only makes me want to word vomit even more, but I bite my tongue to keep from getting ahead of myself.

"She's not what people think she is," he finally answers after washing his bite down with a sip of plain hot tea. "It's an act. The clothes, the voice, the whole aesthetic. It's like an alter ego. It's all fun and games to her. The real Audrina is deeper than that. Smart as hell. Funny too. Doesn't take herself too seriously. Adventurous."

This is the most I've ever heard Burke talk about anything or anyone, and I'm at a profound loss for words.

"A lot of people don't know this—and they wouldn't because she doesn't advertise it—but she's extremely philanthropic." He pushes his sliced bananas around with a fork. "Probably dedicates more time to charities than social media. That should tell you everything you need to know about her."

"Why doesn't she share that with the world?" I ask. "In a world where everyone wants to cancel everyone for every little thing, why not share the good stuff?"

"It doesn't work that way. Not in her world," he says. "The thing is . . . upper echelons of society . . . most people use charitable foundations as tax shelters. It's sort of complicated, but most of the time when you see some public figure doing PR for some charity, it's because they're getting something out of it, like a salary or publicity for themselves, for instance. When I see someone like her—someone from a well-known, well-to-do family—championing some random cause, I know the real reason. They're not donating their time and face to any old clean-water foundation because the issue keeps them up at night."

He's speaking a language I've never spoken before, and yet, it all makes perfect sense.

"Anyway, Audrina didn't want to seem like another one of those people," he continues, "so she kept her charity work private, off of her social media. And she didn't rely on donations to fund her causes. She funded everything herself, with her own money."

"It's too bad the rest of the world doesn't know that side of her," I say. I've seen online parodies and memes of Audrina in the past, and most people tend to put her alongside people like Paris Hilton, Anna Delvey, or whatever socialite or socialite wannabe is trending at the moment.

He squeezes a slice of lemon into his tea.

"I didn't deserve her," he says.

"What happened?" I know better than to pry, but the pain in his tone tells me he's not done unloading.

"I, uh," he begins to say before exhaling. "I almost cheated on her. Got caught. Don't know what I was thinking—actually, I wasn't thinking. I'd been planning the proposal for months, and in the weeks leading up to it, something came over me. Cold feet maybe. I don't know. I downloaded this dating app. I didn't swipe or message or make plans to meet anyone, but I did browse. Somehow, she found it on my phone but didn't tell me. She did, however, tell her best friend—the one who'd been helping me plan the proposal."

"I thought she ran off with some actor."

"That's the story she gave the public. She wanted to control the narrative. Her meeting someone better makes *her* look better. No one wants to be the one who got cheated on."

"So it's better to look like the one who did the cheating?" I lift a brow. It's not that either option is appealing, but damn.

"I'm guessing her PR firm suggested the strategy. They planted blind items all over the gossip sites about her leveling up, though from what I hear, it's a stunt on the actor's end too. He's headlining some new show on Broadway, and they're riding each other's coattails. I don't even think he's straight. It's a whole thing."

It sounds unnecessarily complicated, but I can't relate.

"Have you reached out to her at all? Since she left?" I ask.

He shakes his head. "What would I say? What can I say that I haven't already said? She's not going to suddenly change her mind because I'm apologizing for the millionth time."

"You never know."

I won't tell Burke this, but shitty circumstances aside, this is hands down the best conversation we've had to date. I'm enjoying seeing this broken-down, authentic side of him. I only hope there's more where this came from because something tells me his bark is worse than his bite.

"Think we're all heading to the beach in a little bit," I say when I climb off the bed. "Wish you could join us."

He picks up a triangle of toast before dropping it back on his plate. "Yeah, me too."

Grabbing my tote, I throw in a bottle of sunscreen, a hat, and a book before heading to the bathroom to change into my bathing suit. It's a splashy neon-yellow number with an open back and cutouts on the sides. I found it on clearance online and picked it up because everything else I had was either too revealing or too matronly.

Ten minutes later, I meet the rest of the family in the foyer: Nicola and Dashiell with their matching straw visors and his-and-hers marine-striped bathing suits, the children already slathered in thick white sunscreen, and Redmond in a floral button-down shirt, leather sandals, Wayfarer sunglasses, and navy swim trunks . . .

And then there's Dorian.

Shirtless.

Skin damp with coconut-scented tanning oil.

Hair messy and shoved back with a pair of smudged aviators on top of his head.

Sun-faded fluorescent-yellow board shorts so low on his hips that the thoughts running through my head make me blush.

He looks like he doesn't give a damn what anyone thinks of him—much like the night we met—and I'd be lying if I said it didn't stir something up in the depths of my soul.

"What?" Dorian asks when he realizes we're all staring at him, though I suspect we each have differing reasons.

"Really?" Nicola sniffs as she looks him up and down. Who knows what she's huffing about—it could be anything at this rate. "I thought your luggage finally arrived."

"It did." Dorian slides his sunglasses over his nose, giving her a devil-may-care sniff.

"Can we go now, please, Mommy?" Augustine asks, tugging her mother's hand.

"Yes, my littlest love," Redmond answers for his daughter, gesturing to the front door with his cane. "Our chariot awaits."

We file out, one by one, Dorian walking so close behind me that his suntan lotion scent invades my lungs. It's as if a part of him is touching me, but at the same time, we're a world apart.

There's an awareness on my back, heavy and electric.

I convince myself I'm imagining it.

Outside, a golf cart with six seats idles in the circular drive.

Redmond slides into the driver's seat, and the children squeeze in next to him. Nicola and Dashiell take the center row, leaving the back for Dorian and me.

The drive to the beach is rough once we get to the grassy path, jostling me against my seatmate with every bump. With a death grip on the skinny metal rail beside me, I clutch my tote bag between my knees and ignore the fact that every time my arm brushes against Dorian's I forget to breathe.

Still, we both pretend not to notice.

It isn't until we've arrived at the pristine stretch of private beach—one that serves to remind me of the unforgettable first night we shared—that Dorian finally speaks to me.

"I hope the irony of this isn't lost on you," he says when everyone else is out of earshot.

Before I can reply, he stalks off, his towel flung over his left shoulder.

So many things I'd say . . . if only I could.

CHAPTER ELEVEN

DORIAN

One Year Ago

"What are you thinking about?" Briar sweeps her palm along the sugar-soft sand beneath us and releases a dreamy sigh.

Growing up, I used to hate that question.

It felt intrusive.

My thoughts are private, like a locked diary containing every opinion, secret confession, deepest fear, and biggest regret that's ever passed through my mind.

But for some reason, I'm not annoyed by it tonight.

"All the glitter," I say.

"What?" Briar laughs, confused.

"Your dress for one." I point to the sparkly blue number that hasn't stopped hugging her curves since she walked onto the party bus earlier tonight. "Your purse." I motion toward her little bag next. "The sky." I point up to the twinkling blanket of stars above us. What I don't point out, however, is the glimmer that's resided in her eyes the past couple of hours. I don't want to assume it's for me, nor do I want to sound like some pathetic sap rattling off corny lines in an attempt to get laid.

"I never wear glittery things back home," she says. "In New York, I mean."

"What do you wear?"

"A lot of black. Jeans and sweaters on the weekends. I'm a simple girl at heart."

The ocean laps against the shore, inching closer to us before retreating. This stretch of beach is owned by the resort, and other than a uniformed man raking the sand a few minutes ago, we're the only ones here.

"Glitter suits you," I say.

"How so?" She tilts her head, studying me.

"I can't really explain it," I tell her. And it's the truth. Sort of. I can't explain it without sounding like some philosophical weirdo, and in case this is our last night together, I don't want to leave off on that note.

But she sparkles—truly sparkles.

Inside, outside, and all around.

She's not like anyone else I've ever met . . . in all the best ways.

"Why do you think people really want to get married?" she asks, changing the subject. "Sometimes I wonder if they're just afraid to be alone, you know? And then I think about all these people making these drastic, life-altering decisions from a place of fear instead of love. Obviously, not everyone's scared or whatever. Maybe the ones who married for the wrong reasons are the ones who don't make it. And the ones who married out of pure love are the ones who stand the test of time."

"People get married because they're in love with the fantasy of marriage. The illusion of the happily-ever-after fairy tale we've all been sold since the beginning of time." I dust some sand off my pants. "Why does anyone do anything? Because they want the fantasy of what that thing represents. Why did you move from Nebraska to New York? Was it the fantasy of a glamorous life in one of the most famous cities in the world?

The promise of success? The excitement of a fast-paced life? Somewhere along the line, someone sold you on the fantasy of life in the Big Apple, and you bought it. It's not that much different than marriage, in a way. You just committed to a city instead of a person."

"Wow. You went . . . extra deep with that," she says. Running her fingertips along her collarbone, she says, "I think . . . I think you're not wrong."

"Look, it's not a bad thing. It just is what it is."

"I hate that phrase . . . 'It is what it is.'" She releases a puff of air through her lips. "It's depressing. It insinuates we can't change a situation, so we have to accept it, but a person can change almost every situation—or their attitude surrounding said situation. So in that sense, nothing has to stay being what it is."

"Now you're going deep. I love it."

"You know what else bothers me about marriage?" She sits straighter. "The whole taking-the-man's-last-name part. Granted, I know it's not a requirement anymore, but most people still do it in the name of tradition or romance, completely ignoring the fact that the reason that started thousands of years ago is because women and wives were considered property. Giving them a man's last name showed who they belonged to. I know it was a different time period, and that's not what it means now, but still, I can't get over that. Me, personally? I want someone's heart. Their devotion. Their loyalty. Their love. I don't need their last name."

"Couldn't agree more," I say.

"There aren't a lot of people I can have these kinds of talks with." Her eyes hold mine in the dark. "Okay, that's not completely true. My friends and I can get pretty deep sometimes, but guys . . . men . . . at least the ones I've been around . . . they only want to talk about surface-level things. Anything beyond that and they start squirming and changing the subject."

"You've clearly been around the wrong kinds of men."

"You're telling me." She brushes her shoulder against mine, and a tingling sensation ripples throughout my entire body.

"For the love of God, you have to stay off those dating apps. The guys who'll wax poetic about reality don't waste their time on those."

"So where can I find them?" she asks, her dark lashes softly fluttering as she drinks me in. I'm still buzzing from those mango-vodka shots earlier, and judging by the slower cadence of her voice, she's buzzing too. "If I wanted to find a guy like you in New York, where would I look?"

"A guy *like* me? Why would you want a knockoff when the real thing is right in front of you?" I wink and offer half a smile.

"You don't seem like you're looking for anything right now." She runs her teeth along her bottom lip before directing her attention to the placid ocean waves. There's a hint of bittersweetness in her tone that wasn't there a moment ago.

She's not wrong.

I live on the road with the band.

I'd make a horrible boyfriend, and she deserves better than that.

"I wish I was," I tell her. "I'm not really in a place—"

She shushes me, her finger pressed against my lips. "You don't have to explain. I don't need a speech. It's okay."

Still, I want to tell her that if things were different, if I was spending more time in Manhattan than on the road with the band, then I'd love nothing more than to take her on a proper date and get to know her better.

"Tell me about the girl you sort of loved," she says. "Paint me a picture. What was she like? Why didn't you love her? Why was it only love-ish?"

"I was a shitty boyfriend." It's the first time I've said those words out loud. Drawing in a long breath, I add, "The band was starting to take off, and I was spending ninety-nine percent of my time dealing with that. She got scraps of me. I think I could have loved her, but she didn't want to wait around for that to happen. She told me I was married to my work and she was tired of feeling like the other woman."

"Fair."

"Yeah, she wasn't wrong. And it would've been fine—the breakup and all—but she started seeing someone close to me," I say. "Almost immediately."

"That's shitty," she says. "On both of their parts."

"Yeah."

"How long were you together?" she asks.

"A few years, give or take."

Her mouth forms a circle. "You were with her that long, and you didn't love her? What were you waiting for?"

"Couldn't tell you."

"Do you still think about her?"

"I try not to."

"But you do?" she asks.

"Well, yeah. Not because I want to. Sometimes, a song will come on that reminds me of something she said or some random moment we shared. Other times, I might come across an old picture or one of her T-shirts shoved in a drawer somewhere."

"Does it make you sad?"

"It's a first world problem," I say. "I try not to get down about shit like that. It's not like we were soulmates or something. What about your ex? The one who cheated? You still think about him?"

Briar rolls her eyes. "Every day. And I hate it. Not hate-ish it. But I *hate* hate it. If I could scrub him from my memory, I'd do it in a heartbeat."

"It's tough. Just takes some time. Pretty soon a day will go by, and you'll realize you didn't think about him once. Then that day will turn into two days, then three, then a week, and a month, and before long, he's just someone you used to know a lifetime ago."

"Yeah, you're right."

"Does it bother you seeing everyone so happy here?" I ask. I couldn't help but notice half the people on this trip are coupled up.

"Not at all," she says. "I love it actually. I'm happy for them."

In another world . . .

Under different circumstances . . .

She could be mine.

And she should be.

I've known her all of five hours, but I don't need to spend another minute with her to know she's perfect for me. Everything she believes, everything she stands for . . . it's everything I never knew I could want in a person, and now it's sitting right in front of me, literally within arm's reach.

But it might as well be light-years away.

Quietude settles between us, save for the rolling waves several yards ahead. The warm breeze blows a strand of her hair across her face, and she sweeps it away before closing her eyes and drawing in a long, slow breath like she's trying to capture this moment in her memory.

The slow rise and fall of her chest, the breathy sigh that leaves her parted lips when she exhales, and the burning awareness traveling through me are all but screaming for me to do what I've been wanting to do since the moment I saw her.

Leaning in, I cup her face in my hand, tracing my thumb along her lower lip. Her eyes flutter open, but she doesn't jerk away or act surprised by any of this. Instead, her mouth curls into a sly smile—one that I accept as an open invitation.

Pressing my lips against hers, I kiss her the way a sailor kisses his girl before shipping out. I kiss her the way Connor kisses his pregnant fiancée before he steps on the tour bus. I kiss her the way a man kisses a woman he has no business kissing—with greed, abandon, and blind faith that someday she'll be his.

Our tongues collide, and I take her bottom lip between my teeth before crashing against her all over again.

My fingers tangle in her hair as I steer her mouth back to mine again while time stands still and goes too fast at the same time.

If we could pause this moment, if we could make the rest of the world stop for just a few more hours, I'd be the happiest man on this entire island.

My cock strains against the inside of my pants, swelling with every second that passes.

It isn't until we come up for air that she finally speaks.

"I've been wondering all night," she says with swollen lips as she cups my face with her satin-soft palm, "if you were going to kiss me."

I pull her into my lap, resting my hands on her hips.

Our eyes lock, having a conversation all their own.

"Just promise me something," she says. "Whatever happens next, whatever comes after this, don't say anything you don't mean, okay?"

"I would never."

CHAPTER TWELVE

DORIAN

Present Day

"Your back is burning," I say to Briar.

We've been at the beach for three hours now, and I've managed to do everything I can to avoid looking at her. After going for a swim, I lay on a lounger with my headphones in and my sunglasses over my eyes: my best attempt at blocking out the world around me. But somewhere along the line, between stolen glances and practicing my best poker face, I couldn't help but notice how red she was getting.

I can be an asshole, but I'm not a monster.

She sucks in a startled breath, contorting her hands around her body to check—as if I *lied* about it.

Need I remind her, I'm not the liar in this equation?

"Shoot." She grimaces as she feels the exposed bits of bright-pink skin surrounding her neon-yellow bathing suit—my favorite color, but that's beside the point. She couldn't have known. Once upon a time, my board shorts were the same color. "I must have missed it with the sunscreen."

A year ago, I was untying that same top, kissing the smile that coiled across her lips as her bare chest pressed against mine. She curled against me as if I was her safe place, and our bodies molded together like two pieces of the same puzzle. We were the only two souls on a vacant beach that felt like it existed just for us.

"Where's that fiancé of yours when you need him?" I'm not sure if she can detect the sarcasm in my voice, but it's there. Burke's the last person to lend a helping hand for anything. I'd bet actual cash that if he were here, he wouldn't give a shit about her sunscreen situation. Hell, he probably wouldn't notice.

Me on the other hand? I'm not even engaged to the woman, and I can't help but notice every little thing about her every time we're remotely sharing the same oxygen.

The way her hair smells faintly of vanilla.

The way she sinks back and sighs with contentedness after she finishes a meal.

The way she always tucks a strand of hair behind her right ear when she's really into something she's talking about.

The way she picks at her nails when she's nervous like she doesn't know she's doing it, or the way she doesn't give a shit that she's ruining her manicure.

The way her eyes glint when she steals a glance my way.

They say the body keeps the score, but I'm hopeful one of these days mine will forget the way hers felt on the inside.

Briar digs into her canvas bag, pulling out a bright-pink bottle of Water Babies SPF 50.

"Water Babies?" I snort. "Really?"

"It's a nostalgia thing. My mom always used it on me growing up, so it makes me think of my childhood and summer days at the city pool."

It's funny—the night we met, we exchanged unpopular opinions, painful truths, and everything in between. For the first time in my thirty years, I felt I was truly connecting with someone . . . and like a pathetic sap, I told her that.

We spent three full days together when it was all said and done, but from the moment we met at that sticky nightclub with the terrible music, I felt like I'd known her my entire life.

I'd never believed in soulmates until she waltzed into my life and left glitter everywhere.

Now she's about to marry my brother, and we're talking about sunscreen and acting like the giant elephant in the room is invisible.

Sliding my sunglasses off the top of my head and onto my nose, I turn to leave.

"So that's it?" she calls from behind me. "You're just going to make fun of my sunscreen and walk away?"

Facing her again, I rest my hands on my hips, my fingertips digging into my flesh.

Of all the things I could say right now, only one of them needs to be said.

"I would've waited for you," I tell her. "And I was. I was waiting for you."

Then I leave.

This time, she doesn't call after me.

CHAPTER THIRTEEN

BRIAR

One Year Ago

It occurs to me as Dorian's hands are in my hair and his mouth is claiming mine and his hardness is pressing against my inner thighs that making out with a hot stranger on a Caribbean beach must be the most cliché yet pivotal moment of my life.

I would never do something like this back home.

Mere hours ago, I knew nothing about this man except that he didn't want to be here, but over the course of the night, I've bared my soul to him in ways I never have with anyone else before. At times, there was so much tension between us I thought I was going to burst, tension that subsided only when I convinced myself I was imagining it.

I told myself that the pull I felt between us was all in my head.

After that, I rationalized that it was the alcohol doing the talking.

And then he kissed me.

And then he kissed me again.

And now my lips are so swollen I can hardly feel them, but stopping now would be painful in every sense of the word.

Dorian's lips trail down the side of my neck, pressing hotly against my flesh, before abandoning it for the next unexplored section. The sugar-soft sand beneath me cradles us while a few yards away the ocean waves lap against the shore.

Tugging on his shirt, I pull it over his head, exposing the smooth landscape of his muscled chest and shoulders.

An electric thrill zips through me, followed by an anticipatory surge between my thighs.

"I want you inside me," I whisper against his ear.

He stops, his eyes finding mine under the moonlit sky.

Without a word, he rises, and I'm about to second-guess myself when he pulls me up by the hand and leads me to a nearby cabana where a double chaise longue has our proverbial names on it. Three of the four canvas sides are down, giving us privacy while maintaining the seaside view ahead.

"This okay?" he asks.

I nod. I've heard sex on the beach isn't all it's cracked up to be, but I'm grateful he didn't say those exact words because the last thing I want to picture right now is Dorian hooking up with anyone else. Not that I'm the jealous type—I just want this moment to be unspoiled by reality . . . much like this night has been so far.

Dorian adjusts the backrest of the chaise before lying down and pulling me into his arms. I straddle him, hiking the hem of my dress above my hips.

He cradles my face, biting his bottom lip before looking like he's two seconds from devouring me from head to toe.

"You're so damn beautiful," he says. "From the second I saw you, I wanted to know everything about you."

"You don't have to say that kind of stuff, you know . . ." I stop myself before I sound even more like a pick-me girl. With my palms against his chest, I lean in to taste his lips all over again.

"I know," he says when he comes up for air. "I just thought you should know."

My heart ricochets, and heat creeps through me. I'm usually the type to take my time, to enjoy all the courses one by one, but all I can think about is how badly I want to feel him in the deepest parts of me.

It's an urgency unlike any I've known before.

Dorian slides the straps of my dress over my shoulders before pressing hot kisses down each of them. When he's finished, he runs his fingertips along my inner thigh, stopping when he gets to my panties. Shoving the fabric aside, he plunges a single finger inside me.

Eyes closed, I let my head sink back as I grind against him, breathing slowly and steadily, thinking every unsexy thought I can think of because he's only getting started, and I'm already close.

A moment later, I gently push his hand away and make a move for his zipper. With his cock filling my palm, I stroke his length before bringing my mouth to his tip. His pre-come is salty on my tongue, and the low growl in his moans tells me to keep going.

"God, you're incredible," he says between breathy groans as he gathers my hair in his fist. "I don't want you to stop . . . but I'm dying to have the rest of you."

He pulls me onto his lap once more, tugging the top of my dress down until my breasts are exposed. The tepid ocean breeze feels cooler than it did a few minutes ago, and he takes each pert nipple between his teeth as his fingers dig into my back.

"You're the sexiest thing I've ever seen," he says.

While part of me doesn't want to believe it—I imagine I'm looking somewhat of a hot mess right now with my dress half off, lips swollen, and sand in my hair—every inch of me believes he means what he says.

"Sexiest or sexy-ish?" I tease.

He stops, sniffing a laugh, and then flips me onto my back.

"Why don't I show you exactly what I mean?" Digging into his pocket, he retrieves a condom from his wallet. He rips the gold foil packet between his teeth and slides the rubber down his shaft.

Positioning himself at my entrance, he teases my clit, taking his sweet time before sliding every inch of himself into every inch of me. His generous girth fills me to the hilt, mixing pleasure with pain until it all dissolves into utter wanton desire.

His lips crash against mine as he drives himself deeper, harder, faster into me.

A few hours ago, I told him love was a magical feeling.

But this, too, feels a lot like that otherworldly sensation that washes over a person when they're in the early stages of falling for someone . . .

I remind myself this is sex, not love.

I tell myself that this is all it is and all it'll ever be.

Assuming anything else could come of this would be playing with fire, and I've been burned too many times to count.

CHAPTER FOURTEEN

BRIAR

Present Day

"Oh my god." I sit up in the bathtub that night when I realize my phone has one bar.

When I got home from the beach earlier, the room was dark, and Burke was passed out again. I wasted no time in peeling out of my swimsuit and running myself a tepid bubble bath (would've been hotter if not for my mild sunburn). Out of habit, I took my phone with me, but when I remembered there was no service out here, I decided to listen to an old podcast I'd previously downloaded while deleting old pictures and screenshots from my photo app—a little digital housekeeping.

Pulling up my messages, I fire off a text to Maeve, letting her know I made it, I'm fine, and there's no service here so not to worry if she can't reach me. All the while, the single bar flickers on and off, the signal indecisive.

I press send, hold my breath, and wait.

Five nail-biting seconds later, it shows as delivered.

I compose another message, deciding to make hay since the proverbial sun is shining.

Remember that guy I met last year in the Dominican Republic? I write. He's BURKE'S BROTHER! Pretty sure he hates me now. Dorian not Burke. I wish I could tell him the truth.

Dorian's words have haunted me all afternoon.
I would've waited for you . . .
It's both the best and the worst thing he could've said.

As he walked away, all I kept thinking about was pulling him aside, telling him everything, and hoping he'd understand. But nothing about that would be rational—or smart. Nor do I imagine it would redeem me in Dorian's eyes. If anything, he'll only despise me further for falling for his brother's lies and inserting my feelings into their family tragedy.

The second message to Maeve doesn't go through; it just sits there with an angry, glaring red exclamation point next to it.

I try two more times, but the single bar of service that was there a few minutes ago is now gone.

Placing my phone on the little wooden step stool by the tub, I squeeze my eyes shut tight and sink under a mountain of soft bubbles that smell like magnolias.

"Oh, shit. I'm sorry. I didn't know you were in here." Burke's voice, distorted through the water, steals me from my moment.

I slide up, my sunburned back burning against the tub, and I cross my hands over my breasts despite the protective layer of bubbles obscuring them.

He has stepped out of view, though the bathroom door remains cracked.

"I've seen you throw up; you've almost seen me naked," I say. "It's like we're almost a real couple."

He laughs.

He must be feeling better.

"It's okay, I'm covered," I say.

He peeks his head in, and from here, I can tell his complexion has a little more color than it did this morning.

"Looking alive again," I tell him.

"How was the beach?"

"Relaxing," I say, leaving out the part about his brother ripping my soul from my chest with his bare hands, but it's neither here nor there. "If my family owned this island, I'd never leave. You'd have to cuff me and haul me out of here."

"Visit in January and tell me you still feel the same."

"Is that an invitation?" I wink.

"Sure," he says, though I know he's playing along.

"Did you need to use the bathroom? I assume it's why you barged in here like a man on a mission . . . I'm almost done."

He waves his hand. "I'll use the one in the hall."

Once he's gone, I think about our Audrina conversation from this morning. Without thinking, I reach for my phone to pull up Instagram. That fickle signal bar flashes before disappearing all over again, but I attempt to pull her account up anyway.

It takes a solid five minutes, but I manage to bring up the first nine photos in her grid. None of them are Burke, of course, but none of them are of her with that actor beau either. Each image portrays a vivacious young woman painting the town, living her best life, and looking happier than ever.

While there's no excuse for what Burke did, ending a three-year relationship over it seems . . . extreme. Was there no conversation? No talk of couples counseling? No second chances? The way Burke speaks of Audrina, she has a reason—a good reason—for almost everything she does, and nothing is the way it seems.

I tap the follow button in the seconds before the signal fades for the dozenth time.

Seeing how happy she's trying to look makes me think she's very much the opposite.

Just a hunch . . .

Half an hour later, I emerge from my lukewarm bath, change into a white sundress for our alfresco dinner, and twist my hair into a messy bun before deciding against it. A vision of Nicola's scrutinizing gaze in my mind's eye prompts me to make it sleek and chic instead.

I slick on a tasteful amount of makeup, dab the smallest amount of gardenia perfume behind my ears, and take a second to admire my sun-kissed complexion before making my way to the hall.

I'm lost in my thoughts, rounding the corner to the top of the stairs, when I come face to face with Dorian.

"Oh, sorry," I say after almost running headfirst into him.

His penetrating gaze is as hard as steel, and his jaw tenses while his lips say nothing—lips that once upon a time made me feel like I was falling and floating at the same time.

He simply brushes past me, his shoulder grazing mine—an ice-cold move I'm willing to bet was intentional.

"There you are." Burke's voice sounds from behind me.

I turn to find him striding my way. Behind him, Nicola emerges from her room, stopping to observe our exchange.

"You're joining us for dinner?" I ask him, placing a light of hope in my eyes since I'm under Nicola's watchful stare, a stare that matches Dorian's fleck for fleck but somehow feels even more steeped in loathing than his.

"I am." He leans in, pressing his lips against mine. His kiss is cold and hard, and all I can think about is how grateful I am that Dorian's not here to see this—not that it would probably make a difference.

"Glad you're feeling better, babe," I say, hating how much I sound like one of *those* people, but since we have an audience, there isn't a choice.

"Seriously, Burke? Whatever you have, please, keep it confined to your bedroom," Nicola interjects, her voice laced with disgust. "And honestly, Briar, you should probably stay with him. I'd hate for you to spread Burke's stomach bug to the rest of us . . . especially our father."

Her delivery may be off but her point isn't.

Funny, though, that this wasn't an issue before the beach excursion.

"You're right," I tell her. Nicola's expression softens as I stroke her ego. "I'll stay with Burke until he's feeling better."

"I'll have Yvette bring dinner trays up for you shortly," she says, chin tilted up as if she's satisfied we're seeing things her way. Placing her hand on the back of Burke's shoulder, Nicola hesitates like she's going to say something, then changes her mind and treks off without so much as a never mind.

"What was that about?" I ask him when she's gone.

"Who the hell knows?"

"I was really looking forward to eating outside tonight." The scent of whatever they're making in the kitchen wafts upstairs, making my mouth water.

"There'll be other opportunities. Trust me."

"What are we going to do now? I feel like we've been banished."

He sniffs, half-annoyed, half-amused, I imagine.

"Seriously, though, what are we going to do? No TV upstairs . . . no internet . . . ," I say. I packed eight books for this trip—one for every week. I finished the first in one day. At this rate, I'll run out of reading material by next week unless there's a library on Driftway he forgot to mention. "And you hate talking, so a robust conversation's off the table."

He crinkles his forehead. "I don't *hate* talking."

"Then you must hate talking to *me* because you never say more than you have to." Unless he's talking about Audrina, but I doubt he wants to spend a lot of time waxing poetic with me about his recent heartbreak. "I'm getting the bare minimum from you. Wasn't going to take it personally before, but since you said you don't hate talking . . ."

He snickers as we climb the stairs, head to our suite/prison, and wait for dinner to be delivered. Once back in the room, I head to the bathroom, strip out of my dress, and pull on some pajamas since we're calling it a night.

When I emerge, I see he's done the same thing.

Grabbing a decorative book off the dresser, I curl up at the foot of the bed and page through pictures upon pictures of lighthouses from all over the world.

"I'm getting the sense that if you've seen one lighthouse, you've probably seen them all." I yawn, despite it being too early to be this tired. Then again, yesterday was a long day; sleep was scant last night thanks to Burke's stomach bug, and I spent all day soaking up the sun. My fatigue is warranted and maybe a blessing in disguise given that we suddenly have all this time on our hands.

"There's an abandoned lighthouse on the other side of the island. Think it was built in the late eighteen hundreds," Burke says. "My great-aunt Tillie had it imported from Holland back in the seventies. She was going to restore it. Died before it could happen. It's basically a time capsule now."

I lift a brow. "I take back everything I said. Can we sneak over there tonight?"

My grandmother's house was a time capsule—everything looking exactly as it did in the fifties when she and my grandfather first built the little midcentury modern split-level home. She still had plastic on the furniture and ashtrays on every tabletop (despite the fact that they both quit smoking in the eighties). Even the appliances were original and in perfect working order.

Years after my grandmother passed, some house flipper bought the place and completely gutted it.

To this day, my mother can't drive down Adelaide Avenue without getting tears in her eyes.

"It's not my kind of place," he says with a wince. "Honestly don't even know how to get there anymore. It's kind of off the beaten path. Dorian used to go there all the time as a kid. He'd hide out and listen to his music, get away from everyone."

Sounds like Dorian.

"Maybe he can take you up there this week," Burke says, volunteering his brother, though I can't imagine Dorian saying yes.

The mere mention of Dorian and me doing anything by ourselves turns my skin electric, but I redirect my thoughts before they get off track.

There's a time and place for daydreams and wishful thinking, and this isn't it.

Plus I'd only be torturing myself.

Dorian thinks I'm the worst kind of liar, and I'm legally prevented from telling him otherwise.

"Knock, knock," Yvette calls from the hall.

Burke lets her in, holding the door open as she and another staffer haul in two loaded trays of food while a third follows with a beverage cart. I'm trying to figure out how he got that up all those stairs when it occurs to me that a place of this magnitude likely has an elevator.

"Where would you like everything?" Yvette asks.

"There is fine." Burke points to the writing desk by the window on the other side of the room. "And you can leave the cart. We'll sort everything out. Thank you."

"The chef prepared some chicken bone broth for you, Burke. There's also a Jell-O cup, white rice, and a banana. Just call down if you need anything else or if you decide you'd rather have what everyone else is having," Yvette says before she and her assistants disappear.

Lifting the cloche on my tray, I'm met with a meal that looks like something out of one of those trendy NYC restaurants with the three-year waiting lists. I don't know what I'm looking at, but it smells fantastic, and I'm going to devour every last bit of it, down to the decorative green drizzle.

"I can't believe you grew up living like this," I tell Burke when we're eating. "You're like that Eloise girl in those books, living in some fancy hotel. Only you own the hotel, and you don't have to share your home with strangers. And it's not a hotel, it's a private freaking island. Insane."

"Your Nebraska is showing," he teases. "You've got to get out more."

"Why do you think I moved to New York after college?"

"Because that's what every midwesterner does when they want to look like they did something significant with their postuniversity life?"

"Okay, first of all . . . *ouch.*" I point my fork at him. "But you're not that far off. It's cliché. But it's also the best thing I've ever done. No regrets."

"Yet."

"Yet," I echo, agreeing with him. "But don't jinx me."

I'll never forget going to my ten-year reunion a couple of years ago. Everyone wanted to know what it was like living in Manhattan and if it was as cool as it looked in the movies. I told them it was cooler; then I told them about the rat problem, how much rent is for a decent apartment, and the pure touristy chaos that is midtown 99 percent of the time. The twenty-four-karat luster in their eyes faded pretty quickly—until I told them about the food, shopping, nightlife, shows, concerts, and abundance of other things to do.

"Tell me about your brother," I say.

Burke stops chewing to shoot me a look. "Random."

"You told me about Audrina. Now tell me about Dorian. And don't worry, I'm going to pick your brain about everyone over these next two months," I say. "So has he always had a chip on his shoulder, or what's his deal?"

Burke sips his broth, contemplating his answer.

"Not always, no," he says. "And I'm not sure."

"That's all you're going to give me? No elaboration?"

Burke shrugs. "What else do you need to know about him? He manages some band, basically lives on the road, does his own thing. We're not that close. Not these days."

"So he *is* a band manager . . ."

Lines spread across his forehead.

"Your sister said he was dressed like a roadie at dinner yesterday," I clarify. "I thought she was implying he *was* a roadie. Not that there's anything wrong with that. I was just unsure about what he does."

"Oh. Right. That was just Nicola being Nicola. He manages a band, and it's pretty much the only thing he cares about. Everything—and everyone else—is chopped liver. Kind of sad, honestly. That band's his entire life."

I'm sure someone could say the same thing about Burke and his firm, but that someone won't be me.

"Which band?" I ask. I already know the answer, but I want to see if Burke does. That, and I want to make sure Dorian wasn't lying. Not that I take him for a liar, but you never know.

"I don't know . . . some pop band . . . Symphony something." The scrunched look on Burke's face leads me to believe he knows exactly which band it is, but he's pretending not to.

Is he jealous of his brother's success?

"Phantom Symphony?" I ask.

His expression remains hardened. "Sounds about right."

"If he loves what he does, it's not sad at all. You should be happy for him." I imagine Dorian could say the same thing about Burke and his investment firm, but I don't tell him that. I also don't tell him that, from what I've experienced so far, the two of them are alternate sides of the exact same coin—broody, closed off, and career addicted.

He picks at his plain white rice with a shiny fork. "Guess I've never thought of it that way. We're not one of those happy-for-each-other kind of families."

"It's not too late to try. You obviously care enough about each other to drop everything and spend eight weeks of your summer together. There's got to be some love somewhere in there."

"I wish it were that simple," Burke says under his breath.

"It's never too late to try," I say. "I saw him handing out band T-shirts to some of the staff. Maybe you could wear one of them? Show some support?"

Burke chuffs. "He'd think I was making fun of him."

"Really? I doubt that. I think he'd be thrilled his big brother is proud of him."

"You clearly don't know my brother."

If he only knew . . .

Then again, what would Burke stand to lose by knowing I hooked up with his brother a year ago?

It would change nothing for him.

Absolutely *nothing*.

And it might feel good to get it off my chest.

Before the words have a chance to cross my tongue, Burke pushes his tray off his lap and hightails it to the bathroom, slamming the door behind him.

Two seconds later, the sound of him retching officially ruins my appetite for what remains of this beautiful masterpiece of a dinner.

While he's in the bathroom, I place Burke's untouched container of bone broth on his nightstand and set both of our trays in the hallway, outside the bedroom door, before returning.

A minute later, the toilet flushes, followed by what sounds like a robust handwashing/toothbrushing session.

"Sorry about that," he says when he steps out, red eyed. The scent of mint mouthwash and lemon-honey hand soap drifts off him. Climbing into bed beside me, he flicks off the lamp, folds his hands over his chest, and closes his eyes. "So much for being on the mend."

"It's all good. You get some rest." I tiptoe to the bathroom, run a clean washcloth under cold water, wring it out, and return to place it on his sweaty forehead.

"Thank you," he says. "For the record, you're going to make one hell of a wife someday."

"Appreciate the kind words, but I'm never getting married," I tell him. "*Ever*."

"You sound like my brother," he mutters, his eyelids floating shut. "You know, last summer, he told me he met someone special . . . claimed she was different from anyone else he'd ever met. Said he had no intentions of marrying her, but he was going to spend the rest of his life with her."

My stomach tumbles.

Burke is all but passed out already, but I have so many questions.

I don't want this conversation to end.

Not yet.

Not like this.

Burke adjusts the washcloth over his eyes and nestles his back against the mattress, drawing in a long, deep breath.

"What . . . what else did he say?" I ask because I can't help myself.

Only my question is met by silence.

He's out cold.

CHAPTER FIFTEEN

DORIAN

One Year Ago

She lies in my arms for hours—until the horizon transforms from midnight black to indigo, violet, and then orange.

It won't be long before the shore fills with early-morning fishermen and beachcombers looking for some shells to sneak home in their suitcases.

I've had sex on the beach before—a few times—but it was different with her.

"We should probably head to our rooms, don't you think?" She breaks the hours-long silence with the inevitable.

"Yeah." I exhale, still tasting her on my lips and tongue, still feeling the stinging warmth where her nails dug into my back again and again.

Briar tugs her dress into place, and I cinch my slacks and fasten my belt. My shirt is somewhere on the beach, probably doused in sand, but I'll have to find it as the hotel has a strict dress code.

"I have no idea where those flip-flops are," she says, scanning the cabana before pulling one side of its fabric back. "Oh, I see your shirt."

Without a word, she hops up, traipsing through our footprints from hours ago and returning with the rest of our things.

The walk to the hotel is over in an instant, much like this night. There wasn't a damn thing I could say or do to make each minute with her tick by slower.

"What floor?" I ask when we step into the elevator.

A family of four corrals themselves into one of the corners, causing the two of us to exchange silent laughs. I can only imagine how we look right now.

"Seven," she says. "You?"

"Same." I press the button for the seventh floor.

The family of four gets off on the fifth.

"Oh, good lord." Briar catches her reflection in a strip of shiny metal as she fusses with her hair. "No wonder we scared those people."

I pull her hand away. "Stop. You look fine."

"I look like I stuck my head in an electrical socket and then rolled around on the beach."

"You're welcome," I tell her with a wink.

We must have been going at it for hours.

She's lucky she can even walk after the things we did . . .

The elevator dings and the doors part, dropping us off on the seventh floor.

"What room?" I ask when we reach the sign that points left or right. I suspect our rooms are close together since Vivi and Benson reserved a block of them, but I don't want to assume.

"Seven thirty-two," she says.

"I'm seven thirty-three. Right across from you."

We follow the signs, our paces going slower with each step.

"You hungry at all?" I should've asked earlier.

"Starving," she says. "But I should shower . . . get this sand out of my hair . . . get some rest." She turns to me, poking her finger against my shoulder. "I'm still getting my beach day. I don't care how tired I am."

Stopping outside room 732, I scratch my temple and ignore the heavy sinking sensation in my chest.

If I'm not mistaken, then I think I might be missing her already . . .

"What?" she asks, obviously picking up on something I had no idea I was broadcasting on my face. "What's wrong?"

"Nothing." I try to brush it off with a half smile.

"No, you looked like you were about to say something." She plants her feet firmly against the terra-cotta floor of the hallway.

Exhaling, I drag my fingers through my messy hair and steal a glimpse of her pillow-soft lips, debating if I should kiss them one more time for the road . . .

There's one thing I didn't mention all night—something I probably should have told her before now.

I'm set to fly back later today.

While the rest of the group is staying a few more days, my plan was only ever to fly in for the party and fly out the very next day.

But screw it.

I can't leave now.

I can't leave *her* . . .

Not yet.

"Two o'clock, right?" I ask.

Her sapphire blues light up. "I'll save you a chair."

CHAPTER SIXTEEN

DORIAN

Present Day

"Can I just say, there's something about Briar that rubs me the wrong way." Nicola keeps her voice low. "I can't put my finger on it . . . it's like she's trying too hard or something."

We finished dinner a half hour ago. While Yvette took the kids upstairs for their nighttime routine and my father retired to his room for the evening, I made the rookie mistake of agreeing to polish off a bottle of dessert wine with Frick and Frack.

"For Christ's sake, Nic, she's barely been here twenty-four hours," Dashiell says. "Cut the poor woman some slack. She's got to be nervous as hell, trying to impress us all. Your family can be intimidating, and to someone from the middle of nowhere, she probably doesn't know what to make of all of this."

My sister rolls her eyes. "Here we go again with the whole fish-out-of-water thing that you apparently find so endearing. Please, enlighten us, Dash. Tell us what else you find so charming about this midwestern Kate Middleton."

Shoot me now . . .

"Oh, stop," Dash snips back. "Not playing that game with you again."

Right, because he knows he'll lose . . .

"He doesn't look at her the way he looked at Audrina," Nicola continues. "With Audrina, it was like . . . he was utterly smitten, captivated. With Briar, it's like . . ." Nicola shrugs, making a take-it-or-leave-it face. "I just don't buy it. On top of that, Audrina dumped him not even six months ago, and he's already moving on? It takes him longer than that to order at a restaurant. It took him two years to decide on a college. Eight months to pick an apartment. You can't tell me he got his heart broken and met his soulmate immediately after. I think she's a rebound."

"Be honest, dear. You just don't *want* to like her," Dashiell says. "You can admit it. You didn't like Audrina at first either. You even told Dorian to dump her before she—"

Both of their wine-clouded gazes flick to me.

Just like that, they realize they've invited the elephant we never speak about into the room.

"I'm so sorry." Dashiell looks me dead in the eyes. "I shouldn't have brought her up in front of you."

Nicola is speechless—for once.

I toss back the last of my wine and rise from the table.

"On that note," I say, "good night. And go fuck yourselves, you miserable bastards."

CHAPTER SEVENTEEN

BRIAR

One Year Ago

The gauzy curtains framing my balcony window float on a sea-salted breeze as Dorian and I lie naked in bed, our legs intertwined.

I don't know what time it is, nor do I want to know.

If I had to take an educated guess, I suppose it's somewhere between 11:00 p.m. and 2:00 a.m., though I'm trying not to think about it because, for the first time in eons, I'm living in the moment, and there's no place else I'd rather be.

Dorian runs his fingertip down my arm, leaving a trail of goose bumps in its place.

After he walked me to my room this morning, I managed to shower long enough to wash the grit out of my hair, and then I fell into bed and slept for what felt like years. I woke up just in time to change into a bikini, throw my hair into a messy topknot, and run-walk to the beach to snag a couple of chairs.

True to his word, he arrived at two o'clock on the dot.

For the rest of my life, I'll never forget the vision of the taut, tanned Adonis strutting my way in his bright-yellow board shorts, a towel flung over his muscled shoulder. I swear my stomach climbed into my throat when he flashed me a smile from behind his polished aviators.

We spent most of the afternoon in silence interspersed with the occasional random thought or deep pocket of conversation. It wasn't as intimate as the night before, but everything about it felt like home . . . if that makes sense.

I've known this man a whopping twenty-four hours (give or take), yet somehow, I feel like I've known him forever. Maybe it's cliché, but there's no denying it.

My phone chimes from the nightstand.

"You want to get that?" he asks.

"No," I say.

Until it chimes again.

And again.

"Maybe I should." It takes all the strength I have to sit up. My entire body aches with a sweet kind of soreness thanks to the man who was determined to prove I'm more flexible than I ever thought possible. "It's Vivi . . . she wants to know if I'm alive. And if I'm with you."

Quietude settles between us.

Despite the fun I've been having, Vivi's warning from last night keeps finding its way into my head.

He'll break your heart into a million pieces . . .

While I don't know Dorian as well as Vivi does, the more I get to know him, the more I can't help but notice we're on the exact same page of the exact same book. I've never met someone like him before—so boldly unapologetic, so sure of what he wants, so in step with me on every level.

I text her back, letting her know we're just relaxing and we'll see everyone at breakfast in the morning. I'd feel guiltier about this if we hadn't met the group for dinner earlier tonight. It would've been tempting to hole up in this hotel room after our time on the beach, but we both agreed we needed to make another appearance after missing the majority of the bachelor-bachelorette party.

The instant I set my phone down, Dorian guides me back into his arms. I rest my cheek against his warm chest, listening to the steady thrum of his heart, wondering if I'll ever have a chance to do this again someday or if this entire trip will be some random memory I'll relive in my head a million times on nights I can't fall asleep.

"One more day," I say. "That's all we have until we have to go back to the real world."

Well, one more day and a handful of hours, if I'm being technical.

We both fly out first thing the day after tomorrow.

He interlaces his fingers with mine, exhaling his warm breath on the top of my head as I nuzzle against him.

I close my eyes, dragging the musky, spicy scent of his aftershave into my lungs.

Two days from now, I'll be lying in my empty bed, listening to the upstairs neighbors blaring polka music while the symphony of Manhattan traffic plays outside my window. There'll be no palm trees or sunshine or brightly dressed vacationers smelling like coconut suntan oil. Gone will be the fruity umbrella drinks and happy couples everywhere I turn.

"What city will you fly to?" I ask. "For the Phantom Symphony tour, I mean. What stop are they on?"

"Chicago," he says without a trace of excitement in his voice. "Then Milwaukee . . . Saint Paul . . . Kansas City . . . after that we'll head west . . . Denver . . . Phoenix . . . Vegas . . ."

"You ever get tired of living on the road?"

"All the time." He runs his hand along the tip of my elbow resting above my hip, but for the first time in forever, I don't recoil. In fact, I haven't recoiled at all with Dorian.

My ex used to obsess over my body—and not in a good way. He was never shy about pointing out if my clothes were fitting tighter or if my muscles were suddenly less defined than they were a couple of weeks ago.

Dorian has done nothing but worship every inch of me.

"Any chance you'll be headed east at some point?" I ask. I squeeze my eyes, bracing myself for his answer.

"We kicked off the tour on the East Coast." There's a hint of an apology in his tone.

"I figured as much," I say.

I tried to get tickets to their show at Madison Square Garden last year, but I bought them from some scalper, and they turned out to be fakes. I should've known better. And I'm still embarrassed about the whole situation, but I don't want to mention it to Dorian because the last thing I want is for him to think I'm fishing for handouts.

All I want is a chance to see him again . . . whatever that entails.

"So where do you live when you're not on the road?" I ask. I could've sworn he said something about being from New York that first night, but it also could've been wishful thinking on my part. And I never did clarify if he meant New York State or New York City.

"I have a place in Manhattan," he says. "I'm subletting it right now."

"So where do you go when you have off time?"

My questions are becoming more obvious by the second.

I should quit while I'm ahead.

His chest rises as he draws in a long, slow breath, and he pinches the bridge of his nose when he lets it out.

"Look," he says in a way that makes me instantly want to harden my heart. Nothing good ever comes after that word. "I'm not in a position to date anyone right now . . . not with this insane schedule . . ."

"You don't have to give me a speech. I get it." My cheeks flush, cherry hot, as I stare at the ceiling, wishing I could melt into the covers and take back every question.

"No," he says. "You didn't let me finish."

I swallow the hard lump in my throat, realizing our fingers are still intertwined and he hasn't moved an inch. Most guys retreat when they give you "the talk." At least they do in my experience.

"Things are going to be crazy for me for the next couple of years," he says. "I'm working on outsourcing a lot of what I do so I don't have to be on site with the band all the time . . . I'll still manage them, but I'll be able to do what I need to do remotely. At least, that's the plan."

Dorian rolls to his side, resting his head on his hand as he studies me.

"Will you wait for me?" he asks.

I'm too stunned to give him an answer.

This is not the direction I thought this conversation was headed . . .

"I know it's asking a lot for you to put your life on pause," he elaborates, "but I just . . . if I leave this place and never see you again, I'm always going to wonder."

Me too . . .

"Give me two years, and we'll pick up right where we left off," he says.

"Y . . . yeah," I finally manage. "Yes. Okay. I can wait two years."

Taking a break from the exhausting dating scene and focusing on my career wouldn't be the worst thing in the world for me to do, and having something to look forward to—like knowing we're going to pick up where we left off—would make the anticipation half the fun.

"No texting," he says. "No phone calls. No emails. It'll turn into some long-distance thing, and I don't want that for us. I don't want to waste those first two years living for the rare trips home and missing out on everything we could be doing together. All the firsts. I don't want to be calling you from backstage in Seattle to tell you happy birthday, and I don't want to be FaceTiming you from Ontario on New Year's Eve."

Waiting for him for two years is one thing . . .

Radio silence is something else.

But before I have a chance to talk myself out of it, I'm nodding and kissing him and agreeing to his crazy little idea.

How could I not?

This man is everything I never knew I wanted.

CHAPTER EIGHTEEN

BRIAR

Present Day

"I'm sorry, I need to sit down for a second." I run my hand along the curved brick wall inside the Driftway lighthouse and take a seat on one of the narrow steps. As someone who has never been inside a lighthouse before, I had zero expectations. Turns out, I should've done more research besides looking at pretty pictures in a coffee-table book.

Most lighthouses are composed of circular rooms on top of circular rooms. Aside from the tiny windows or the occasional crack in the wall, there's not much airflow in here. That, coupled with the dark, narrow space, is making me claustrophobic and breathless.

Still, I don't want to seem ungrateful for the fact that Dorian miraculously agreed to give me a tour. I'm not sure what Burke said to him, but I'm willing to bet there was some kind of bribe or ultimatum involved, because never in my wildest dreams did I expect Dorian to say yes.

"You okay?" He sighs like he's annoyed he has to ask, which is a step up from earlier today when we ran into each other in the hallway, and he told me through gritted teeth that I was like glitter because I was everywhere. I drag three stale breaths into my lungs, close my eyes, and nod.

"You want to keep going?" he asks.

I rise from my step, grip the skinny metal banister, and continue the climb. We're only three levels up—past two oil rooms and a coal room. We haven't yet reached the actual light, and I'm not leaving here without checking out the living quarters.

I didn't endure an awkward, silent, ten-minute ATV ride for nothing.

Dorian stops when he reaches the next doorway, leaning in and giving the rusty-hinged door a good shove with his shoulder.

"Living room," he says, continuing his pattern of saying the fewest number of words as possible to me.

We step into another brick-walled room, this one with a saggy orange couch that looks like it's from the set of an *Austin Powers* movie, as well as a dusty rocking chair, a crooked bookcase chock full of tomes that are falling apart by the second, and a pile of knitted blankets as old as the universe.

Burke wasn't exaggerating when he said this place was a time capsule.

I peruse the tiny space, soaking up every detail, imagining life as a lighthouse keeper.

A grimy picture in a frame on the wall shows a man and woman standing in front of what I can only assume is this very lighthouse in another time, another place. When Burke said Maurice maintained this place, he must have meant structurally? Mechanically? It's clear there hasn't been a broom, mop, or feather duster inside this thing in years.

"Do you know who these people were?" I point at the photo.

"Previous owners."

I move on to the next filthy picture frame, using the hem of my shirt to wipe off the foggy glass. I'm about to ask him who is in this photo when I recognize the woman as the same Carolyn Bessette-Kennedy blonde from the photos in the main house.

Dorian keeps his gaze trained on the floor, then the window.

Anywhere but on me.

"Burke said you used to come out here and listen to music," I say. "I can see why. Feels like a world away from everything, almost like time stands still here. You can be alone with your thoughts in a place like this and forget about everything else."

He says nothing as he positions himself in the doorframe.

I take it as a hint that he's ready to head to the next level.

Giving the circular living room a final perusal, I meet him by the stairs and follow him to another section of the lighthouse, which appears to be a former kitchen turned catchall room. Cardboard boxes are stacked on top of an old stove, spilling over onto a small kitchen table with two bistro-style chairs. A handful of aprons hangs from a hook on the wall, and a dismantled faucet lies lopsided in a cast-iron sink.

It's a depressing sight, but I try to picture it the way it probably was in its former glory—maybe filled with laughter, music, and traditional Dutch cooking.

The next room is a bedroom—this one notably less dusty than the rest of the place. A double bed is shoved against the curved wall, leaving a gap of space. Two wingback chairs are positioned beside a window, and next to them is a record player and an impressive collection of vinyl.

"Are these yours?" I point.

Dorian nods.

"Does this thing work?" I lift the lid off the top of the player. It's immaculate inside. He doesn't answer my question, so I press the red button, and the needle springs to life. Crouching, I gently flip through his vinyl collection before selecting an album. "The Cars? You're speaking my language."

A second later, I'm placing the needle on the record, and a distinct guitar riff followed by Ric Ocasek's trademark tenor telling us to let the good times roll plays over two crackling speakers that give the song a gritty, vintage quality.

I wanted something fun, something up tempo, to hopefully help Dorian out of his miserable mood.

Grinning, I turn to see if there's any light in his eyes, only to find him leaning against the wall, his arms folded, looking even more annoyed than when I had to take a break on the stairs earlier.

Without a word, I cut the music and place the record carefully back inside its cardboard sleeve.

"You have great taste in music," I say.

As expected, he continues to give me the silent treatment as we head to the next level, which is some sort of mechanical room. Above that is the actual lantern room, complete with a 360-degree view framed by a row of windows encapsulated in steel, wood, and brick.

From here, the main house looks tiny and the guesthouses tinier still.

"I bet the sunrises are breathtaking," I say. "You're lucky you had a place like this to retreat to growing up. I had a basement family room with wood-paneled walls. Smelled faintly like cigars and gin. Not from us but from the people who lived there before us. My mom never had the money to renovate it, but that was where I escaped to when I needed some space."

His lips press flat as if he's acknowledging that he heard me but has nothing to add.

"I won't take up any more of your time." I head to the top of the spiral staircase. "Thanks for showing me this place. I appreciate it."

It isn't until we're outside that he stops midstride on our way to the ATV and turns to me.

"What else did Burke say about me?" he asks.

"What?"

"When he was telling you about the lighthouse," he adds. "What else did he say?"

Frowning, I think back to our conversation last night. There wasn't much Burke said other than the two of them weren't very close and they weren't the kind of family who cheered each other on.

It wouldn't do either of them a favor by sharing that.

"Nothing much," I say. "Just that this was always where you hung out when you needed space."

He jangles the ATV keys, stuck in a moment.

"That's all he said?" he asks. "About the lighthouse?"

I'm confused, but I'm not going to elaborate or add fuel to their already burning fire.

"Yeah, pretty much," I say. "That, and he said he wouldn't even know how to get here if he tried."

A slow smile claims half of Dorian's full lips before disappearing completely.

"What?" Now it's my turn to ask questions. "What's that mean? That face?"

"Nothing," he says as he treks through tall grass to our waiting ATV.

I trot behind him.

We're buckling in when I ask him again.

"What are you not telling me?" The irony of my question isn't lost on me.

He starts the engine. "Maybe you should ask your fiancé what he's not telling you."

Burke has no reason to lie to me given that we're not in love and we're not actually getting married. Why would he lie about something as trivial as not knowing how to get to the lighthouse? In retrospect, all one has to do is go over the big hill in the middle, and the thing sticks out like a sore thumb among the tall pines and skyscraping oaks.

I ponder this during the entire bumpy, scenic ride back to the main house, and by the time we arrive, it bothers me more than I thought it would.

Nevertheless, I suck it up because, at the end of the day, does it matter?

Would it change anything?

"Thanks again for the tour," I tell Dorian when we're heading in, though calling it a tour is a bit of a stretch.

He stops short outside the front door, turning my way. Stepping closer, he narrows the space between us.

"Can you stop?" Dorian asks.

"Stop what?"

"The fakeness, the formality." He gestures with his hands, though I'm not sure what he's gesturing at. Me? This? Everything? "The prim-and-proper act. I get that you're trying to make a good impression on my family, but you don't have to do that around me. That ship has sailed."

"All I said was thank you . . ."

The storm brewing in his teal eyes tells me this goes deeper than my politeness.

He wouldn't despise me so much if he wasn't hurting.

And you don't feel hurt over people you don't care about.

He still cares about me—even if he doesn't want to.

"It's what you're not saying," he says. "It's what you're not doing. It's what you're pretending to be, pretending to care about." He starts to say something else, then stops, gathers a deep breath, and looks me dead in the eyes. "You're not who I thought you were."

My lips part, but nothing comes out.

"So that's all you have to say for yourself?" he asks. "I don't even get an explanation?"

"Do you . . . *want* one?" My words are slow and careful, and half of me prays he says no because it'll make this complicated situation a lot simpler—though it'll do nothing to anesthetize the emotional pain.

He pinches the bridge of his nose, taking a step back.

"I don't know. No," he says. "I think your reason's pretty obvious actually. It's pretty clear why you're here."

My skin flushes cold as the color is draining from my face, and I can do nothing to stop it.

"What are you talking about?" I ask.

"You don't love him," he says. "That's plain to see. When he kissed you at breakfast this morning, it was like he was kissing our grandmother. And you bristled."

I don't recall bristling.

If I did, then it wasn't intentional, and Burke didn't notice, either, or he'd have said something.

"Forgive us for not slipping each other the tongue in front of the whole family," I say.

"He doesn't love you either." He won't look at me. "Not that you probably give a shit. I think we all know why you're marrying him."

"It's not like that."

"You realize you're a rebound, right?" His words are rushed, like they've been weighing on his mind for days and now they're spilling out faster than he can control. "For crying out loud, he's only been single since earlier this year—which means you've known him less than six months."

His eyes search mine as if he thinks he'll find the truth somewhere in there, or he's trying to make sense of something that doesn't make an ounce of it.

I avert my gaze to break his hold on me.

"What happened to the woman I met a year ago who was antimarriage, who proudly proclaimed she didn't need a piece of paper to show she was committed to someone?" he asks.

"People are allowed to change." I hate that I have to give him this answer.

"Right . . . they see dollar signs, and suddenly, everything they stand for goes out the window."

"That's not . . . I'm not . . ." I struggle to pick my words in such a way that they won't violate the NDA. I could stand here and swear up and down that I'm in love with his brother, but the last thing Dorian deserves is another unnecessary lie that won't fix any of this. "I wish I could explain this to you in a way that makes it hurt less."

"Give me a damn break." He runs his hand through his hair, tugging a fistful. "I thought you were different, Briar. Turns out you're just one of those people who tell everyone what they want to hear because it sounds good in the moment. At the end of the day, you're nothing but a liar. A fraud. And if you ask me, that's worse than being a pick-me girl."

"Dorian, I—"

"Spare me."

"No," I say.

He huffs, refusing to look at me.

"You got to say your piece, now I get to say mine." I hold my head high, despite every part of me crumbling inside. "You should know, I was going to wait for you too."

"But you didn't."

With that, he disappears inside.

I wait, gathering my composure and blinking away the hot sting of tears clouding my vision.

"Briar?" a voice asks from behind me.

It's Nicola. Wearing a wide-brimmed hat and a swimsuit cover-up, she tucks a hardback copy of *Malibu Rising* under one arm and pulls her sunglasses off her face.

"What was that about?" Her pinched expression tells me she's not going to let this go without an answer.

"Dorian took me to see the lighthouse." I force a smile, knowing full well she's too observant to buy such a simple answer. "Something must have upset him. I'm sure you know how he is . . ."

Nicola squints before looking me up and down.

"It looked like you two were fighting," she says.

"Mommy, Mommy!" Augustine skips up the circular drive in her soaking-wet Lilly Pulitzer swimsuit. Behind her are Dash and Remy, carrying pool floaties and cabana towels. "You said we could watch a movie after the pool."

As if flipping a switch, Nicola's sour demeanor turns saccharine sweet. Bending, she cups Augustine's pointy chin and presses a slow kiss against her forehead.

"I did promise that, didn't I, darling?" she asks. "Run inside and get changed. I'll meet you in the family room."

"I should probably go check on Burke," I say.

"Yes." Her lips press into a hardened line as she straightens her posture. "You probably should."

CHAPTER NINETEEN

DORIAN

One Year Ago

"Now boarding United Airlines flight 1270 with nonstop service to Chicago O'Hare," a woman's semimuffled voice announces over the intercom.

"That's me," I tell Briar.

Our hands remain interlocked as we soak up these final seconds, a line beginning to form behind us.

I drag a final breath of her amber perfume into my lungs, wishing I could keep it there forever.

When I stepped off the jet bridge Saturday morning, a haphazardly packed duffel bag slung over my shoulders, the only thing I felt was antipathy at the fact that I had to travel thousands of miles to drink alcohol in celebration of my college roommate's impending nuptials—something we easily could have done in the States over the course of a single night.

I never could have anticipated that three days later I'd be about to step back onto that same jet bridge with a gnawing heaviness in the pit of my stomach because I'm not ready to leave . . . this.

Her.

"I meant what I said." I brush a strand of dark-blonde hair from Briar's face before cupping her cheek and running my thumb along her rose-colored lips. "In two years, the tour will be over. I'll be back in New York."

I realize I'm asking a lot of someone I only met three days ago, but if I didn't ask, I'd spend the rest of my life wishing I did.

They say fortune favors the bold.

I never fully appreciated that sentiment until now.

From getting stranded twice in one night together, to hooking up on a private beach and watching the sun come up together, to sneaking away between group activities every chance we got on Sunday and Monday, to now . . . it all seemed to happen in a vacuum.

A surreal daydream that started and ended in the blink of an eye.

Another announcement plays. "Now boarding all United Airlines flight 1270 passengers in zone two."

I squeeze her hand in mine and kiss the top of her head. Her hair is still slightly damp from the shower we took together this morning.

"Will you wait for me?" I ask.

Her lower lip trembles, but she bites it away and replaces it with her gorgeous smile—one I'll have permanently etched in my mind every time I close my eyes from here on out.

Hell, every time I open my eyes.

All I'll see is Briar.

The next announcement comes over the speakers. "Now boarding zone three."

"I'll wait for you," she says, her ocean-blue eyes filled with both excitement and bittersweetness.

My heart hammers as I study her. "Promise?"

Briar nods, rising on her toes and pressing her mouth to mine before throwing her arms around my shoulders.

"I promise," she says.

Her words are music to my ears.

I play them on a loop in my head the entire flight to Chicago.

CHAPTER TWENTY

BRIAR

Present Day

"You can talk about her if you want," I say to Burke. We're seated on the back of a speedboat, en route to the mainland Saturday morning, when I catch him looking at photos of Audrina for the tenth time today.

He clears his throat, shoving his phone away.

"I know what it's like to have your heart broken," I add. "Sometimes it feels good just to get it out, you know? Vent or whatever. Get it off your chest."

I peek over my sunglasses toward the same young boat captain from the other day. The engine's loud enough that I doubt he can hear us back here anyway.

We were almost done with breakfast this morning when Redmond mentioned sending Yvette to pick up his prescriptions in town. Burke wasted no time volunteering the two of us under the guise of wanting to show me around town. Redmond didn't protest. In fact, he seemed to like the idea, telling him to make sure to take me to the candy shop on the square for some sea-salted-caramel taffy.

Burke didn't bother inviting his brother (thank goodness) or his sister and her family (also thank goodness).

Ever since Nicola caught the tail end of the exchange I had with Dorian the other day, she hasn't looked at me the same. Then again, her facial expressions are almost always pinched and sour. Still, I can't help feeling like an ant under the molten-hot, refracted light rays of a magnifying glass whenever she's in the room.

"It's fine," Burke says after what feels like two years of silence. "No point in dredging up the past."

I don't believe everything's "fine," but I don't press it.

He's finally feeling better after that stomach bug, and we're still getting to know each other.

The boat slows as we approach the marina. As soon as we're docked, I finger comb my messy hair into a topknot and secure it with a white silk scrunchie that matches my eyelet sundress.

This time, Burke waits to help me off the boat rather than leaving me in the lurch. He's getting better about remembering we're supposed to look like we actually love each other, though with all the money he's spending on this endeavor, I find it odd that he needs a reminder at all.

"We should be back around three," Burke tells the captain.

"I'll be here, sir," the young man replies. "And if you decide you want to return earlier or later, just give me a call."

Burke slips his hand over mine and leads us down the dock toward the parking lot, though there's no waiting Escalade or town car.

"You okay walking?" He nods toward the quaint and colorful business district ahead.

"Of course," I say, despite having donned platform espadrilles. I was about to toss a pair of tennis shoes in my tote bag when I found myself face to face with Dorian by the back door. He was coming inside from his morning jog after breakfast, his muscled shoulders glistening with sweat and his messy dark hair shoved off his forehead with a thin elastic headband.

Our eyes caught in a moment that felt much longer than it was.

Inevitably, I lost my train of thought, forgetting about the task at hand.

A second later, Burke strolled around the corner, placed his hand on the small of my back, and asked if I was ready to go.

We were halfway to the dock when I realized I forgot the sneakers.

"You're doing great," Burke says out of the blue when we reach the main drag. The walk from the waterside to here was silent save for a couple of hobby planes circling overhead and a handful of cars cruising past. "I know my family can be intense, but you're really holding your own."

"Just . . . doing my job." I don't know what else to say.

He sniffs a laugh. "Yeah. I guess."

We stop at a little pharmacy around the corner, one between a barbershop with one of those red-and-blue spinning poles and a gift shop with a window display chock full of marine-themed trinkets.

"I'm going to check out the cards," I tell him once we're inside. "My roommate's birthday is next week. Should probably send her something since I won't be able to text her."

I'm browsing greeting cards when I steal a glimpse of Burke as he's waiting in line. It isn't but a handful of seconds before I catch him reaching for his phone again. He thumbs through screen after screen of what I can only assume are photos of Audrina, though I could be wrong. He certainly doesn't look like he's checking his email or responding to texts, despite the fact that it's the first time he's had cell service all week.

I turn my attention away from my heartbroken employer, select the cheesiest birthday card I can find—one with a pair of old ladies riding mopeds on the front and a god-awful one-liner only Maeve would appreciate—and then I meet Burke in line.

Just as I suspected, he's in Audrina mode, only now he's scrolling her latest Instagram posts.

"Does she know you're still pining away for her?" I startle him.

He darkens his phone screen.

"I mean, yeah, you messed up, but it's not like you actually went through with anything," I say, referring to his story about how he almost cheated on her. "Does she know how sorry you are?"

I try to put myself in her shoes. While I'm sure she could have just about any man she wanted, she must have loved Burke enough to spend three whole years with him. I can't imagine that kind of love just evaporates into thin air.

"I doubt she cares," he says. "I've already apologized a hundred times."

"Talk is cheap. If she saw what I've seen . . . I wonder if she'd change her mind?"

We step up to the counter, and the pharmacist greets Burke with a friendly smile and some small talk about Redmond. It's strange seeing my boss—a man who makes interns shake behind their cubicles—in such a normal, everyday exchange.

He pays for Maeve's card before I can protest, lumping it in with the six bottles of prescription meds we're picking up.

I continue our conversation on the sidewalk outside. "Maybe you should reach out to her again. You clearly still love her. She should know."

"Oh, yeah?" he asks, though I think he's only humoring me.

"I would want to know . . . if it were me."

Not to mention, seeing a powerful man with his tail between his legs is a rare sight.

It's a shame she's not around to witness it.

He says nothing, only trudges ahead like a man on a mission, though I've no idea where we're headed. We pass a trinket shop, a blow-dry bar, and a chowder bistro before I break the silence again.

"Don't let your pride steal your happiness," I say.

Burke shoots me a look. "This isn't about pride."

"What's it about, then?"

His lips press flat as he contemplates his response. "It doesn't matter now. It's not like it'll change anything. I messed up. She moved on."

"Was she the One?"

He exhales. "And only."

"Then suck it up and do what you have to do to get her back."

"Don't you think I've tried?" His tone is snippier than it's been all week. Without warning, he stops in his tracks and turns to me. "She has me blocked . . . my number, my email, everything. I had to make a fake Instagram account just to see her pictures. It's pathetic." Dragging his hands through his neatly combed hair, he says, "I can't believe I said that out loud."

"No, this is good," I say. "Get it out."

"She wants nothing to do with me. Ever again. I have to respect that."

He's not wrong.

But still, I can't help but wonder if she'd feel differently about this whole thing if she knew what was going on behind the scenes. Any sensible woman would. And from what he's told me about her, she sounds like she has a good head on her shoulders.

"You want a coffee or anything?" He points toward a little café straight ahead. "Head's pounding. Could use some caffeine."

"I'm okay." I take a seat on an empty bench. "I'll just wait here."

He disappears inside, where the line is at least ten people long, and I take a second to catch up on texts and emails now that I have a stronger signal.

But halfway through my mission, I take a detour to Instagram, pulling up Audrina's profile. Her most recent photo was posted yesterday—a candid shot of her strolling along a gray city sidewalk, Buckingham Palace in the background. Her effervescent smile is contagious even from the other side of a phone screen, even from another corner of the world.

I bite my lip and start composing a message to a woman who'll probably never see it anyway.

> Audrina—you don't know me, but I'm engaged to your ex . . . Burke Rothwell. I think he's still in love with you, and I don't want him to make a terrible mistake by marrying the wrong woman. I realize how insane this sounds, and I wouldn't blame you if you deleted this and wrote me off. But if you're available to talk, I'd love a minute of your time. You can reach me at 555-272-7719.—Briar

It's a shot in the dark, and even if she calls, I'll likely not have service, but it's worth a try.

I'm a sucker for a happy ending, even if it's someone else's.

Besides, if Burke gets Audrina back, maybe he'll let me out of my NDA.

And maybe—just maybe—Dorian won't hate me anymore once I tell him I'm still waiting for him . . . and that I never stopped.

CHAPTER TWENTY-ONE

DORIAN

Present Day

"You've been hard to pin down lately." Nicola slides a bookmark into her hardback and places it beside her on the poolside lounger. "Every time I try to get a minute alone with you, you disappear."

I yank my earbuds out and pause the music I was listening to—some demo tracks the band has been working on for their upcoming sophomore album. With their debut being such a hit, the pressure is on, and judging by this new shit, they're bringing their A game like never before, but half of these songs sound like they're trying too hard.

"Why? What's going on?" I sigh, waiting to find out what kind of drama she's manufacturing now.

She slides her long legs over the side of the lounger, angling herself toward me. A few yards away, Dash and the kids splash in the pool. Leave it to my sister to invest the time and energy into getting herself pool ready with her SPF 100 sunblock, her oversize hats, and her carousel of designer resort-wear swimsuits . . . only to never so much as dip her toes in the water.

"The other day," she begins, chin tucked, "I could've sworn I saw you and Briar having some kind of heated argument outside."

I remember everything about that day—except seeing my sister, apparently.

"No idea what you're talking about," I lie.

"Really? Because I asked Briar about it, and she said something must've upset you at the lighthouse."

"Not sure why she would say that. I gave her a tour and we came back."

Nicola cocks her head sideways, her mouth half-open as if she doesn't buy a word of this.

"You have the worst poker face, just so you know." She adjusts the floppy brim of her hat, studying me.

"Okay." I shrug, letting her words bounce off me. She can call bullshit until she's blue in the face. It won't change anything. And it sure as hell won't get me to tell her a damn thing about those three fateful nights one year ago, when I made the biggest ass of myself, thinking I'd met someone special.

Someone different.

I'll take that to the grave.

"You don't like her, either, do you?" Nicola asks, taking a surprising left turn with this conversation. "You hardly look at her, and when you do, it's like . . . I don't know, like you're disgusted or something."

"That's a strange thing to notice."

"You realize who you're talking to, right?"

She has a point. Nicola never misses a thing, especially when it concerns other women treading on Rothwell soil. Whether her astuteness is coming from a place of protectiveness or self-interest is anyone's guess, though I have my suspicions.

"Is this about Burke being happy?" Nicola continues, "I mean, let's be honest, he's been happier. But does it bother you or something? I'm married, Burke's getting married, and you're alone."

I refuse to justify her ridiculous question with a response, so I steer my focus to Dash, who's carrying Remy on his back in the deep end of the pool while Augustine teeters on the edge of the diving board, working up the courage to take the plunge.

"Marriage isn't everything, you know," Nicola says, keeping her voice low. "I don't know why Dad's so obsessed with it. I mean, I *know* why. We *all* know why." She pauses, glancing at her family for a split second. "Don't get me wrong. I love my husband. I do. But sometimes I want to kill him . . . and I think that about sums up marriage perfectly."

This is exactly why I'll never exchange vows with anyone.

I'd hate to have the woman that I promised to spend the rest of my life with feel like she wants to strangle me half the time.

"He's not so bad," I say. He's more hands on than our own father ever was. And despite my sister's petulant attitude most of the time, he still looks at her like she hung the moon. "You could've done worse."

"Talk to me after you've spent almost twenty years with someone." She rolls her eyes while the man who sired her children and promised to love her until the day he dies is over there being father of the year.

"Why stay with him, then?"

She sniffs. "Do I even have to answer that?"

"You signed a prenup. It's not like you're walking away with nothing." From what I know, they have five properties between them, his trust fund, and a portfolio of successful business ventures they've invested in over the years. Nicola could walk away right now, and her lifestyle wouldn't change a bit.

"And give up half of our family's estate to Burke? Yeah, no." Nicola's failure to mention the emotional well-being of her children is disappointing, but it's no surprise.

"I've never understood this family's obsession with money." I rise from my chair, not about to let Nicola ruin this perfectly good afternoon with more Nicola-isms.

"Where are you going?"

"I don't know yet."

"Is it something I said?" Nicola shields her face with her hand, squinting up at me from behind an oversize pair of designer sunglasses.

"Yeah, actually," I say. "You just sat here and told me you want to kill your husband half the time, but you're willing to stick it out until our dad dies so you don't miss out on your share of the inheritance."

Her nose wrinkles. "So?"

"Not once did you mention your kids. Screw them, right? Who cares how any of this affects them as long as you get your millions."

"Oh, come on. It's not like that. The kids . . . that goes without saying."

"Keep telling yourself that. And when you're done, why don't you work on convincing yourself that people like you aren't everything that's wrong with the modern-day institution of marriage."

I leave, silently hating how triggered I am . . . and how triggered I've been since I watched my brother head to the dock this morning with Briar in tow.

As much as I want to loathe her, as much as I resent being played for a fool, I can't stop wishing things were different.

Wishing, much like looking back, is nothing more than a waste of time.

And there's nothing I hate more than wasting time.

CHAPTER TWENTY-TWO

BRIAR

One Year Ago

I've been back from Vivi and Benson's trip a mere eight days—hardly enough time for my tan to fade—when I stop in my tracks on my way inside Sunrise Coffee Co.

Seated with his back toward me at a table for two is a man with silky brown waves, white AirPods in his ears, and his nose buried in some thick book.

It isn't until someone brushes past me that I realize I've no idea how long I've been standing here, staring at the back of some random guy's head. And it isn't until the same person who brushed past me takes a seat across from the dark-haired mystery man that I realize it isn't Dorian.

With flushed cheeks, I take my place at the end of the line and quietly chastise myself for getting my hopes up. It isn't the first time this week. Or the second, for that matter. In fact, I've been seeing Dorian everywhere since the second my flight touched down at LaGuardia.

I'm on the subway fifteen minutes later, en route to the office, when I grab my phone and pull up Dorian's number.

We weren't going to exchange numbers at first.

We didn't even exchange last names because we didn't want to be tempted to google each other—save for the one time I googled the band, but there was no mention of him anywhere.

The plan is to get to know each other in person, sans internet assistance, when the time is right . . . which apparently is two years from now when Phantom Symphony's worldwide tour is over.

Then—and only then—are we supposed to reach out.

But my self-control is paper thin these days.

Dorian is all I think about; he invades my thoughts, my daydreams, my every waking minute, and everything in between.

Holding my breath, I type out a text telling him I spotted his doppelgänger in a coffee shop. It's a desperate attempt to open up some kind of dialogue between us. Or maybe I only want to see if he'll respond, if he'll prove Vivi wrong about the whole heartbreaker thing.

Only before I press send, I delete the whole thing.

We made a promise.

We have an agreement.

And I'm nothing if not a woman of my word.

CHAPTER
TWENTY-THREE

DORIAN

Present Day

The house is silent when I come in from the pool. I'm halfway to the kitchen to grab a bottle of water when I spot that the door to my father's study is wide open, a green-tinted light spilling out.

"Hey." I rap on the doorframe before stepping in.

He glances up from his newspaper, placing his magnifying glass aside. The old banker's lamp that he's had since the beginning of time is aglow beside him, making his gray eyes shine brightly.

"Dorian," he says. "Come on in. Take a seat."

For a minute, I'm sixteen again. It's the summer after Mom died, and Dad is forcing us to hole up on this godforsaken island because he still can't bring himself to spend a single night back in Manhattan, where our lives were in full swing before the tragic night that took her from us.

"Where's everyone?" he asks.

"Nicola, Dash, and the kids are swimming. They were talking about taking the horses for a ride later," I say. "Burke and Briar are still in town, as far as I know."

"How are you doing?" He leans back, his chair creaking, and he folds his hands over his thin belly. His eyes are squinted, laced with concern.

"I'm . . . fine." I'm not sure why he's asking.

He never asks.

"No, how are you really?" He sits straighter, resting his elbows on his desktop. "Can't help but notice you've been in a bit of a mood since you arrived. More so than normal."

"Just have a lot on my plate," I say, quickly adding, "with work."

His mouth forms a hard line, and he forces a hard exhalation through his nostrils.

"I know how that goes," he says. "All too well, unfortunately. It's taken me eighty-one years to learn the most valuable lesson this life had to give me."

"And what's that?"

"That time is the most precious commodity there is," he says.

I nod. "Couldn't agree more."

He lifts a finger. "But that's not all."

"Okay . . ."

"The quickest way to burn through time is to prioritize the wrong things." He leans back in his chair again, hands clasped. "I can't tell you how many days, nights, weeks, months, years I squandered away working when I should've been spending that time with my family."

"You can't beat yourself up over the past."

I imagine that facing one's impending demise makes them think about regrets and all the things they would do differently if given another chance, but what's done is done. My father worked his life away—despite having the financial means to not have to work a single day in his life.

He made his choice.

There's no changing it now.

"I wish I'd thrown a ball with you boys a little more often," he says. "I wish I hadn't missed so many of your sister's dance recitals. I wish I'd taught you how to play chess, rather than hiring someone else to do it. I should've taken us on more family vacations instead of shipping you kids off to every summer camp under the sun."

"You don't have to say any of this."

He lifts a flattened palm. "I do, though. And you need to hear it."

I bite my tongue, knowing there's no arguing with Redmond Rothwell once he gets going.

"Your sister, she's a fantastic mother. Much like your mother. I'm not worried about her. Those kids are her whole world," he continues. "And Burke. Burke can't be alone for longer than two seconds without panicking. I'm not worried about him—he'll always have someone to keep him company. But you. All you have is your job. A man needs more than that if he truly wants to be happy."

"I'm the happiest I've ever been," I say, though I'm lying. The statement would've been the truth had I said it over a week ago. I was happier then. Hopeful. I had something—or rather, someone—to look forward to.

"You say that, but I don't think you mean it." His gray eyes hold tightly on mine. "Just a hunch."

"I don't think happiness is the point of life."

"It's the only point," he says. "The only point that matters."

"Agree to disagree. Not trying to be some hedonistic trust fund nepo baby."

Dad chuckles. "And I admire that about you, but I'm not talking about that. I'm talking about love. Finding someone to spend your life with."

"If you're about to give me another lecture on marriage, I'm going to have to stop you right there." We've had this conversation more times over the years than I can begin to count. "Save your breath. Save your energy. Save your *time*."

"I know you're probably a bit gun shy after the whole Audrina thing." His expression turns somber. "You know how much I adored that woman. She'd have made a fine Rothwell."

I nod. He wasn't shy about singing her praises any chance he got, and she took a liking to him as well. Their bond was wholesome, if rather unusual.

"I don't agree with the way things went down with Burke. It was awful on both of their parts. Selfish. But I think we can all agree, she was a better fit for him than she was for you."

"Why are we talking about this?" Digging up painful memories has never been my thing. Chaining them to cinder blocks and drowning them in the sea has always been more my style.

"Right." He clears his throat. "I guess what I'm getting at is, don't let the hurt from the past steal the happiness of tomorrow."

"Did you get that from a fortune cookie?"

My father rolls his eyes. "I'm being serious here. I hope one day you'll be able to find someone who'll make you forget Audrina ever existed. It'll make that whole thing look like playground love."

I say nothing because there's nothing to say.

While I was able to get over Audrina relatively quickly all those years ago, I've yet to get over the betrayal by my own flesh and blood.

In a roundabout way, Burke did me a favor by stealing her out from under me.

But it doesn't change the fact that I'll never be able to look at him the same way again.

Or trust him.

Or feel an ounce of happiness for him, particularly where his love life is concerned.

"I'm curious to hear what you think of Burke's new fiancée." Dad steeples his fingers. "We haven't had a chance to talk about her yet, just us two."

I hate everything about that word . . . "fiancée."

It's pretentious and assuming and old fashioned.

"I think she's crazy," I say.

Dad chuckles like he thinks I'm joking.

I always thought anyone would have to be insane to want to settle down with Burke. He's a workaholic with the personality of a piece of white paper or a mouthful of sand. He has no hobbies or interests, at least none that make him stand out from the sea of Brioni-suit-wearing, New-York-financial-district lemmings he associates with.

I'm still not sure why Audrina chose him over me.

I was the fun one, the adventurous one, the one who could actually carry on a conversation that didn't revolve around the stock market, T-bonds, international trade treaties, or the petrodollar.

"Burke seems content around her, don't you think?" Dad asks. "A little more at ease than usual."

"Sure." He's probably at ease because he's already counting the fat stacks of cash he's going to collect in the near future. That's enough to put even the most harried New Yorker in a Zen-like state.

"He doesn't quite light up the way he did before with Audrina, but I like this one. She's down to earth, and I think that could be good for him."

I gaze out the wall of windows, watching the rolling ocean waves crash along the dock in the distance. Any minute now, the two of them will be back, and my brief refuge from this shit show will be over.

Drawing in a long breath, I count to seven before letting it go.

Seven more weeks—if I can last that long. And I will, but only for my father's sake. He might be set in his archaic ways, but he's the only dad I have, and this will likely be our final summer together.

"I want to talk to you about the inheritance clause," he says, clearing his throat.

Here we go . . .

"You don't have to—" I begin to say before he slices his hand through the air.

"I want you to understand my reason behind it. I'm not just some old man losing his marbles, trying to steer a sinking ship before it goes down forever," he says. "I just want to know that when I'm gone, each one of you will have someone to weather life's storms with."

"I appreciate the intention, but you don't have to worry about me."

"I do, though." He cocks his head, his eyes softening. "You're my youngest. My most fiercely independent. Sometimes you're too independent for your own good. You need someone to soften you. To make you smile. If I could give you that, my son, I would do it in a heartbeat. But I can't. All I can do is guide you in that direction—and that's exactly what I'm doing."

"Again, I appreciate the sentiment, but that's not the way it works."

"I just want you to keep your eyes open. Keep your heart open. Keep your mind open—there's someone out there for each of us," he says. "And when you find them, you'll know. Believe me. You'll feel it in the deepest part of your soul."

I had those soul-stirring feelings the night I met Briar.

Turns out, my soul is a terrible judge of character.

"Noted," I say, but only so we can wrap up this painful TED talk.

"I want you to be happy," he says. "It's all a father could ever want for his child."

"I can be happy without signing some papers and wearing a tuxedo in front of hundreds of people."

"You're missing the point." He splays his fingertips across his desk. "There's something extraordinary about making a commitment to someone and promising them—in every way imaginable—that you'll be there for them, come what may. That you'll be theirs and they'll be yours forever. That's the sort of promise money can't buy. Look at Dash and Nicola—happy, in love, committed, building a beautiful life together. I'd hate for you to miss out on a lifetime of beautiful memories and purpose."

I save my breath and decide not to tell him that his one and only married child feels like she wants to murder her husband half the time—to the point where she's practically counting down the days until our father croaks so she can be a free woman again.

"I know I say a lot. And I've said a lot just now. But if there's one thing you take away from this conversation, it should be that there is someone out there for you, and I hope you find her sooner rather than later. Who knows, you'll probably find her when you least expect it. Or it could be someone you already know. Maybe the one for you has been in front of you this whole time, waiting for you to make a move."

He's always been deeply romantic at heart. I'll never forget the weekly delivery of red roses my mother would sign for every Friday when I was a kid. On Saturdays, he would take her out on some sort of special date. Sometimes they'd go to the symphony. Other times they'd sneak away to some jazz concert or rooftop restaurant. They would always dress to the nines and come home long after the three of us had gone to bed for the night.

That said, I suspect he wasn't always that way.

Long before my siblings and I were a twinkle in his eye, he was married to another woman. They had two daughters—Emily and Hannah—and they lived in some countryside estate in Vermont.

The four of them were coming home from a Christmas tree farm one December night when they ran into a freak snowstorm. The roads were slick and winding, and there wasn't a star in the sky to light the way home.

The newspaper articles I've found say they hit a snowplow head on, coming over the top of a hill. The station wagon my father was driving spun several times before flipping upside down into a nearby ravine.

Everyone perished that day except my father, who somehow walked away with some bruised ribs and a few cuts and scrapes.

The number of times my father has spoken about that night I can count on one hand.

He said it took him years to find peace with what happened, though last I heard, he never fully forgave himself.

He wasn't looking for love when he met our mother.

He was shopping for a new wallet for himself one random August day, and she happened to be the sales associate who rang him up. She was funny, he said, making one-liners and cracking jokes the whole time. He recalled that it was the first time someone had made him smile in years. Before he left her shop, he asked what her favorite restaurant was, and then he asked her out on a date, taking her to said restaurant later that week.

The rest, as they say, is history—until twenty-five years later, when my mother suffered a brain aneurysm in her sleep. Earlier that same night, he held her in his arms as she drifted off, breathing peacefully, neither of them knowing that one of those breaths would be her last.

She was only forty-five.

"You still haven't told me," he says, "what you think of Briar for Burke."

"I think they're all wrong for each other."

He chuffs. "What makes you say that? They're perfect together."

I shrug, picking at a loose thread in my board shorts. "You asked for my opinion. I gave it to you."

"Care to elaborate?"

"Not really."

"I see." He adjusts his posture. "When I'm gone, all you three will have is each other. I hope someday you'll be able to forgive Burke for what he did, and that you'll all be able to be happy for each other as you move forward in this life."

"Mm-hmm," I say to appease him.

His brows knit as he studies me.

"If this is about Audrina, you have to let it go. If not for them, then for yourself. For your health. Anger only ever hurts the one who holds it."

"God, no. It's not about her. That was a lifetime ago." While it wasn't ideal at the time—my older brother stealing my fiancée out from under me—it taught me a barrage of invaluable lessons . . . a diamond ring is meaningless, your own flesh and blood is perfectly capable of screwing you over, and placing your happiness in someone else's hands is a stupid and reckless move.

Though that last lesson I didn't learn until last week, when I watched my brother introduce the woman of my dreams—a woman I had every intention of spending forever with—as his future wife.

CHAPTER TWENTY-FOUR

BRIAR

Present Day

"Wow . . . I . . . I'm so sorry." I swipe a generous tear from my cheek as I offer Redmond a bittersweet smile. An hour ago, I came downstairs to grab a glass of water before bed, not expecting to bump into Burke's father doing the same thing. He invited me to pull up a stool to the island, and we made small talk. Only somewhere along the line, the conversation detoured, and he ended up giving me a rundown of his life's tragedies—beginning with his first wife and daughters dying in a car accident and ending with his second wife dying in his arms in her sleep. "I had no idea about any of that."

"Burke doesn't tend to dwell in the past," he says. "Sometimes you have to pry these sorts of details out of him with your bare hands."

"I've noticed."

"The thing about us Rothwells is, when we love someone, we love them with everything we have, even if it isn't always obvious," he says. "We tend to hide our emotions under our sleeves instead of wearing them on the outside. I wasn't always the way I am. My second wife is the one who brought out this side of me. I'm hopeful that you'll one day do the same for Burke. He needs that, you know. Someone to make him smile the way his mother used to make me smile."

Thinking back to the events of the past week, I can only recall Burke smiling a small handful of times, and even then, I don't think it was because he was charmed by any stretch of the imagination.

"You seem like you still have so much love to give," I say. "Did you ever try and move on again? Or can a person move on at all after losing the love of their life twice in a row?"

His gray eyes dampen as he purses his lips.

"I thought about it from time to time," he says. "But I was still too in love with both of them to seriously consider finding someone new. And even then, I knew myself. I knew I'd keep her at arm's length, afraid to lose someone yet again."

By my calculations, Dorian, Burke, and Nicola's mother passed a little less than two decades ago.

That's an awful long time to spend alone.

"My mom always likes to say there are different kinds of love," I tell him. "Friendship love, romantic love, soulmate love, companionship . . ."

"She's a wise woman, your mother." He sips his water. "And to that, I would add, love . . . is priceless. It's the one thing money can't buy."

If he only knew . . .

"Genuine love, that is," he clarifies. "When it's real, you can't put a price tag on it. You can't bargain it or sell it or trade it. The only problem is, this world is full of people who think differently. People who marry for money or prestige or survival."

"You're not wrong."

"Why do you want to marry my son, Briar?" His question comes out of left field and nearly makes me choke on my drink.

I take a generous gulp, swallowing away the irritation in my throat.

"What do you love about him?" His head is tilted to the side as he waits for my response. "How did you know he was the One?"

Redmond is a kind man, and he may be in his eighties, but he's as sharp as a tack.

This is nothing more than a test.

In an unfortunate turn of events, my mind turns blank, providing zero assistance whatsoever as I try to think about what I like about Burke.

In the weeks leading up to this, Burke seemed to be more focused on the two of us memorizing the paper versions of each other rather than trying to forge any kind of real connection.

"I'm sorry." I give him a nervous chuckle. "No one's ever asked me that before."

"It's all right, dear. Take your time."

I run through my earliest memories of Burke, which are all just a few months old at best. The first time I saw him was in a staff meeting shortly after I started working at his firm. There was no denying the man could command a room, but there's nothing sexy about making your employees cower in fear.

All the times I saw him after that were in passing mostly.

In hallways.

By the elevator.

Coming and going.

He always looked through me, never at me.

Last month when he called me into his office, I was 100 percent convinced I was being let go for some unknown reason. My hand trembled as I pushed his door open, and heat crept up my neck as I strolled toward his oversize mahogany desk.

There's nothing about Burke that puts a person at ease.

He isn't warm or welcoming.

He's damn near impossible to get to know.

He isn't funny or romantic or charming.

But more than any of that, he's not Dorian.

With Redmond waiting patiently for my response, I make an executive decision to describe how I fell for Dorian, without making it obvious.

Despite only having spent three days with that man, I could wax on about him until the sun comes up and never run out of things to say.

"The day I met your son," I begin, "I wasn't looking for anyone. Isn't that how it always goes?"

He smiles, nodding and listening.

"Anyway, he seemed to have this chip on his shoulder," I continue, "not exactly approachable, you know? But then we started talking. And he was funny. Sarcastic funny, not ha ha funny. That told me he was intelligent. And he had this way of looking at me that made the rest of the world fade away. It's hard to find someone like that. It's like he was present. Truly present. Most of the time, you're lucky to get half of someone's attention on a good day, but he gave me all of his."

Redmond's expression is tender, much like his heart, and I hate lying to him in this way, but in a roundabout way, I'm also telling the truth.

I'm in love with his son . . .

Just not the son he thinks.

"That first night, we never ran out of things to talk about," I go on. "And the more we talked, the more we realized how much we had in common. We shared a lot of the same opinions about things, like love and relationships and commitment. And when we weren't talking about those sorts of things, he was telling me about his work. I knew right away how passionate he was about his job, and that's another thing that's hard to find these days. So many people are afraid to chase their dreams, but he was living his."

"He's always been ambitious," Redmond says with a proud gleam in his eye.

"We were walking home one night, and I was wearing high heels," I say. "He went up to a total stranger and paid her to trade him her flip-flops. Paid her a hundred dollars for them too. I didn't even have to ask. He just did it. Like it was nothing. Because he wanted me to be comfortable."

"They don't make them like us anymore," he says with a wink.

"I've kissed a lot of frogs in my life," I say, "so to speak. But your son? He was the first one who actually turned out to be a prince."

Redmond chuckles. "Don't tell him that. It might go to his head."

I smile. "I don't think it would."

Dorian is anything but arrogant—unlike Burke.

"Anyway, your son is the first person who ever made me feel seen and heard and valued and wanted," I say. My throat tightens with the gravity of those words, with the gravity of everything I'm giving up because of this arrangement. "I think about the night we met all the time. It was one of the most profound experiences of my life. And no matter what happens, no matter which way our lives take us, we'll always have that. What we shared will forever be ours and no one else's."

Redmond straightens his shoulders, exhaustion and contentedness washing over him.

"Well," he says. "I think that's the perfect way to end a lovely conversation, don't you?"

I yawn, covering my mouth with the back of my hand.

It's been a long day, and it's going to be a long seven weeks.

"Good night, dear. Sleep well," he says before shuffling off, his glass of water in his hand.

I linger a moment longer in the dark kitchen, the space lit only by the light over the stainless steel range along the far wall. I let my words play in my head, wishing Dorian could've been there to hear me but knowing I'll never be able to speak these words out loud for the rest of my natural life.

Only the last thing I expect is for my wish to come true.

"*Ohmygod.*" I gasp, clutching at my chest, when I spot the masculine shadow seated at the breakfast nook in the corner. "How long have you been sitting there?"

He rises, slowly, stepping out of the shadows in his white V-neck shirt and navy-blue sweats, slung low on his hips. But it's his piercing turquoise gaze that steals the remaining air from my lungs and anchors my feet to the cold marble floor.

"Long enough," he says.

And with that, he disappears into the next room.

He heard everything.

CHAPTER TWENTY-FIVE

DORIAN

Present Day

"I didn't know you were in here." I stop short in the doorway of the sunroom where Briar is curled up near a window, paging through some paperback as rain pelts the glass beside her.

True to her glittery self, she's everywhere.

Even with all the square footage on this island, I can't seem to get away from her no matter where I go.

She closes her book and sits up. "I can leave."

Lightning flashes and an angry growl of thunder follows, rattling the windowpanes and reverberating through every inch of the space around us.

We lost power half an hour ago. Burke and Maurice went to find out why the generator didn't kick on, and Nicola took the kids to the family room to distract them with their iPads.

I thought I'd find my father in here. He tends to pass the time in this room during storms, calling it the "best view in the house" with its three walls of floor-to-ceiling glass.

"No, stay," I tell her. Hooking my hands on my hips, I draw in a sharp breath.

Last night, I was sitting in the kitchen, alone with my thoughts—minding my own business—when my father and Briar wandered in without so much as glancing toward the breakfast nook where I sat in the dark.

What began as idle chitchat and general pleasantries morphed into a full-on heart-to-heart where Briar described all the things that made her fall in love with my brother.

Only she wasn't describing Burke.

She was describing me.

"Why are you here?" I ask her.

She tucks a wispy strand of hair behind one ear, studying me from the other side of the room through a fringe of dark lashes.

"The house is dark . . . I just wanted a little bit of light so I could read, so—"

"No." I cut her off. "I mean, why are you really here? What do you want? Is it money? Is that why you're marrying my brother? Because you're sure as hell not in love with him."

A bolt of lightning tears through the dark sky behind her.

She fixes her attention on the carpet, her full lips pressed together.

"You going to answer me or . . . ?" I let my words taper, though my feet are firmly planted. I'm not leaving until I get a response.

"I'm here because your brother and I are engaged," she says, though she still won't look at me. With one hand grasping her book, she grips the edge of the sofa cushion with the other. This topic clearly makes her uncomfortable.

Is it because I see through this act?

Is it because I'm calling her out on her bullshit?

"We're in love," she says, though her tone is anything but convincing.

"Huh. Could've fooled me." I play dumb. "When's the wedding? Want to make sure I'm out of the country that day."

"We haven't set a date yet." She ignores my sarcasm, though this time, her gaze flicks up to mine.

"Really? No mad dash to the altar?"

"There's no reason to rush."

"I don't disagree with you on that. On the basis of principle, I mean. I couldn't give a shit if you marry him tomorrow or five years from now. I'm just curious, is all," I say. "Especially given the fact that a year ago, you were adamantly opposed to the idea of marriage."

She swallows. "Not everything in life is cut and dry. Love is complicated. I never expected for this to happen."

"Happen? It hasn't happened yet. There's still time to walk away, still time to not marry a man who looks at you like you're some consolation prize. A participation ribbon."

Her mouth falls open, though she doesn't speak.

Maybe I took it too far, but it's true.

I know my brother.

I know what he's like when he actually gives a damn about a woman.

There's no love between those two.

"Tell me one thing, and then I'll never ask you another question again." I keep my voice low. "Why him? Why Burke?"

She begins to say something when the lights flicker on.

Nicola's kids cheer from down the hall.

"I'm sorry," she says.

"That doesn't answer my question."

"I'm sorry I can't give you an answer," she says. "I wish that I could."

I'm about to roll my eyes and give her yet another piece of my mind when a warm hand on my shoulder steals my momentum.

It's Yvette.

"Have you seen your father?" she asks.

I turn to face her. "No, why?"

She toys with the gold pendant around her neck. "I was passing by the dining room and noticed his medication was still sitting out where I left it for him at lunch. He should've taken those pills four hours ago. I've been looking all over for him. Thought maybe he was in here, but . . ."

Briar tosses her book aside and pops up from the sofa. "I'll help look."

"Thank you," Yvette says. "I've already been in every room of the house, but I haven't checked the outbuildings yet. Briar, if you could double-check upstairs, that would be great. I'll take the main floor. Dorian, would you mind running to the guesthouses and horse barn? I can't imagine why he'd be outside in this weather, but something's off."

My conversation with Briar takes an immediate back seat as I sprint outside in the thunder and rain to search for my father, assuming the worst and hoping to God I'm wrong.

CHAPTER TWENTY-SIX

BRIAR

Present Day

The smell of hospital antiseptic fills my lungs as monitors beep and machines whoosh and whir around us. There's a rhythm to it all, yet it's all discordant, out of sync.

Not unlike the Rothwells themselves.

The ICU room is compact, filled with more wires and apparatuses than a person should ever have to be hooked up to.

Four hours ago, we were frantically searching for Redmond in the midst of a torrential downpour.

Dorian sprinted outside while Yvette and I checked every closet, nook, and cranny of their impossibly large home, eventually enlisting the help of Nicola, Dashiell, and the kids.

Ultimately, it was Nicola who found him collapsed on the floor of the potting shed, a few stalks of freshly trimmed larkspurs in his hand.

When Dashiell questioned why Redmond was cutting flowers in the middle of a thunderstorm, Nicola was quick to point out that today would have been her mother's birthday.

And larkspurs were her favorite.

Everything that happened after we found him seemed to happen in slow motion, every second longer than the one before. While Dorian located an emergency satellite phone, Nicola calmed the crying children. Dash stood around, looking as if he wanted to help but mostly taking up space. I clung to Burke in the midst of it all, an attempt to offer him comfort that he clearly didn't need since his arm was limp in my grasp.

The rain cleared in time for the Life Flight helicopter to land on an open patch of the island. While paramedics worked to get Redmond stable enough for the flight to Boston Medical Center, the rest of us piled into the boat at the end of the dock, with nothing more than the damp clothes on our backs. When we reached the shore, an SUV was already waiting to take us to the hospital.

Now here we are.

Gathered around a dying man's hospital bed, watching him sleep while machines keep him alive.

It feels wrong to be a part of this. Inappropriate, even, to be taking part in a moment so intimate for this family. I shouldn't be here.

But leaving Burke's side also feels wrong given everything we've led his family to believe about us. Adding drama on top of tragedy would be traumatic for the Rothwells, and I'm not about to touch that with a ten-foot pole.

I remind myself it's not about me, it's not about Burke, and it's not about our arrangement.

Not here, not now anyway.

This moment is about Redmond, his family, and their potential final goodbyes—nothing more, nothing less.

"Can I get anyone anything?" I break the silence that's been weighing us down for the past hour. I'm not sure any of them have so much as looked at each other since the doctors let us in the room. In fact, we're lucky they're allowing us all to be in here at the same time. Hospital policy typically allows for only two visitors at a time in ICU rooms, but I suppose they make exceptions when there's an entire wing named after you.

"No." Burke glances down, acknowledging me for the first time. His nose twitches when he realizes I'm holding on to him, as if he finds it annoying.

I let go.

"Nicola?" I ask. "Dash?"

Nicola ignores me as she takes a seat on the edge of her father's bed. Dashiell shakes his head no, though he offers a grateful, tight-lipped smile.

Heat creeps up the sides of my neck as I turn my attention to Dorian.

"Dorian, can I get you anything?" I offer, knowing he'll likely ignore me the way Nicola did.

Between the search for Redmond and the commotion that ensued, I've yet to stop thinking about our unfinished conversation. He wanted an answer that I couldn't give him, and while I was grateful for Yvette's interruption at that moment, I never expected it to lead to this.

"I should check on the kids," Dash says. We'd only been here a few minutes when one of the floor receptionists offered to let them wait in a private office, with crayons and coloring books to distract them from what was going on. "They're probably hungry. And tired. If it's okay with you, I'll get us a room at the Marriott down the way."

Nicola says nothing, only nods. Turning to her brothers, she says, "I'm staying. And you two better stay as well. We're not leaving his side."

A neon-yellow sign fixed to the door states that visiting hours end at 8:00 p.m.

I imagine, much like the other rules in this hospital, that won't apply to the Rothwells.

Dash gives his wife a peck on the cheek before departing, though she doesn't seem to care or notice. Her tired eyes are glued to her father as if she's worried his heart will stop beating if she takes a break from watching.

"I'm going to grab some coffee," I say after Dashiell leaves. "I think there's a vending machine down the hall."

My words are met by silence, though I don't blame any of them.

It's been a traumatic day, and the three of them are facing the reality of losing their last living parent.

I only wish there was something more I could do for them.

I'm halfway to the vending machine when I remember I don't have my purse. We left the island in such a hurry that there wasn't time to grab anything. Reaching into my pocket, I feel for my phone, which I happened to have on me by chance when everything happened.

Gathering a breath, I take a seat in the waiting room.

Those three need a moment alone with their dad anyway.

The TV mounted in the corner is muted on some cable news channel—one with a never-ending scroll at the bottom that makes the viewers feel like the country is one headline away from collapsing once and for all.

With a strong cell signal and nothing but time on my hands, I catch up on text messages and emails and mindless social media scrolling, grateful for the much-needed distraction.

"There you are."

I glance up to find Nicola standing before me, her hands on her narrow hips as she peers down her angular nose.

"Thought you were getting coffee?" she asks.

I place my phone down. "I forgot I didn't have my purse with me."

"There's a beverage station in the hall for visitors. Free coffee and ice water." Her tone is neutral, but I can't tell if she's being kind or facetious. The woman's impossible to read. "You've been out here a long time. Thought maybe you got lost."

"I was just giving you guys some space."

She sniffs, her lips half-cocked on one side. "How gracious of you."

I'm still not sure what she wants or why she's standing here, pretending to be friendly when her eyes are shooting daggers my way, but I straighten my shoulders and do my best to appear as unfazed as possible.

"Hospitals are so depressing." She collapses into the seat across from me. Pulling her phone from her pocket, she folds her long legs and exhales. "Dash got us three side-by-side rooms at the Marriott. That man never misses a meal. Or a good night's rest. I don't know about you, but I don't plan on sleeping tonight."

If these minutes are so precious to Nicola, I've no idea why she's wasting them on me, but I don't dare mention that.

"Burke and Dorian are going at it in there," she says as if she read my mind. "I needed a breather."

"Going at it?"

"I always thought if I had a sister, she'd be my best friend." She ignores my question. "Sure, there would be fights. That comes with the territory. But I always thought she'd be my ride or die, you know? Do you have a sister?"

I shake my head. "Only child."

"I was supposed to have two of them," she says. "Well, I had two of them. Before I was born. Though, if they were still around, I probably wouldn't be here. It's weird to think of it that way, but in that regard, I guess we were never meant to be sisters. Not in this lifetime anyway."

"Redmond told me about them last night. Such an awful tragedy."

"He probably didn't tell you he'd been drinking the night of the car crash, did he?" She sits straight, darkening her phone screen as she directs her full attention to me.

I frown. "No . . ."

"Of course not. He likes to leave that part out." She rolls her eyes. "I love my father. I do. He's a brilliant, loving man. But he has his demons. We all do." She swallows, pressing her lips into a hard line. "The men in this family, they like to rewrite history sometimes. My father does it, my grandfather did it, and his father before him."

I don't know what she's getting at, but I'm all ears.

"Burke is no different," she continues. "You should know that before you marry him."

"If you're trying to talk me out of marrying him, Nicola, with all due respect, this isn't the time or place—"

"If not now, when?" she asks with a shrug. "If my father passes, I have a feeling my brother's going to rush you off to the nearest chapel, use this tragedy as a way to lock you down."

"I don't think he's like that."

"Then you don't know him very well." She arches a brow. "I just find it convenient that as soon as he loses one fiancée, he picks up another—just in time for our father to take his last dying breath. Never mind that he has to be engaged or married in order to collect his third of the inheritance."

My jaw falls.

Burke has only ever told me that his father was getting older and that it was his wish to see his children happy and committed; he mentioned his father's health wasn't the greatest, but he never once mentioned his inheritance or any such clause.

"What? Like you didn't know . . ." She swats her manicured hand at me. "For all I know, the two of you are in on this together. Lord knows he doesn't look at you the way he used to look at his ex. And don't think

I haven't noticed the way you look at Dorian when you think no one's watching."

"Nicola, I—"

"I'm guessing Dorian's your backup plan? If it doesn't work out with Burke, you'll set your sights on his little brother. Good luck with that." She chuckles. "Dorian is too free spirited for his own good. The day that man marries is the day hell freezes over."

I'm processing all this as fast as I can, rendering me speechless.

The fact that Dorian's willing to stand up for his own convictions and bypass an enormous inheritance only makes me appreciate him more.

"Why do you look so shocked?" she asks. "I pegged you as a terrible actress from the moment you walked in, but you're *this close* to getting a Razzie Award."

"I'm sorry, I'm just . . ." I collect my thoughts, careful not to let anything slip. Despite originally being led to believe I was simply helping Burke give his elderly father a summer to remember, I realize now I was nothing more than a pawn in a sick and twisted inheritance game.

Burke lied to me by omission.

Even if our arrangement was nothing more than a transaction with a million-dollar price tag attached to it, it has cost me *everything*.

On top of that, if the truth ever comes out, I'll look just as self-serving as him, something that I imagine might make Dorian hate me more than he already does—if that's possible.

I hate that I was blinded by all those zeros, that I took Burke's word at face value and agreed to help him because I was convinced it was a sweet and innocent endeavor and not a chess move.

"Speak of the devil." Nicola paints a lukewarm smile on her face when she spots Burke on the other side of the waiting room. "Your ears must have been burning."

Burke ignores her, rubbing his tired eyes with his thumb and index finger.

"You doing okay?" I ask, rising to take his side. I rub my palm along his tension-filled shoulder, not because I'm trying to make a convincing show of this in front of Nicola but because the man before me looks more tired and browbeaten than I've ever seen him.

Maybe he doesn't need my comfort, but he's getting it anyway because the last thing I want is for Nicola to rain even more drama onto this already tragic situation.

"I think we should turn in for the night." Burke feels his pockets for his phone before remembering he doesn't have it on him.

"Dash got you a room at the Marriott," Nicola chimes in. "Feel free to get your beauty rest. I'll be here all night."

"The doctor said he's stable," Burke says. "And he needs his sleep. We all do. I'd rather be rested for tomorrow . . . and the next day. He's not getting out anytime soon."

Nicola shoves herself up from her seat, straightening the hem of her blouse.

"Suit yourself," she says, strutting off.

"If they're both staying, maybe we should too," I suggest. "I'm fine pushing some chairs together in the waiting room . . ."

He bristles as if the idea of sleeping in a fluorescent-lit hospital waiting area is akin to sleeping in a dark alley in the meatpacking district.

"Do you have your phone on you?" he asks. I nod. "May I borrow it?"

I hand it over, and he taps in a number he knows by heart. We're halfway to the elevator and he's midconversation when I realize he's talking to Yvette, rattling off all the things he wants her to pack in his overnight bag as well as telling her to throw a few things in for me. We're riding down to the main floor when he tells her to call the boat captain to have him make the delivery.

Never mind that it's getting late.

And forget the fact that Yvette likely had one of the most traumatic afternoons of her employment.

Burke doesn't say a word during the entire walk to the hotel, nor does he say more than a handful of words as we settle in for the night in a room with two queen-size beds. He takes the one by the air-conditioning unit, cranking it to the coldest setting before rolling over on his side.

It's impossible to know if he's being distant because his father is, quite literally, on his deathbed . . . or if he's no longer concerned with putting on a show because his inheritance is pretty much in the bag now, thanks to me.

In the hour that follows, I shiver under my icy blankets, attempting to chase sleep while Nicola's words take up residence in my head.

Every last one.

CHAPTER TWENTY-SEVEN

DORIAN

Present Day

"They're faking it," Nicola says from the other side of the ICU room.

"Chrissake, Nic, it's two in the morning. What the hell are you talking about?"

"Briar and Burke. They're faking it. This is about the inheritance."

My eyes are dry and burning from this stale hospital air, and my father's breath rattling in his chest is the stuff nightmares are made of, but Burke's engagement is the last thing on my mind.

"I just don't buy it." She shrugs, crossing her legs and leaning forward. "It's phony. Everything about it. It's an act. I mean, this woman has been in our lives for hardly a week. We've spent every day with her, and all we know is she's from Nebraska, and she's so agreeable it makes me want to poke my eyes out with a rusty razor blade."

Nicola and her theatrics . . .

"Can we talk about this some other time?" I point my gaze toward our dying father, whose heart is failing with every beat.

Five years ago, he was diagnosed with congestive heart failure, which was kept at bay with vasodilators, ACE inhibitors, aldosterone, and lifestyle changes.

But a few months ago, it got worse.

He's been living on borrowed time ever since.

The last thing he deserves is to go out with the two of us bickering across him.

"Believe it or not, not everyone gives a shit about our inheritance." I pinch the bridge of my nose, shutting my eyes to give them a break from watching this shit show unfold.

"We should test them." She ignores me, and her foot is bobbing up and down. I'm inclined to believe this is a coping mechanism, but I've got half a mind to head down to the twenty-four-hour gift shop and buy myself some noise-canceling headphones and her a book of *New York Times* crosswords. "I have an idea, but you have to be on board with it."

"I'm not," I say. "I'm not on board with anything. I just want to spend time with my dad before he dies. Can we focus on that? Please?"

"You've always been Dad's favorite, you know that, right?"

"If you're trying to guilt-trip me, it's not working."

"I was always so jealous." She huffs. "Who are we kidding, I still am. But it's like you could do no wrong in his eyes."

As the eldest living Rothwell sibling, Nicola has no doubt been held to a different standard.

My father got his mini-me in the form of Burke, who accomplished all the things that gave him ample material to brag about with his country club friends on the golf course.

But I've always been his wild card.

The one who went against the grain.

Still, Nic's not wrong—everything I ever did to push him away only made us closer.

Sometimes I think it's because I was the only one who ever told him how I felt, what I believed, what I stood for . . . when everyone else was telling him what they thought he wanted to hear.

"It's just fucking money," I tell her.

My grandfather once told me that when we die, all that remains is a dash on our tombstone between the day we were born and the day we took our final breath. It's up to us to make that dash count.

While his way of leaving a lasting legacy involved donating obscene amounts of money to various hospitals, libraries, and civic centers in exchange for them chiseling his name on well-placed placards, I'd prefer to make my dash count by living it to the fullest and on my terms.

"I want to reach out to Audrina," Nicola says.

I open my eyes, my vision blurry as I glare in her direction.

"Now why the hell would you do that?" I ask.

"I want to see how Burke reacts when he sees her. It'll tell us everything we need to know," she says.

Standing, I rake my hand along my jaw, conjuring the right words to say to her in this ridiculous moment that shouldn't be happening.

"Invite her," I say, "and I'll *never* forgive you."

CHAPTER TWENTY-EIGHT

BRIAR

Present Day

I wake to the buzz of my phone, my temples throbbing after a stressful and sleepless night and my head still occupied by unresolved thoughts and unanswered questions.

The caller ID reads "Restricted," sending me shooting out of bed with a sharp gasp, convinced it's someone calling from the hospital with bad news.

The other bed is empty, nothing but a mess of tangled white sheets. On the opposite side of the wall, the shower is running.

Clearing my throat, I tap the green button and answer the call.

"Hello?" I ask.

"Hi, yes, is this . . . Briar?" a woman's voice asks. My heart races, sure that it's a nurse or doctor from Boston Medical trying to reach Burke via my number since he doesn't have his phone.

"This is she." I can hardly hear the sound of my own voice through the whooshing heartbeat in my ears.

"This is Audrina Fairchild," she says. "My assistant was going through my DMs yesterday, and she found yours . . ."

Oh my god.

With everything going on, I completely forgot I'd messaged her when we were in town last Saturday.

"Is this . . . legit?" she asks.

"One hundred percent," I answer without pause. I'm not sure how long Burke's been in the shower or how much time we have left, but if he walks out and finds me talking to his ex-fiancée, he's going to have questions, and it's far too early in the morning to answer them.

"I'm sorry. I get a lot of crazy DMs . . . but I heard he was engaged," she says. "And I heard her name was Briar . . . I just . . . can you send me proof?"

The two of us have yet to take a single photo together.

I could give her a play-by-play of everything that's happened over the past week, but Burke might hear me and wonder who the hell I'm talking to.

"I can . . . just not right now. We're in Boston," I say, peeling my phone from my ear. My battery is at 17 percent. "Redmond's in the ICU at BMC. Things are a little . . . unsorted right now. Can I call you later today? Once I have more time to explain?"

"Redmond's in the ICU? What happened?"

"We found him collapsed in the potting shed yesterday." I keep my voice low while listening to make sure the shower's still running. "His heart is failing. He's stable for now, but we don't know how much time we have."

The other end is silent for a few beats, followed by a muffled sob.

"I'm sorry," she eventually says. "Redmond was like a second father to me. I knew he had some health problems, but I didn't know . . . you never think . . . no one's ever ready for this kind of thing, you know?"

"I understand."

"I'm flying into New York right now—we're supposed to land in half an hour. I'll see if we can detour to Boston instead. I'd never forgive myself if I didn't get to see him one last time."

Shit.

I simply wanted to talk to her about Burke—I didn't expect her to be making a surprise appearance.

I'm about to tell her that I should check with the family first when the shower handle squeaks on the other side of the wall, and the water stops running.

Burke will be stepping out any second.

"I'll call you when I land," she says between sniffs.

"Okay," I say because it's not like I can tell her not to come. She's beside herself.

"Can you text me the hospital room number when we hang up?"

"Sure. I need your number, though."

"I'll text it to you when we hang up. But one more thing before I let you go." She pauses for a few beats. "Is . . . Dorian . . . there?"

The silence lingering between us spans an entire ocean, literally and figuratively.

"Of course," I say, wondering why she'd ask such a thing. "Nicola and Dash are here too."

She's quiet once again before exhaling into the receiver.

"All right," she says. "I'll get there as soon as I can."

I remember Nicola's words last night about Rothwell men having a tendency to rewrite their histories.

She was referring to Redmond at first and then Burke.

But Dorian's a Rothwell man too.

What other details have been omitted from this entire thing?

Why would Audrina specifically ask if Dorian would be there?

"You're up. Finally." Burke emerges from the bathroom, a white towel cinched low on his hips. "I'm ordering room service. You hungry?"

I can't possibly think about food at a time like this, not when it feels like the world is about to blow up in all our faces the second Audrina's flight touches down.

They say no good deed goes unpunished.

"Sure." I climb out of my bed, the soles of my feet pressing against the cool, short-pile carpet. My appetite is gone, but if I don't have something to settle my stomach now, I'll be dry heaving later when shit hits the fan. "Eggs and toast, please. Coffee."

He cradles the landline receiver on his shoulder, whistling to himself as he scans the room service menu. I'd ask him how he's doing, but he seems unusually chipper given the situation with his father.

I'm beginning to realize that maybe I had him all wrong from the start.

He intentionally misled me about his father's condition.

And his emotional distance and detachment were never about his broken heart or his ailing father—he was nothing more than annoyed about having to go through some dog and pony show to collect his inheritance.

I don't want to believe it, but the past ten hours have shown me he's not who I thought he was—not even close.

All the things I want to say to him dance on the tip of my tongue, but I swallow them down. This isn't the time or the place. Even if he's a horribly self-centered excuse for a human being, he's about to lose his father, and the last thing I want to do to anyone in this family is insert myself more than I already have.

That aside, Audrina's question about Dorian stands out in a sea of bitter thoughts.

Why would she specifically ask about him?

What else don't I know?

What other details did Burke leave out when it came to his broken engagement?

I lock myself in the bathroom, change out of yesterday's clothes, and pray I didn't ruin *everything* for *everyone.*

Especially Dorian.

CHAPTER
TWENTY-NINE

DORIAN

Present Day

"That was bleak," I say to my sister after the doctor briefs us. It's barely past 8:00 a.m. The stale stench of yesterday's clothes and coffee breath fills the air. My back throbs from sleeping in a chair all night.

But I'm not leaving.

"Just because they're giving up hope doesn't mean we have to." Nicola exhales, sinking back in the seat she placed beside Dad's bed. Dr. Calloway all but told us to start making funeral arrangements, but leave it to my sister to plant her feet firmly in the soil of denial. "Mind if I use your charger?"

At some point in the middle of the night, a staff member from the house dropped off a few essentials for each of us: phones, charging cords, changes of clothes, toiletries, even some boxed meals—though who can eat at a time like this?

I tug the cord from the socket and hand it to Nic before returning to my post and burying my face in my hands. Inhaling through my fingers, I gather a long, hard breath of bleach-scented air and let it go.

Staring at the man isn't going to prolong his life.

Wishing and hoping and praying he'll pull through won't either.

"Dash is supposed to bring the kids by around nine o'clock," Nicola says after checking her phone, though I suspect she's talking to herself. "I'm debating on whether I should just send them all back to the island."

I don't answer. It's not my decision to make, and I don't give a damn either way.

"It isn't good for the kids to see their grandfather like this, you know?" she continues. "This shouldn't be their last memory of him."

Again, I stay silent.

"Ugh," she sighs. "I'm not getting a signal in this room. Are you?"

"I wouldn't know." I haven't made a call or checked my phone since it was dropped off.

"I'll be right back." Phone in hand, Nicola trots to the hall.

My father's chest rises and falls as the monitors beep—slow and steady, then sporadically fast for a handful of beats. His face is swollen. Fingers too. The nurse said that's common with heart failure patients. I just hate the way it distorts him.

Eyes closed, I try to imagine living in a world where Redmond Rothwell III no longer exists, only instead, my mind is rattling off all the ways I could have been a better son.

I could have visited more than once a year.

I could have called on days that weren't birthdays or holidays.

I could have stayed longer than eight weeks in the summer instead of ticking off each day like a kid at sleepaway camp biding his time until it's over.

I could have listened to his stories without interrupting him and reminding him that he'd already told that one before.

The old man and I have had our share of differences over the years, but the love was never lost . . . I just did a shitty job at making that clear to him.

I hopped on a tour bus, lived a dream life that was only afforded to me because of my last name, and I made excuses.

"I'm sorry, Dad," I say because this might be the last time I'll ever have a moment alone with him. "And I love you."

Those three little words have never come easily to me. My mother used to say them so much that I convinced myself they lost their meaning, and I went out of my way to avoid saying them after that—until Audrina came along.

Saying them to him now feels like too little, too late.

A light rap at the door shakes me out of my despondent reverie. I sit straight, unfurling my tight back, and slide my palms against the top of my jeans as I wait for the nurse to come in and do her thing.

Only it's not a nurse.

It's Audrina.

Her white-blonde hair is twisted into a neat bun on the top of her head; her face is scrubbed free of any trace of makeup, and her long-limbed body is covered with coordinating beige sweats, but it's her.

"What the hell are you doing here?" I keep my voice low. Heat stings my veins as I recall Nic's idea from last night. I made it crystal clear that if she invited Audrina to the hospital, I'd never forgive her. Not unsurprisingly, my words fell on deaf ears.

Guess she'll learn the hard way that I made a promise, not a threat . . .

"This space is for family only," I add, rising. "You can't be here."

She gives me an apologetic half smile, before striding toward the bed and taking a seat on the edge.

"I didn't come here for you," she says to me while concentrating on my father. "Or your brother. I'm here for Redmond and only Redmond."

Audrina swipes a tear from her cheek before cupping her hand over my father's.

"Jesus Christ," I mutter under my breath as I turn to leave. I can't watch this shit show another second longer. That, and I need to find my sister and have her take care of this problem she created.

"Redmond, it's Audrina," she says to him, her voice as soft as cashmere. "I just wanted to thank you for . . ."

I don't stick around to listen.

My father was good to her. That much I know. She reminded him of his first wife, he once told me. Outgoing. Adventurous. Worldly. Captivating. Easy on the eyes. Every time I'd bring Audrina by, my father would light up like Christmas and the Fourth of July had come all at once.

And I couldn't blame him . . . because I did the same thing.

Once upon a time, I was smitten with her—so smitten that I got down on one knee and proposed marriage because she wanted a commitment and a ring—and my biggest fear was losing her. I was willing to put aside my personal beliefs on the outdated institution of marriage as long as it meant keeping her.

And she was mine . . .

. . . until the summer I brought her to Driftway and she met Burke.

I turn right at the end of the hall and find my sister leaning against the wall, her phone pressed to the side of her face as she barks orders to someone I can only assume is her husband.

"What the hell?" I throw my hands up as I stalk toward her.

Her manicured brows knit as she presses her phone against her chest and mouths "What?"

"Don't play dumb. You know what you did."

"Dash, let me call you back . . ." She ends the call and slides her cell into her back pocket. "What's wrong? Is Dad okay?"

"Why is Audrina here?"

Nicola's expression turns ashen as she squints. "What?"

"You heard me."

"Audrina's here? As in . . . at the hospital?"

Exhaling, I hook my hands on my hips, jaw clenched.

I don't have time for these little games.

"She's in Dad's room right now. Sitting on his bed. Holding his hand. Talking to him. How the hell did she know where he was?" I ask. "You called her after I specifically told you not to."

Nicola pushes past me, striding back to the room as if she doesn't believe me—which doesn't bode well for my theory about Nic being the one who extended the invitation. Now that I think about it, Nic didn't even have her phone until a few hours ago. Unless Audrina happened to be in the area, there's no way she could've gotten here that fast.

I follow my sister back to the ICU, where she stops cold in the doorway.

She's as shocked as I was a couple of minutes ago.

"Audrina," she says, arms crossed as she walks into the room like she owns the place. "What are you doing here?"

Audrina glances up. "Nic. Hi. It's been a while . . ."

"Did Burke invite you? I'm so confused." Nicola turns to me, her hand splayed on her chest. "I swear it wasn't me. You can look through my phone. I wouldn't do that to you . . ."

My sister is famous for meddling, and a few minutes ago, this had her name written all over it, but for some reason, I'm inclined to believe her now.

Audrina uncrosses her long legs and clears her throat before rising and slinging her monogrammed bag over one shoulder.

"I know I'm not exactly welcomed in this family anymore," she says, "but I wanted to say goodbye to Redmond while I still could."

"You still haven't answered me," Nicola says. "Who invited you?"

"Audrina?" Burke's voice from the hallway steals our collective attention. "What are you doing here?"

I don't tell him he's the third person to ask that question because I'm too busy wondering why he's asking it at all . . .

If it wasn't Nic and it sure as hell wasn't me who invited her, it had to have been him.

My brother pushes between us and makes his way to our ex. From the corner of my eye, I spot Briar standing in the hallway, one hand gripping her opposite arm and her eyes fixed on the cream tile floor.

"Burke." Audrina's eyes light up when she sees him. "Hi."

I steal another look at Briar. Despite the fact that this is beyond disrespectful to her, she doesn't seem the least bit bothered.

"I wanted to see your father one last time." Audrina places her hand on Burke's arm. "I hope I'm not upsetting you by being here."

I choke on a laugh.

Funny, she didn't apologize to me a few minutes ago.

"No, it's fine," Burke says. His back is to all of us now, and I'm 99 percent sure Briar's the furthest thing from his mind. "I'm glad you could make it."

I'm sure he is . . .

"I'm just confused," he continues. "How did you know we were here?"

Audrina's eyes flick to the doorway, where Briar had been standing just moments ago—only now she's gone.

CHAPTER THIRTY

BRIAR

Present Day

"This must be weird for you." Nicola takes the seat beside me in the waiting room. She's speaking slowly and softly, though frigidity remains in her cool green eyes.

While Burke was processing the fact that Audrina was standing before him, I got the urge to leave. Not because I wanted anyone to think I was upset but because I wanted to give him a moment alone with her, a moment where he didn't have to worry about how his siblings would perceive the entire exchange with me watching.

Ten minutes passed before Nicola came out to check on me, though I can't decide if she's checking on me or digging for dirt.

"Are you upset?" Nicola asks, settling into her chair. She folds her arms. "Because you have every right to be. If Dash's ex showed up here . . . I don't know what I'd do, but it wouldn't be pretty."

"It's fine," I say.

From the corner of my eye, I spot Dorian making his way to the elevator. He glances in our direction, and our gazes lock for half a second before he continues.

"It's fine?" She repeats my words as if they leave a salty taste on her tongue, and then she reaches for a copy of *Town & Country* magazine from the coffee table in front of us. "You must be a bigger person than me, then."

I shrug. The less I say, the better.

"None of us can figure out who invited her," Nic says through a yawn as she flicks the glossy pages. "Wasn't me. Dorian swears it wasn't him. Burke looked shocked when he saw her, though who knows. He could've been acting for your sake." She nods toward the wall clock. "I think it's strange that you've been out here quite a while and he hasn't once come to check on you."

"He doesn't have to check on me. I'm a grown woman."

"She broke his heart," Nic says. "And the second she's back in his life, you're chopped liver. All I'm saying is I'd be livid."

"You and I are pretty different."

"Fair." She sniffs. "I guess the entire thing doesn't sit right with me."

"I'm sorry, Nicola, but I really don't want to have this conversation with you." I cross my legs, take a deep breath, and pray she doesn't bite my head off. There's a contentiousness emanating off her in waves, and I don't want any part of it.

A familiar-looking nurse with thick crimson curls piled on top of her head trots into the waiting room, scanning the sea of unsmiling faces until she finds Nicola.

Abandoning the shiny magazine—and our conversation—Nicola races over to her. Their words are too soft for me to hear from this side of the room, but three seconds later, they're both gone.

Whatever it is . . . it can't be good.

Several minutes pass before I decide to head back to the room to see if Burke needs me, but before I so much as get out of my chair, I spot Audrina passing by.

She must have noticed me at the same time because she makes a beeline in my direction.

"Briar?" she asks when she's closer.

"Yes?"

"I'm Audrina." She extends her hand, gifting a soft smile that contradicts the pain behind her bright-blue eyes. "Thank you for letting me know about Redmond."

"Of course," I say, though it was never my intention.

"Do you mind?" She points to the seat beside me.

"Not at all."

Tucking a loose strand of platinum hair behind her ear, she cups her dainty fingertips over her nose and mouth and breathes out.

"Did you see the way he looked at me?" she asks.

I didn't—because I was behind Burke and his back was to me the entire time. From the moment we left the hotel and climbed into the Uber (to take us a mere three blocks because Burke didn't want to walk in the early-morning drizzle), Burke shut me out emotionally, physically, and otherwise. After breakfast, he said maybe five whole words to me. And once we arrived at the hospital, he walked at least three steps ahead of me from the main entrance to the elevator to the ICU.

After learning about Burke's inheritance situation—and witnessing how lifted his spirits have been since his father's medical crisis—I'm realizing I've pegged him all wrong. The only reason I contacted Audrina at all was because I felt sorry for Burke. Now I'm beginning to think he wasn't heartbroken over this woman so much as he was licking his wounds.

Men like him aren't used to rejection because they're usually the ones doing the rejecting.

He wasn't devastated. He was nursing a bruised ego.

"He seems angry that I'm here," she says with a bittersweet sigh.

"Burke?" I shake my head. "I didn't get that at all."

"No, Dorian," she says.

"Why would Dorian care?"

Her full lips press flat as her eyes search mine. "You don't know?"

"Know what?"

"Before I was engaged to Burke . . . I was engaged to Dorian." Her lips flutter into the faintest smile as she says his name, but it vanishes in an instant. "I ended things with Dorian when I met Burke. Dorian's schedule was so different than mine. We were both too invested in our careers to put our relationship first." She pauses as if she's reminiscing in a silent memory. "And then I met Burke. He was like the suit-and-tie version of Dorian. And he was always in New York—which is where my primary apartment is. Burke felt like home base, I guess. He felt solid. Like a sure thing. Driven as hell too. And as much as I hate to admit this, I found his arrogance charming—at first. Dorian acted like giving me a ring was like imposing some kind of death sentence on him. I swear when he proposed, he had tears in his eyes and not the happy kind."

The idea of Dorian getting down on one knee seems farcical given what I know, but I'm too busy attempting to digest all this information to form a sensible response, so I simply nod and listen.

"Anyway. I suppose I don't need to get into the dirty details of how everything went down," she says. "It wasn't pretty, I'll say that. I wish it could have been different."

"So you broke off your engagement to Dorian . . . to be with Burke?" I ask, wanting to ensure I'm getting this right.

"Regretfully."

"And then you broke it off with Burke when you found the dating app on his phone?"

Her mouth bunches at one side. "What dating app?"

Nicola's mention of the Rothwell men's tendency of rewriting their own histories plays in my mind.

"He told me you found a dating app on his phone, and that's why you called it off," I say. "Is that not what happened?"

"Wow. Yeah, no. That's not what happened at all." She narrows her gaze for half a second. "I ended it with Burke because I was still in love with Dorian. He told you it was because of a dating app?"

"Yeah." I swallow. "He did."

If Dorian and Audrina reconnect because of the situation *I've* orchestrated, the irony of that will haunt me for the rest of my life.

"For the record, Burke lied to you," she says, chin tipped high, arms crossed. "Which is honestly another reason I ended it with him. He was always lying about little, inconsequential things. Like what he had for breakfast or how many miles he ran or whether or not he'd read a certain book or seen a certain play. I didn't want to spend the rest of my life wondering what else he was lying about . . . or waiting for him to lie about bigger things."

Audrina gasps, placing her hand on my forearm.

"Oh god. I'm sorry." She bites her bottom lip, her pretty face wincing. "I know you're engaged. I don't mean to speak badly about Burke. I know you love him . . . he's just not for me."

"I don't understand," I say. "When I spoke to you on the phone earlier, you were calling because of the message I sent you about Burke still being in love with you."

"Right."

"If you didn't want to be with him anymore, why did you contact me at all?"

Folding her hands, she slides them between her knees, letting her shoulders fall. "Well, to be honest, someone told me he was engaged again, and I guess I was curious . . . but when you mentioned Redmond being in the hospital, I threw my curiosity out the window. All I could think about was getting here as fast as I could."

"You asked about Dorian before we hung up."

"Yeah," she says. "I figured he'd be here, too, but I needed to prepare myself. I've reached out to him several times over the past six months. He finally called me back a month ago, but only to tell me to stop contacting him because he's in love with someone else."

My heart stops cold.

He could have had the gorgeous, well-traveled, and adored-by-millions woman who shattered his heart into a thousand pieces—but he turned her down . . . for *me*.

"He hates me now." She waves a manicured hand as she rolls her eyes, though her voice breaks with the pain of a woman in the throes of regret. "And he should. He has every right to after what I did. And I had a lot of nerve asking for a second chance. I know that. I guess part of me was hoping if he saw me again . . . maybe he'd reconsider. But the look on his face when I walked into the room . . ."

Her voice trails off, though her words are better left unsaid.

I've seen that look.

I've *felt* that look.

It's enough to make the world tilt on its axis before screeching to a halt—in the worst way.

"It's so strange, isn't it?" Her ethereal eyes search mine. "Life, I mean."

She can say that again.

"You love Burke. Burke loves me. I love Dorian. Dorian hates me," Audrina says. "Meanwhile, the patriarch of the Rothwell family is dying. It's like our own little messed-up real-life soap opera."

None of this is entertaining to me, but I don't disagree.

It's messed up from every angle.

"Dorian wanted to show me the world," she says, "but Burke wanted to *give* me the world. Those are two very different things, two very different futures. I know now that I chose the wrong one, and I've spent every day hating myself for that."

"You couldn't have known." It's strange, offering sympathy to a woman who would swipe Dorian out from under me if she had the chance. Not that he's mine to begin with. Not anymore anyway. But if she could, she would. She's still in love with him.

And when you love someone—truly love them—you do whatever you can to be with them.

"I should probably get going." Audrina rises and adjusts the strap of her oversize bag over her lithe shoulder. "Thank you for reaching out to me, though. I'm grateful for the opportunity to see Redmond one more time. And I got the answer I was looking for with Dorian." Her lips arch into a soft smile. "Congrats on your engagement."

"Thank you." I'm too stunned by all this to say anything more; then again, what more is there to say?

"Could you do me a favor?" she says before she leaves. "I hate to ask you this because you've already been so gracious to me, but if you ever get the chance . . . if it ever comes up in conversation someday . . . could you tell Dorian that I still love him? And that I always will?"

My eyes turn hot, and I blink away the threat of tears.

"Sure," I say, though I imagine I'm the last person Dorian would want to talk to about that topic.

On that note, Audrina's gone, her long legs striding toward the elevator bay outside the waiting room. From here, I watch her step inside, her eyes glued to the floor, and in the seconds before the doors close, I swear I see her swipe a tear away.

That woman could have anyone she wants.

Anyone in the world.

And she wants Dorian.

I knew he was special when we first met, but learning I'm not the only one who feels that way is the gut punch I wasn't expecting today.

I wallow in my thoughts for a few more minutes before Burke appears in the doorway. He scans the room until he spots me, then makes his way to the chair beside me—the exact one Audrina sat in just moments ago.

"How's he doing?" I ask.

Despite the fact that I'm displeased with his lies, I'm not heartless.

He slumps back, his fist half covering his mouth, and then he exhales.

"He's gone," Burke says.

I begin to say something before I realize what he said.

"Oh, Burke." I place my hand on his arm—a knee-jerk reaction—and offer him some comfort. Comfort he hasn't needed and arguably doesn't quite deserve. "I'm so sorry."

When the nurse came out earlier to grab Nicola, there was a sense of urgency about the whole thing, but I didn't expect this.

At least, not so soon.

"You doing okay?" I ask after a bout of silence.

He sniffs, though there aren't any tears, so I don't think he's crying.

"Yeah," he says.

"What can I do?" Sitting here makes me feel useless. I can't imagine that going to the room is an option, but what wouldn't I give to throw my arms around Dorian and offer him my heartfelt sympathies—even if he doesn't want them?

Burke straightens his posture, and I release my hand from his forearm.

"How did Audrina know we were here?" He angles his head my way, his eyes pointed and dark. "Nic and Dorian claim they didn't tell her. Dashiell doesn't have her number, and he's not on social media. The staff at Driftway are all under strict NDAs. *You* were the only other person who knew."

His father just died, and *this* is what plagues him right now?

"It was me," I say, "but before you get upset, please hear me out."

His stoic, unreadable expression is unnerving, but nevertheless, I continue.

"You know when we went into town? And we had cell service?" I ask. "I messaged her on Instagram. I told her I was your fiancée and that I was worried you were still in love with her."

Burke leans forward, his elbows on his knees and his head in his hand. "For fuck's sake, Briar. Why the hell would you do that?"

"Because I thought I was . . . I don't know . . . reuniting you with the one that got away?" I shrug. "You were always looking at pictures of her on your phone—I just thought—I don't know—I thought you were brokenhearted, and I thought I could help."

He pinches his nose before sitting straight again and rubbing his palms on the tops of his thighs.

"I'm sorry," I say. They say the worst thing you can do is justify an apology with an excuse, so I'll leave it at that.

"You didn't mention our"—he scans the room before leaning closer—"arrangement, did you?"

"Of course not."

He studies me as if he's some sort of human lie detector all of a sudden.

"I would never," I say. Voice low, I add, "Why didn't you tell me she's the one who dumped you? That she was with Dorian first? That she still loved—"

"Because none of that was any of your concern."

"You didn't have to make up a story about some stupid dating app. You lied to me."

"I'm not discussing this with you." He rises from Audrina's chair, turning to face me. "If you don't mind, I just lost my father. I'm going to be with my father. And you should come with me, seeing as how you're my *fiancée*."

The jig isn't up simply because Redmond's gone.

I imagine I'm still obliged to play this part until he collects his portion of the Rothwell inheritance.

I follow Burke to the ICU, and we stop in the hall outside Redmond's room, where Nicola, Dashiell, and Dorian are huddled.

Nicola's eyes are bloodshot, yesterday's makeup smeared beneath her lower lids. Dash slips his arm around her, pulling her against him.

Dorian wears a shell-shocked expression on his face, his gaze averted.

"I'm so sorry," I say to them. "This is so awful."

Nicola shoots me a look.

Dorian ignores me.

Burke slips his hand into mine and steers me closer to him, a silent hint for me to console him, I suppose. I imagine he feels the desperation to sell "us" now more than ever.

"If there's anything I can do, please let me know," I say. But again, my words fall on deaf ears. I don't hold it against them, though. They're in mourning. They're devastated. They don't owe anyone anything. "I'm happy to make phone calls if you'd like."

Nicola peels her cheek from her husband's cashmere-sweater-covered chest and shoots me a cold look. On second thought, I imagine they have people who can do that for them . . . people who've known the family longer than a couple of weeks.

Two nurses exit Redmond's room with somber faces, pulling the door closed behind them.

One of them places a magnet on the door, one depicting a single burning candle.

The five of us stand in silence for what feels like forever, nothing but beeping monitors and nurses'-station chatter filling the background.

From the corner of my eye, I steal a glimpse of Dorian, replaying my conversation with Audrina in my head. His hair is messy, and his clothes are wrinkled, and he's still the most beautiful, broken thing

I've ever seen. For a second, his lower lip trembles, but he reins it in. A moment later, he walks away without uttering a single word to anyone.

My heart breaks for him.

But also for us.

A month ago, he loved me.

If only he knew . . . I never stopped loving him.

CHAPTER THIRTY-ONE

DORIAN

Present Day

I hang the rented suit on the back of my guest room door for Yvette to return, and I tug the zipper around my suitcase. Crazy to think this might be the last time I'll set foot on these grounds. I'm on the fence as to whether that's a good thing or a bad thing. This place haunts my dreams when I'm not here, filled with some of the happiest moments of my life—but also all the worst moments.

A shadow passing by the doorway catches my eye. I turn to look when said shadow stops moving.

"Hi." It's Briar. She rests her cheek against the whitewashed trim as she studies me. "You're leaving already?"

Her voice is cashmere, and her eyes are glimmering, and she hasn't stopped staring at me all week, though she's yet to say more than a handful of clichéd lines, asking if I'm okay.

I don't know why she cares. Burke should be the recipient of her unneeded sympathies.

With my back to her, I do whatever it takes to appear like I'm too preoccupied with my luggage to pay her any mind.

The floor creaks as she makes her way to the bed, taking it upon herself to curl up on the foot of it. She draws her knees against her chest, wraps her arms around them, and sighs.

"You've been so quiet," she says. "I just want to make sure you're okay."

"You've asked me that a million times already. Kind of getting old . . ."

"I know," she says. "Nic has Dash. Burke has me. Who's checking on you?"

"For the record, you're under no obligation to be that person."

"Why didn't you tell me you were engaged before? When we first met?" she asks. "You were all antimarriage from the second you sat down. When Audrina told me what happened . . ."

Her voice tapers off as if she expects me to fill in the blanks or take the lead, but I have nothing to say. Audrina is neither here nor there, and while Briar is here, she might as well be there too.

"Audrina told me why she broke it off with Burke." Briar traces her fingertip along a pattern in the quilt before flicking her bright gaze to me.

"I don't mean to interrupt." Yvette knocks on the open door, then clasps her hands at her hips. Despite her bloodshot, swollen eyes, she's still as put together as always, still running a tight ship, as if the old man were here to supervise. "But your boat's at the dock, Dorian."

She spots the rented suit hanging behind the door and adjusts the plastic cover until it's perfectly protected.

"Thank you," I tell her.

She gives a terse nod and some semblance of a smile before disappearing. I've tried to check on her a handful of times this week, but all she does is assure me she's fine before changing the subject to something related to her duties.

"You're really leaving?" Briar asks. "Now?"

In a few hours, I'll be flying out of Boston, en route to Jacksonville, to meet up with the band and rejoin the tour. After Jacksonville, we're heading to Atlanta, then making a few other stops up the coast in the days that follow. As long as I'm anywhere but here, I'm golden.

I slide my suitcase off the bed, letting it land with an angry thump on the hardwood floor.

Briar rises off the bed, wrapping her arms around her sides and taking small, reticent steps in my direction.

"I'm sorry it didn't work out for us the way we wanted it to." Her bittersweet tone is apologetic and as low as a whisper. "I wish it could've been different."

I say nothing . . . because nothing I say will change any of this.

The damage has been done.

It is what it fucking is.

"There's so much more I wish I could say to you right now," she adds, keeping her voice low like she's worried someone might hear it. Burke perhaps. This entire exchange has been a mere ten seconds, but it's already reminding me of a similar conversation I had with Audrina when she handed over the vintage three-carat yellow diamond I gave her—her supposed dream ring—and informed me she'd fallen in love with my brother.

I'm not interested in reliving any of that shit again, so I wheel my bag into the hall, leaving her to wallow in her own self-pity—as she should.

"Regardless of what you think, Dorian," she says, following me, "I care about you. Deeply. More than you could possibly imagine. And maybe you hate me . . . and that's fine . . . but I could never, would never hate you. I just want you to know that."

A door down the hallway creaks open, and out steps my brother with shower-damp hair, wearing linen shorts and a crisp white button-down. Never mind that we just buried our father yesterday; Burke's clearly back in vacation mode.

"You leaving already?" he asks.

"Yep." I roll my bag to the top of the stairs, although I'm half-tempted to linger a bit longer to see if Burke questions why his fiancée is stepping out of my room. Changing my mind, I carry on.

My boat is waiting.

And so is the rest of my life.

Everything else I'm leaving behind.

CHAPTER THIRTY-TWO

BRIAR

Present Day

"Is this you?" I hand Burke a photograph of a dark-haired child standing beside a snowman three times his size. His smile is wide, with a gap where his two front teeth should be, and he's grinning so hard his eyes look like slits.

He sniffs beside me on the sunroom sofa. "Yeah. I must have been six or seven. We were having a competition to see who could build the biggest snowman. It was Dad and me against Mom, Nic, and Dorian. Dad brought out the snowplow so we could push the snow into huge segments."

"Safe to say you won?" I ask.

"Of course." Nicola rolls her eyes. "Burke won everything, always."

His gaze lingers on the photo for another moment before he turns his attention to the next pile.

Earlier today, Nicola brought out every photo album she could find, wanting to place them all in chronological order so she could send them to an archivist. Somewhere along the line, the task at hand lost some steam, and instead, the two of them were reminiscing about old times.

It is nice to see them laughing and enjoying one another's company for once.

It's too bad that isn't the norm.

People with siblings have no idea how lucky they are to have someone to weather these storms with.

"I should see if Dash needs help putting the kids to bed." Nicola closes the photo album in her lap and places it gently on the coffee table.

Taking a break from sifting through these old Rothwell family memories, I curl up under a blanket on the sunroom sofa and watch the sky turn from tawny orange to indigo before settling on a deep-Atlantic-blue shade.

This island's history, views, and isolation set it a world apart from reality.

I can see why it meant so much to Redmond and the staff who have dedicated their lives to maintaining its unparalleled New England charm.

The instant Nicola's gone, Burke slides farther away from me, leaving an entire sofa-cushion-size space between us. I'm not sure if it's an unconscious move or if he needs a break from being in my atmosphere. Since Redmond's passing, Burke has dialed up the intensity of our phony romance to a fever pitch, playing up the brokenhearted-son act while making up for lost time with the fake engagement he thought he'd have all summer to milk.

Either way, I'm not complaining about the space between us.

In fact, I welcome it.

This past week has been nothing short of eye opening, and I've come to realize Burke truly is as insufferable as he pretends not to be. Everything about him is fake. Everything he does is for self-preservation.

He's the worst kind of human, and now that I've seen it, I can't unsee it.

"Have you heard from Dorian?" I ask.

Burke scoffs. "No. Why would I?"

"Just wondering if he made it to where he was going safely." I didn't get a chance to ask where he was headed. Earlier, I attempted to google the band's tour schedule, but my signal was weaker than ever.

He could be anywhere.

But all that matters is he's not here.

"We don't do that." His handsome face is shriveled with disgust. "We just assume everyone makes it to wherever they're going unless we hear otherwise."

"I see." I adjust the knit blanket over my chilled feet and focus on the crashing waves in the distance, watching them splash against the very same dock Dorian stepped from eleven hours earlier when he boarded his boat back to town.

Maybe I'm imagining it, but the house feels emptier without him. Even though his company wasn't mine to enjoy, his presence was quietly comforting. In a way, it made me feel complete. Like all the parts of me were here and in working order. Now that he's gone, there might as well be a cannonball-size hole in my chest.

"How do you think he's doing with everything?" I ask next because I can't help myself. He's haunting my every thought. In fact, I miss him so much it hurts. There's an ache in my middle and a void in my soul that weren't there until this morning.

Earlier in the week, all three siblings had decided to stay as long as necessary to help tidy up loose ends with the staff and the estate and anything else. I thought we'd have at least another week, maybe two, together.

When I walked past his room this morning and saw him zipping his suitcase, it was like the bottom dropped out from under me.

Despite knowing how it could look if Burke found me sitting on Dorian's bed talking to him, I took my chance in case it was the last time I'd ever see him again.

"Dorian's clearly fine if he's already back to work." Burke flicks through a stack of Polaroids, most of which appear to be of his sister, and judging by his heavy breathing, that fact annoys him. He tosses them aside and moves on to the next pile. "It's just like the bastard— skirting any real responsibilities."

"Maybe his band needs him."

Burke snorts. "More than his family needs him?"

"Do you . . . do *you* need him?" I ask. "Because the two of you didn't say more than a handful of words to each other all week."

Nicola clearly doesn't need him. She has Dash. Plus her hands are full with the children. She didn't seem the least bit bothered by the news that Dorian was jumping ship early.

"It's called moral support," he says. "He should be here, and he isn't. I think that speaks volumes, and I don't know why you're defending any of that."

"Everyone handles grief differently. Maybe he needed a change of scenery. Maybe he wanted to immerse himself in something that didn't . . . I don't know . . . didn't make him sad. You can't assume everyone is like you."

He squints, scratching at his temple. "And what am I like exactly?"

I want to say cold . . . unfeeling . . . self-centered.

But I think better of it.

"You're . . . you." I shrug. I don't know what else to say that wouldn't offend him. "The two of you are night and day."

"Clearly."

"I just think maybe he's more sensitive than you, and maybe, as his big brother, it wouldn't be the worst thing if you reached out to him to make sure he's okay."

Burke slowly turns to face me, his eyes laced with a searing incredulity.

"Forgive me for not taking your advice on account of you knowing my family a mere hot minute," he says. "Thanks, but no thanks. And I'll pass on any other unsolicited advice you feel so inclined to give."

I shoot up, tossing the blanket onto the sofa arm.

"Where do you think you're going?" His brows narrow, and he waves a photo in the air. "We're not finished."

As much as Dorian hated me during the past weeks, he never once spoke to me with such utter condescension. And he sure as hell didn't treat me like a piece of property. On top of that, not once has Burke asked if I'm okay. Maybe I didn't know Redmond as long as anyone else, but I still knew him. I enjoyed his hospitality and his conversations and the way he welcomed me into his home. His death has affected me, too, though Burke wouldn't know that because he hasn't troubled himself to so much as care.

Folding my arms, I choose my words carefully. I don't want to go rounds with him. I'm too exhausted. In fact, I might sleep in another room tonight. The last thing I need is Burke's toxic energy seeping into my skin and plaguing my dreams.

"I'm tired," I say.

"Going to bed already?" He checks his watch. "It's not even nine o'clock. There are children who stay up later than this."

"Again, I'm tired," I repeat. "And I'm sleeping in another room tonight."

"Yvette's gone for the day. She won't be here to make up another bed for you."

"I'll just use Dorian's."

"Ah." His lips slide into a cockeyed sneer. "And there it is."

"What's that supposed to mean?"

"What were you doing leaving his room this morning?" He asks the question I've been waiting for all day. He happened to be in the hall when Dorian was leaving, and despite watching me walk out of that bedroom, he didn't breathe a word about it. Not at breakfast. Not at lunch or dinner. Not in the hundreds of seconds and minutes that have since passed.

"I was saying goodbye."

"You went into a man's room—a man you hardly knew—to personally tell him goodbye?" The contempt in his voice is laid on thicker than Tammy Faye Bakker's mascara. "That, coupled with your concern for his safety and well-being, makes me think you've taken a liking to my brother."

"I'm not sure where you're going with this, but I'm tired, and I'm going to bed." I turn to leave, but he tuts.

"I can already tell you, even if you were free to date someone else, he wouldn't be interested in you. He's still hung up on whoever that girl was from last year."

My stomach plummets and my mouth runs dry. "What?"

"I told you before . . . he met someone last summer . . ."

"Yes, I remember. But how do you know he still loves her?"

"Because." His nose wrinkles as if he finds my question annoying and pointless. "He told me."

"When?" My voice is breathless, and Burke is two seconds from seeing through me, I'm sure of it, but I have to know.

"Oh my god. I was right." He tosses a stack of photos onto the coffee table, sinks back, and threads his fingers behind his head as he scrutinizes me from across the room. "You *do* have a thing for Dorian."

I consider telling him he's wrong.

I could brush this off, insist he's imagining it, maintain that Dorian's not my type.

But doing any of that means I'd lose the opportunity to press this issue further—and I *have* to know.

"You forget I'm not technically taken," I say. "I have eyes. I have feelings. I'm not saying that I have a thing for your brother, but if things were different . . . if our arrangement was off the table . . . I could see myself being interested in someone like him."

His dark eyes flick to the ceiling and back. "God, you sound like Audrina, and we both know how that worked out for her."

Audrina chose Burke, and Dorian never forgave her.

"When did he say he was still in love with that girl?" I try my damnedest to sound casual. "Just out of curiosity."

"I don't know." Lines cover his forehead as he ponders my question. "As recently as a couple of days ago, I think. I'm telling you, Briar, you don't stand a chance. Dorian would spend the rest of his life as a celibate monk before he settled for my sloppy seconds."

Sloppy seconds.

We haven't done more than kiss or hold hands.

But probably in Dorian's mind, we've done it all.

Rarely do I agree with anything Burke says, but tonight? He might have a point—a point I'll never be able to argue against because I'm legally sworn to secrecy.

Burke yawns, then returns to the photo project in front of him.

I head upstairs without another word, stopping in our shared room to grab my pajamas and a toothbrush before making a beeline to Dorian's room.

Ten minutes later, I'm under his sheets, my cheek pressed against a pillow that smells faintly of him.

This may be the closest I'll ever get to being with Dorian Rothwell ever again.

CHAPTER
THIRTY-THREE

DORIAN

Present Day

"Dorian!" I'm greeted by the scent of sex, spilled beer, and groupie perfume the second I step onto the tour bus. "You're back!"

We're parked at some truck stop outside Jacksonville.

"Dor-man, hey." Connor appears from behind a curtain that separates the living quarters from the sleeping quarters. His fly is up but the top button of his jeans is undone. His hair looks like he either just got up from an afternoon nap or he's been entertaining one of the leggy blondes he always snags from the pit at each show, unbeknownst to his devoted fiancée back home. "How's it going?"

I don't like attention and fanfare of any kind, so I shrug and give a simple "Ready to be back."

"We missed you," a groupie says. I can't remember her name . . . Charla, Charlotte, Charley maybe? We picked her up sometime after our Red Rocks show, and no one's had the heart to ditch her yet. I have to hand it to her, though; she's made herself indispensable. She sews, and she cooks or handles ordering food. She keeps the bus fridge well stocked with everyone's favorite beers, makes a mean whiskey sour, and personally sees to it that the bus doesn't perpetually reek of vomit and stale food.

All that, and she's yet to ask for a single dime.

If I knew her better, I'd tell her she's being used, but then again, that's probably the whole point. This is a once-in-a-lifetime opportunity for her, and if it was so awful or if she was expecting to be on the payroll, she'd have bounced five states ago.

"Sorry about your dad." Charla or Charlotte pouts her lower lip and takes a seat beside me on the bus couch.

"Thank you."

How I missed it before, I'm not sure, but Charla-Charlotte is wearing a Phantom Symphony T-shirt that has been bedazzled with rhinestones and glitter, making her sparkle every time she shifts around.

"Oh, you like this?" She tugs on her shirt when she sees me noticing it.

Her innocent smile and big sky-blue eyes make it difficult for me to tell her I hate it.

I hate glitter.

Glitter reminds me of Briar.

And Briar is the last person I want to be reminded of.

She's the reason I couldn't leave Driftway fast enough. The whole place was dripping with tears. Everywhere I looked there were puffy eyes, crumpled Kleenex, ancient photos of better times forever captured. It was as depressing as hell. And on top of that, I had to watch my brother receive undeserved comfort and sympathy from the woman I can't stop wanting, no matter how much I try.

"I can make you one," she offers after my silence.

"No, thank you."

Her smile vanishes.

"Appreciate it though," I add.

Connor swipes a can of Voodoo Ranger IPA from the fridge, pops the top, and chugs it in one go. We've got a show in about six hours, and downing a six-pack has always been part of his preshow ritual.

Fans go crazy over his stage presence, but they'd never know that, deep down, he's an anxious wreck before each and every performance. That's the thing about guys like him. All that over-the-top confidence is simply overcompensation for their lack of confidence.

Billy, our bassist, steps out from behind the curtain next.

"Thought that was you, man." He gives me his usual high-five-half-hug combo before plopping down in the seat across from me. "Glad you're back. Sorry about your old man."

"Thank you."

There are four other members of the band, a handful of girlfriends, and an entire second bus full of stage crew, which means I'm going to have to hear about my dead dad the rest of the night. Not ideal, but nothing I can do about it other than get through it.

Last week, the band offered to cancel their Baton Rouge show and come to the funeral, but I told them not to.

The show must go on.

It's the number one rule in the entertainment industry, but I ought to adopt it as my personal mantra from here on out.

When Audrina left me for my brother, I was crushed, confused, heartbroken, but I hardened my heart, pushed her out of my mind, and went on my way.

The world didn't end then, and it's not going to end now.

All it took was time.

Someday, there'll come a time when I'll be able to write Briar off once and for all.

Hopefully sooner rather than later.

Then, and only then, the show will go on, and the intensity of what we had will fade like a vivid dream that's turned into some misty, long-forgotten, watercolored memory.

CHAPTER THIRTY-FOUR

BRIAR

Present Day

"Wasn't expecting you back so soon." The glossy-haired, baby-faced intern I'd just begun to train before I left last month places a mug of coffee on my desk. "You have a good time?"

"I did," I say.

"Go anywhere fun?" Her enthusiasm is forced, but I can't blame her. I remember the days of being an underpaid office nobody and wanting everyone to like me in the hope that my internship might one day turn into an actual job.

"Stayed with some friends at their beach house." It's the version closest to the truth I can give due to my NDA.

"Oh, fun! Like, in the Hamptons?" She perks up as if she loves the Hamptons and goes all the time.

"Not the Hamptons, no," I say, "but similar vibe."

Give or take a private island and significantly fewer people . . .

My email dings with an iCal invite from Burke. After Redmond's funeral, we spent another week on Driftway, tying up loose ends. We've been in the city a few days now but back at the office for a mere two.

While we didn't discuss how things were going to be once we were back in the proverbial real world, I didn't expect that we'd go back to being two passing ships in the night.

The man has walked past my desk no fewer than seven times, and he hasn't so much as coughed in my direction.

I can't say that I'm surprised—nor am I disappointed.

We're not friends . . . and after everything that came to light, it's safe to say we never will be.

It was nothing more than a business arrangement.

I double-click on the iCal invite—some meeting at a downtown law firm this Friday morning. A quick Google search of the law firm's name tells me they handle estates, wills, and trusts.

I can only imagine this has to do with the settling of the Rothwell estate, and as his fiancée, he needs me by his side to keep the gig going.

Red-hot annoyance flushes over me, replaced with the zing of anticipation when I realize that there's a chance Dorian will be there too . . .

Once the intern sashays off to chitchat with someone else, I take the opportunity to sneak my phone out. I tap on the colorful Instagram icon, type "Phantom Symphony" into the search bar, and pull up their account. According to the most recent photos, they've been in Jacksonville and Atlanta, and the concert-tour schedule pinned at the top of their page shows they'll be in Nashville next.

Holding my breath, I zoom in on all the recent photos, hoping to spot Dorian somewhere in the background, preferably smiling.

He's been through the wringer.

All I want is for him to be happy . . . the man at least deserves that.

But alas, he isn't showing up in a single one.

I scroll down, farther and farther, diving deep into posts from the late teens, until I find one with him in it. My chest tightens when I see his chiseled face, intense turquoise irises, and devil-may-care smirk. He's standing in the middle of a group of guys, with a green beer bottle in his hand, wearing ripped jeans low on his hips.

In this image, there's no question he's content.

But this was a lifetime ago.

Like a weirdo, I screenshot it because this might be the only image of Dorian that exists online, and I want something to refer to when I'm fueling my melancholy daydreams.

Days before Dorian left Driftway—and just before he buried his father—Dorian confessed to Burke that he was still in love with me. Since Burke told me that, I've thought about that fact more than I care to admit, at times seeking solace and comfort in it and at other times wondering if he was being intentional in his actions and hoping his brother would inadvertently pass that tidbit along.

If he didn't want me to know, I can't imagine he'd have breathed a word of any of that to Burke.

Maybe it's foolish of me to keep this death grip on hope, but I'm not ready to accept that this is the end of the road for us.

There's this unsettled sensation that gnaws through me at 2:00 a.m. sometimes when I'm lying wide awake in bed. Other times, it's a jolt of electric hope zinging through me without warning. Whatever it is, it doesn't want to let go. Not yet. And neither do I.

There's got to be a way.

Pulling up my contacts, I search for Dorian's number. We'd exchanged our numbers a year ago in the Dominican Republic, swearing we'd wait two years before using them per our agreement. But now that things have changed, I'm feeling inclined to reach out sooner rather than later. That, and if we're going to see each other at the attorney's office later this week, I don't want things to be more awkward than they already are.

I begin to type: Hi, it's Briar. I know I'm probably the last person you want to hear from, but I just wanted you to know I'm thinking of you and I hope you're doing well. Also, Burke told me what you said . . .

My thumb hovers over the send button until I have a change of heart and delete the last sentence of my text. We need to talk about that, but not like this.

"I'd think you'd be absolutely buried in work after being gone nearly a full month." A man's voice sends a jolt to my heart, causing me to drop my phone on the floor. Burke chuckles as if he finds amusement in scaring the daylights out of people.

I retrieve my phone and set it face down on my desk. "Just settling back into a rhythm."

"Did you get my calendar invite?" He sips his coffee, his piercing eyes homing in on me.

"Yes, I'll be there." I wouldn't miss it for the world—not because I'm contractually obligated to appear as his fiancée but because there's a chance I could see Dorian again.

"You can ride with me."

"As opposed to taking the subway?" I wink, entertained by the thought of him showing up in his chauffeured town car and me stepping over subway rats to meet him at some fancy law firm downtown. If Nicola happened to see any of that, the jig would be more than up.

Burke looks me up and down, clearly finding zero humor in my question.

My contract with him is up at the end of July, and it can't come soon enough.

The NDA, though? That's unfortunately forever.

CHAPTER THIRTY-FIVE

DORIAN

Present Day

"Right this way, Mr. Rothwell." A perky paralegal with red-soled shoes leads me to a conference room at the end of a long hallway. When my father's attorney reached out to me earlier this week about coming in for a meeting, I told him I'd have to Zoom or Skype or whatever the people are using these days.

There was no way I was going to set foot in the same room with my siblings only to watch them wipe the drool from their faces as they cash in on my third of the estate.

Unfortunately, I was informed that I was required to attend in person, that there were documents to sign, a video to watch, and a bunch of other legal-babble bullshit I didn't attempt to understand, and this was the only way.

So here I fucking am.

"Would you like a coffee, sir? Water?" the paralegal asks before I go in. She bats her lashes at me, though in no way is she attempting to flirt. I literally rolled out of bed at 4:00 a.m. in last night's clothes, brushed my teeth, finger combed my hair, and took the cheapest Uber to the airport to hop on some shitty commuter jet that didn't offer Wi-Fi or snacks.

I look like ass.

And I feel like it too.

Good thing I have no one to impress . . .

"Coffee'd be great," I tell her before shoving the door open.

I spot Nicola first—seated at the head of an extralong table, Dash at her side. Dash gives me a nod. Nicola, dressed in head-to-toe black, crumples a tissue in her hand. Either she's still in mourning or she's a typical New Yorker fighting a bad case of seasonal allergies.

Either way, I couldn't care less.

On the opposite end of the table are Burke and his devoted fiancée.

I don't bother turning my head in their direction. I can see them from the corner of my eye just fine. Though I can't help but notice they, too, are dressed like they're going to a funeral. Don't they realize we already did all that?

Grabbing a seat in the middle of the table, equidistant from both couples, I stare at the plaques of various legal awards that adorn the wall.

"And here you are." The paralegal places a mug of coffee before me along with a spoon and packets of sugar and powdered creamer folded inside a napkin. She takes the chair beside mine before laying out a yellow legal pad, a thick folder of papers, several pens, and a notary stamp. How she managed to haul all that in one armful is beyond me. "We're just waiting for Mr. Giannotti. He's finishing up a phone call, and then we'll get started."

They mentioned earlier there'd be a video to watch. Something my father recorded before his death. For some reason, I didn't have it in me to admit I didn't want to watch it. Not yet. I'm still processing the fact that I can't call him up or that I'll never wander up from the dock at Driftway to be greeted by a frail old man with Santa Claus hair and a smile as wide as his whole face.

Seeing him on video is something I'd rather not do—if given the choice.

"How's everyone's morning going so far?" The paralegal's tone is far too chipper for a meeting about a recently deceased man's estate.

Collectively we answer her with dead silence.

Before she can make another attempt at awkward small talk, a man with salt-and-pepper hair at his temples and who's wearing an expensive suit strolls in.

"Apologies, all," Mr. Giannotti says as he sets up camp across from me. Cracking open his laptop, he taps in a short password. "All right. Just pulling up my notes here. Natalie here has all the paperwork you'll need to sign, but first, I'm going to read off the allocation of the estate per your father's last will and testament—dated May fifteenth of this year."

The silence in the room is deafening, though I'm not sure why everyone's so tense. We all know how this is going to go. Nicola and Burke are in committed relationships, and I'm not. They'll split everything fifty-fifty. Half of me wonders if he left me something to remember him by . . . his baseball-card collection or his prized fully restored 1957 Studebaker, which he only drove twice in his life.

"This should be fairly straightforward." Mr. Giannotti slips a pair of wire-framed glasses over his nose and clears his throat. "First, your father has designated one percent of his liquid assets to be divided equally among the following individuals: Yvette Barstow, Maurice Barstow, Gladys Pimpernel, Debra Knox, Candace Kenworth, Tate Tucker, Ron Sandler, and Monte Redburn."

I nod. Those are all longtime employees of my father. Dedicated. Loyal. True-blue types. One percent of his liquid assets divided eight ways will be more than enough for each of them to retire and live happily ever after.

"To his children, Nicola, Burke, and Dorian, the rest of his liquid assets will be divided equally between them," the attorney continues.

My sister sucks in a gasp, small yet audible.

I don't waste my time or energy looking in Burke's direction.

I don't have to.

His shock and displeasure are radiating off him in waves so turbulent they can probably be felt in Hoboken.

"Are you sure?" I ask. "He always told us we had to be married or engaged in order to inherit anything. I'm single . . ."

Mr. Giannotti nods as he leans closer to his laptop screen. "I'm absolutely sure. In fact, I remember the day he came in here last month, wanting to change his will. He said he had a change of heart." He slides his glasses off. "Particularly where you're concerned, Dorian."

I don't understand.

Racking my mind, I think back to May—and that's when it hits me.

Every Mother's Day, I make sure to call my father. It's been an unofficial tradition of ours to reminisce about my mother that day, to share the same old stories that never fail to put smiles on our faces, to honor her, to show that, although she might be gone, she could never be forgotten.

This past Mother's Day, however, our conversation forked off in an unexpected direction. While I can't recall exactly how it happened, I remember admitting to him that I'd met someone, that I was head over heels in love with her, that we agreed the timing was off, and that we'd wait two years to be together.

"This is absurd," Burke chimes in. "This was never the plan. All my life, my father made it crystal clear to each of us what the expectations were."

I steal a look at Briar, whose full lips are dancing as if she wants to say something to quell his anger. Our eyes lock, and she remains silent.

She's bright enough to know that not being one of us—yet—means it's best if she stays out of this.

"Shall I continue?" Giannotti asks, scanning the table from end to end.

"Please," I answer, because Nicola is apparently too stunned to speak, and nothing nice is going to come out of Burke's mouth in the foreseeable future.

"I have a list here . . . approximately three pages' worth of hard assets. Jewelry. Real estate. Cars. Various collections. Artwork," he reads off. "Your father wishes for the three of you to keep the items that are priceless to you—heirlooms and such. The rest is to be auctioned off via an estate sale or private broker of your unanimous choosing. Any proceeds are to be split three ways, minus one percent, which will be allocated to the eight individuals previously mentioned."

"I'm keeping Mom's wedding ring," Nicola chimes in.

"Actually . . ." Giannotti lifts his finger. "That particular item has been willed to Dorian."

My stomach drops.

"Are you kidding right now?" Nicola's voice rises, and she leans forward. Dash places his hand on her back, but I doubt she feels it. "Dorian doesn't even want to get married—why should he get her ring?"

"Seriously?" Burke shoots her a deadly look from the opposite end of the table. "That's the battle you're choosing here? Not the fact that we did everything right, and Dorian's making out like a bandit here?"

The paralegal beside me taps her pen against the legal pad, biting her lip as she watches the two of them bicker over something none of us have an ounce of control over.

"You don't even like money." Nicola directs her anger at me. "You've always hated being a Rothwell."

Giannotti splays both hands in the air. "Listen, I know these situations can bring up a lot of emotions—oftentimes unpleasant ones—but if you don't mind, I'd like to get through the remainder of this process, and then you guys can take this somewhere else. I'd let you use the conference room, but we have another client coming in after this. So. In the interest of saving everyone's precious time, can we continue?"

"Of course," I answer for us all.

"Natalie," he says with a nod to the paralegal. "Did you bring the USB drives?"

She flips open the folder and reaches into an interior envelope, then produces three thumb drives, each of them white, each of them labeled with our individual initials.

"You don't have to watch this now," the attorney says. Thank God. "But your father recorded these messages for you the last time he was here, and it's his wish that you have them and watch them at some point. Now, back to the division of liquid assets. As of May fifteenth, the amounts came out to approximately seventy-eight million apiece. That number is an estimate, as some of this money was held in interest-bearing savings accounts, CDs, and the like."

Seventy-eight million?

I don't even know what I'd do with that kind of money.

I knew my father was loaded, but I never so much as attempted to assign a number to it. It was never going to be mine anyway.

Or so I thought.

Natalie slides away from the table, then places packets of paperwork in front of each of us along with a shiny pen that feels weightless in my hand the instant I pick it up.

Or maybe my hand is numb.

Either way, I feel nothing as I sign these forms.

A hush blankets the room in the minutes that follow, coming to a halt only when Burke slams his pen down and leans back like a kid who finished a timed test first. He sinks back, arms crossed, a sullen, sour expression on his face.

Briar's gaze is fixed on the window.

Perhaps she's wondering what she's going to do with all that money now that she's marrying a multimillionaire whose biggest passion in life is turning cash into even more cash.

As much as I want to believe she's marrying him for superficial reasons, I can't reconcile that with the person I met a year ago. I want to believe she lied to me—it'd make hating her a lot easier. But deep down, I can't. No matter how hard I try.

"Your father has listed ten properties here," Giannotti continues, "all of which are eligible to be sold except for one. His wish is for Driftway to remain a family property, co-owned by the three of you, and maintained as a Rothwell estate for each of you to enjoy with your family, friends, and loved ones. He also requested that the three of you spend two weeks there each summer . . . together . . . in his memory."

Burke sighs.

Nicola pulls a clean tissue from her purse. "Of course he would want that. I just don't know if that's realistic."

It's the one thing I'm willing to agree on here—getting the three of us to spend fourteen days together by choice is going to be damn near impossible. Not to mention, I don't want any part in watching Burke and Briar run off into the sunset, marry, have babies, and live happily ever after.

"We'll make it happen." Dash rubs circles on my sister's lower back. "I think it's a great way to honor the man who's done so much for us. Two weeks a year is nothing."

Oh, Dash . . . ever the optimist.

If Nicola has it her way, they'll be in the midst of a messy divorce by next summer.

"We've made copies of everything for each of you," Giannotti says as Natalie stamps and notarizes document after document. "And as soon as we finish up, Natalie will scan all of the signed forms and email them to you for your records. Should you have any questions throughout this process, we're only a phone call away."

"So that's it?" Burke asks. "Just like that, we split everything three ways, and that's it?"

"Feel free to contest it if you want to be that guy." I shrug, fighting a tight smirk. I don't want this money. I never did. Nicola was right about that. But I'd be lying if I said it didn't bring me a bit of pleasure to take it away from Burke.

"I'm sensing some sarcasm from your end, Dorian, but Burke, you should know that contesting an ironclad will like your father's will be lengthy, stressful, not to mention devastatingly expensive, and the outcome will likely not be in your favor. But you do have that right." Giannotti closes his laptop, rises, and tucks it under his arm. "Anyway, we're all done here. Like I said, any questions, give me a call. In the meantime, we'll begin working on the disbursements."

With that, Giannotti is out, with Natalie trailing after him with her armful of folders.

We all make a move to leave at the same time, though walking out together feels like the last thing any of us want to do.

Screw it.

I have to take a piss, and I'm not about to sit here like we're a bunch of midwesterners at a four-way stop.

Slipping the thumb drive with my initials on it into my pocket, I get the hell out of that sorry conference room.

I'm halfway to the hall restroom when someone calls my name from behind.

Glancing over my shoulder, I find Briar trotting up to me. What she could possibly want now is beyond me, but for whatever reason, I'm curious enough to stop and find out.

"Yeah?" I ask, trying my hardest not to appreciate the way her subtle curves fill out her navy-blue dress or the way her shiny dark-blonde hair bounces with each step like she's a model in a damn shampoo commercial.

A year ago, those curves were mine, and that hair was tangled around my fist as she called out my name, but I digress.

"I just wanted to make sure you're okay. You never replied to my text," she says.

Really? *That's* all she wanted?

I can't decide if I'm annoyed that she's wasting my time or suspicious that she's got an ulterior motive. She's clearly aware that I'm seventy-eight million dollars (and change) richer than I was when I walked into that room half an hour ago.

Still, something tells me I'm wrong on both accounts.

Raking my hand through my messy hair, I exhale. "I'm fine. Do I not look fine or something?"

Her eyes flicker, and she bites a smile that fades before it has a chance to mean anything.

"That was intense in there," she says.

"Welcome to the family."

"I'm sorry Burke behaved that way. Embarrassed for him, actually . . ."

"You don't have to apologize for him. The sooner you learn that, the happier your marriage will be." I almost tell her she's getting a preview of what her marriage will entail, but I decide to rein in my contempt.

"Can I tell you something?" Her voice is pillow soft, and she worries the inside of her lip. Narrowing the space between us, she sucks in a slow breath. "I don't want to marry him."

Before I can stop myself, a shit-eating grin claims my face.

I knew it.

I fucking knew it.

This is Audrina all over again.

I've seen this movie before, and I know how it ends.

"You want me to feel sorry for you or something?" I release an incredulous laugh. While I understand what she's getting at and I want to be the one she wants, it doesn't make this entire thing any less fucked up. "I'm sorry you chose the wrong guy, but that's not my problem."

Her eyes turn glassy. "I know. I just . . . I wanted you to know that. For whatever it's worth."

"Why are you telling me this? What are you trying to do here?"

"I . . . I don't know." Her lower lip trembles. "I just feel awful for everything you've been through, and I don't want to be another thing on a list of things that make you angry at the world."

"Is that what you think I am? Angry at the world? Just because I don't think the way everyone else does, doesn't make me angry. If anything, I'm happier than most of you people. So please, do me a favor and take your sympathy and your crocodile tears somewhere else."

"I'm sorry. I didn't mean to upset you." She places her hand over her chest. "I just . . . Burke told me what you told him the week of the funeral."

"Which was . . . ?" I said a lot of things that week; half of them I can't recall because I was too busy numbing myself with expensive wine. What started as a toast to my old man became a drink in his honor and then another and another. I can only imagine the shit that came out of my mouth, especially around Burke.

"You told him you were still in love with the girl from last summer." Her bright-blue eyes search mine, and I know exactly what they're looking for, but she won't find it.

"I said that, did I?" I pretend like I don't remember, but the truth is, that's the one conversation we shared that sticks out like a sore thumb.

We were talking about love, for some reason. Burke brought it up, but I think his intention was to see if I was going to magically produce this mystery woman so I could claim my third of the inheritance. He was testing me, though in retrospect, it was all in vain.

"So you didn't say it?" She blinks.

Half of me wants to lie to her, tell her I can't recall or deny it altogether.

The other half of me wants her to know the truth, for a myriad of conflicting reasons.

"I thought I was," I say. "Turns out, that girl? She was just an illusion. Some pick-me type, you know? Telling me all the things she thought I wanted to hear."

Her pretty face falls, but she doesn't argue.

I almost wish she would.

Then again, I'm exhausted. I have a flight to catch. And there's nothing I hate more than wasting time.

An argument about whether I'm still in love with her would be the biggest waste of time because, at the end of the day, it doesn't mean a damn thing, and it won't bring us together again.

"We had a plan." I shrug before shoving my hands in my jeans pockets and turning to leave. "All you had to do was *wait*."

CHAPTER THIRTY-SIX

BRIAR

Present Day

I'm hiding in the law office's ladies' room when Burke texts to tell me he's in the lobby and that the car is on its way. Splashing water on my face, I pull myself together and wipe away any smudged mascara remnants before heading down to meet him.

He's got his nose buried in his phone when I find him standing in a sea of people coming and going. His position in the dead center of the vast, open space forces everyone to go around him.

"I want out of the contract," I tell him. "What do I have to do?"

Burke darkens his phone and meets my pointed stare. "What?"

"You heard me. How do I get out of this? You don't have to pay me a dime, I just want out."

"It doesn't work that way."

"You got your inheritance. You got the one thing you wanted. And you didn't even need me. I don't see why it matters now."

He chuffs, rolling his eyes. "Of course you don't see why it matters, and that's exactly why I can't let you out of that."

"I don't want the money."

"Then don't take it. But I'm not ripping up the contract. We had a deal. You signed on the dotted line."

"I signed without knowing exactly what I was getting myself into," I say. "I didn't know . . . I didn't know your father was dying. You told me you wanted to give him a memorable summer, put his mind at ease."

"Everyone's dying. That's part of life. Every day we're twenty-four hours closer to death."

"You lied to me about the reason Audrina left you."

"I don't see how that has anything to do with the agreement you and I made." The smug tone in his voice makes me want to slap him across the face, and I don't have a violent bone in my body. "Look, if you want to sit here and tell me what an insufferable bastard I am, go ahead. You wouldn't be the first, and you sure as hell won't be the last. If you want to walk away from your million-dollar payout, be my guest. But I'm not letting you out of that NDA. And that's what you're getting at, right? You want out of the NDA so you can chase after my brother."

His astute perception steals the oxygen from my lungs and the words from my mouth.

"I already told you," he continues, "Dorian would *never* go for you. You're my sloppy seconds in his eyes. You're damaged goods. You're Audrina all over again. Do yourself a favor—take the money, walk away, and forget you ever knew either of us. Your future self will thank you— and that advice is on the house."

"I don't understand why it matters." I refuse to back down, not with my future on the line. "You're getting your inheritance whether or not you're with someone. Why would it matter if Dorian and Nicola know that this was fake all along?"

Raking his hand along his angled jaw, he tilts his head and sighs.

"Not that I owe you an answer to that, but my brother and sister would never let me live that down," he says. "That's why. The whole thing reeks of desperation, and I'd never hear the end of it. I'd be the laughingstock of the Rothwell family."

"So this is about your pride? Your ego? I have to sacrifice everything just so you can save face?" I close the distance between us, unafraid to get in his face so he can hear me crystal clear. "That woman he met last summer? The one he was waiting for? The one he still loves? *It's me.*"

He begins to respond—only before he says a single word, his eyes skim over my shoulder, and his mouth presses flat.

"Fuck," he says under his breath.

I'm confused . . . until I turn around and find none other than Nicola standing behind me, arms crossed, an expression on her face that tells me she heard everything.

CHAPTER THIRTY-SEVEN

DORIAN

Present Day

"You should put your phone in airplane mode if you're just going to ignore all those texts." The middle-aged woman beside me on an extremely packed flight to Nashville points to my lap. "It's been going off like crazy since you sat down."

We're still in the boarding process, and the center aisle is packed with travelers all waiting to find their seats, all being held up by some neck beard trying to shove his overpacked carry-on into an already crammed compartment. It isn't until a flight attendant appears out of nowhere that the proverbial roadblock is dislodged, and the line moves again.

"I will once we take off," I tell her.

"What's the point of leaving it on if you're just going to ignore it?" She rips open a travel-size bag of white cheddar Cheez-Its and tosses a couple in her mouth.

"It's just my sister. She does this whenever she wants attention. She'll stop eventually," I say, quietly recalling a time when I woke up to eighty-seven text messages, sixteen missed calls, and four emails. I thought someone died, but it was just Nicola being Nicola. When she wants something, she *really* wants it.

"What if it's an emergency or something?" The woman digs her hand into the bag of crackers once more, this time coming out with a bigger handful than before. "You want some?"

"No, thank you."

Digging into my pocket, I pull out my AirPods, hoping this well-meaning but nosy woman gets the hint. I'm not one of those fellow passengers who will sit and chat for a full two hours and twenty-one minutes. I'm a close-my-eyes-put-some-music-on-and-bide-my-time kind of passenger.

Waking my screen, I pull up my music app and tap the shuffle option. It's been the longest day of my life, and I'm too tired to make decisions of any kind right now, so I'll let the universe decide for me.

But before I have a chance to darken my phone, another text from Nicola fills the screen.

NICOLA: SERIOUSLY CALL ME RIGHT NOW—IT'S ABOUT BRIAR.

Rolling my eyes, I sniff a laugh. If she wants to talk shit about Burke's fiancée or wax poetic with another one of her crazy theories, she's going to have to bark up Dash's tree, not mine.

NICOLA: WHERE ARE YOU??

NICOLA: IT WAS FAKE. I WAS RIGHT THE WHOLE TIME. IT WAS FAKE!!!

NICOLA: DORIAN! HELLO?

NICOLA: I KNOW BRIAR'S THE WOMAN YOU MET LAST SUMMER!

My stomach drops. How would she know that? I made damn sure no one knew.

The line in the center aisle grows smaller and smaller, and the flight attendants are closing all the full overhead bins. A few minutes from now, we'll be taxiing to the runway. But I'm too curious not to engage in this conversation, so I call her in the interest of saving time.

"What are you talking about?" I ask when she answers.

"Oh my god. Where are you?"

"On a flight. About to leave. What's going on?"

"You have to get off that plane." She's breathless, more insistent than ever. Then again, Nicola has always had a penchant for being dramatic. She once threw a funeral for a dead plant and petitioned our father to let her skip a day of school so she could mourn it properly, arguing that she'd nursed it from a seedling to a fully grown spider plant. Never mind that her neglect of the very plant she claimed to love was the reason for its demise. "It was fake. The engagement. All of it. He paid her to pretend to be his fiancée! He wanted Dad to think he was engaged so he'd get his inheritance. A million dollars, can you believe that?"

"Wait, wait, wait . . ."

I'm attempting to wrap my head around this when the woman beside me nudges me with her elbow and mouths, "Is everything okay?"

"How do you know this?" I ask Nic.

"Because I heard their conversation. All of it," she says. "And I heard her say that she was the woman you met last summer, the one you still love."

I have to admit, I didn't expect Nicola to want anything to do with me after today, on account of me "stealing" the inheritance she was anticipating.

I'm not sure what's more shocking here . . . that or learning Burke and Briar's engagement was a ruse.

"You have to get off that plane," she says.

"Why?"

"Because you should go to her. You should be with her. She told Burke she didn't want the money. She begged him to let her out of some NDA he made her sign," Nic says.

A flight attendant's voice plays over the speakers. "Ladies and gentlemen, as we begin . . ."

"She chose you over money," Nicola says. "*Briar loves you.* You'd be an idiot to walk away now."

Dragging in a long, hard breath, I eye the front of the plane before unfastening my seat belt and heading to the jet bridge.

Nashville's show will go on without me.

But I can't go on without her.

CHAPTER
THIRTY-EIGHT
BRIAR

Present Day

I was going to take the afternoon off after the whole incident in the lobby with Burke—until I decided to quit.

If I ever see that man's face again, it'll be too soon. And as far as I'm concerned, I fulfilled my part of the contract that he refuses to cancel, so I'm looking at a bit of a financial windfall (relatively speaking) next month.

Until then, I can subsist on my paltry savings and little orange packets of ramen while I figure out my next move.

I unfasten my bra, toss it in a hamper, and change into the softest T-shirt and shorts I can find in my pajama drawer. Never mind that it's only one o'clock in the afternoon—this day is over.

After Nicola heard everything, she and Burke had words, and when their little spat grew too private, he insisted they take it outside.

I sat on the ledge of the lobby water fountain as I watched them argue outside. It was like watching a TV show on mute. I had no idea what they were saying, but their animated gestures and beet-red expressions kept me glued.

After a few minutes, his town car rolled up, and they disappeared inside, along with Dash, who didn't seem to have a part in their conversation whatsoever.

I walked home, taking my heels off halfway after they started pinching the sides of my toes. Strolling barefoot for two miles along dirty New York sidewalks is not my finest moment, but I was too busy basking in something that felt akin to freedom to care.

The secret's out.

Nicola knows.

And while I'm still technically bound to the NDA, she isn't.

I can only hope she tells Dorian all the things I never could—and that he realizes my hands may have been tied and my lips might have been sealed, but my heart was always his.

CHAPTER THIRTY-NINE

DORIAN

Present Day

"Damn, that was fast." A pink-haired woman in a faded Led Zeppelin T-shirt and denim overalls answers the door to apartment 3C, a five-dollar bill in her hand. "I literally ordered, like, not even five minutes ago."

"I'm sorry . . . is Briar here?" I ask. "I was told this was her address."

I'm lying—I technically googled it. And then I paid some shady website fifty bucks to unblur her information. But I don't want to sound like a stalker.

"Uh, who are you?" She braces herself against the door, keeping one foot on the other side like a human doorstop.

"Dorian. Is she home?"

Her pointed expression softens. "Holy shit. *You're* Dorian?"

I frown, unsure if this is a good "holy shit" or a bad one.

"Yes." I steal a quick glimpse into the apartment, only from here, all I can see is a mirror hanging on a wall behind her. "Is she here? I need to talk to her. It's important."

I could have called, I suppose, but texting or calling over something like this feels wrong. Plus I want to see her face. I want to hear the truth from her lips, with her voice, her eyes on mine.

"I'm sorry." Her lips tuck to one side. "She just left, actually."

Damn it. "Where'd she go?"

"For a walk?" The woman lifts a shoulder. "She moped around the apartment for, like, a solid hour when she got home, and then she changed her clothes and said she needed fresh air."

This city is nothing but sidewalks.

She could be anywhere.

I could wander these streets for days and not come close to finding her.

"Thank you," I say.

I head downstairs, phone clenched tightly, ready to call her despite the fact that it isn't how I wanted this to happen.

Once outside, I take a seat on the steps to her building, stopping to gather my thoughts. I'm queuing up her number when something catches my eye.

No, not some*thing*.

Some*one*.

Half a block away is a vision in gray sweats and dad sneakers, her hair stuffed under a Red Sox cap and her eyes hidden behind mirrored aviators.

My heart knocks inside my chest with every step that brings us closer.

"Oh my god," she says when she realizes I'm outside her apartment building. "What are you doing here?"

I rise to meet her.

"Is it true?" First things first.

"You're going to have to be more specific than that . . ."

"Nicola overheard your conversation at the law firm. She said you signed some contract to pretend to be engaged to my brother. That he was paying you. That none of it was real." While the entire thing feels like something only a psychopath could dream up, it all reeks of Burke and his prideful desperation. The man has always had a sense of entitlement a mile wide and infinitely deep. Couple that with his inability to feel guilty about anything, ever, and it's the perfect recipe for this pathetic little scheme.

Not to mention, what woman in her right mind would turn down the opportunity to make a million dollars by hanging out on some private island for eight weeks . . .

I could never fault her for that.

Briar slides her sunglasses down, revealing eyes that turn glassier by the second. "I wanted to tell you . . . so many times . . . I couldn't. Legally. I-I tried to think of so many ways to get around it, hoping somehow you could read between the lines . . . I didn't know what to do. I would have walked away from the money, from the contract, but Burke said—"

I close the distance between us, cupping her face in my hands and grazing my thumb against her quivering lower lip.

A single tear slides down her cheek.

I swipe it away.

And in the middle of a crowded midtown sidewalk, I kiss my girl.

"I've loved you from the moment I saw you," I tell her. "And I never stopped. Even when I wanted to. Even when it killed me."

"I love you too."

In the moments that follow, the busy world around us disappears, becoming nothing but background noise until an old man with a Brooklyn accent yells for us to get a room.

Briar's mouth curls into a smile against mine.

"Know some place we could go?" I ask.

"Just so happens that I do." Sliding her hand into mine, she leads me back to her apartment.

In a hazy blur of an instant, we find ourselves bypassing her confused roommate and stumbling backward into her bedroom. She kicks the door shut as I taste her mouth all over again, and I pin her against the wall, pressing my hardness into her hips.

She exhales as I work my way down, pressing fevered kisses along her neck before tugging her shirt over her head.

Briar's hands work my belt and zipper, fumbling as if we're chasing the clock despite both of us knowing there's no need to rush.

"You came back," she says as if she's just now realizing what's going on, like it's hitting her for the first time.

"How could I not?" I cup her pretty face, tracing my thumb along her bottom lip.

"Did you mean it?"

"Mean what?"

"When you said you loved me?" She blinks, her voice soft as clouds.

"Of course." I tamp down any hint of insult in my voice. "I don't say things I don't mean."

"But it's not, like . . . love-ish? It's actual love?"

I flash an amused half smile her way. "I *love* you. There's no ish about it."

Slinking her arms over my shoulders, she rises on her toes and nuzzles against my neck, breathing me in.

"If you need more convincing, though, I'm happy to show you . . ." Gliding my hands down her sides, I cup her ass before lifting her in my arms and carrying her to the bed. I lay her down gently in the center of her plush mattress and press my mouth against her bare stomach.

"If you insist . . ."

Running my fingers along the waistband of her leggings, I tug them down along with her panties and toss them aside before turning my focus to the delicate arousal between her thighs.

I'm a goner with the first taste.

Hoisting her thighs over my shoulders, I devour her like she's my last meal, my hands gripping her hips as she arches the small of her back in the moments before she comes.

"Oh my god," she exhales, her body limp beneath me. "That was . . . I didn't think I could . . . I don't normally come that quickly . . ."

Crawling over her, I silence her with a kiss that tastes like everything that's right in this world.

"I'll let you rest," I tease her, "but only for a minute. We've got lost time to make up for."

CHAPTER FORTY

BRIAR

Present Day

"I still can't believe you're here." I'm lying in Dorian's arms, every atom in my body electric, and I'm pretty sure I haven't stopped smiling since he kissed me on the sidewalk mere hours ago. "That you came back for me."

"I can't believe we have Nicola to thank for this moment . . ." He sniffs a laugh.

"Ah, true. We'll have to send her flowers or something," I tease. "Though honestly, I'm pretty shocked by that move. Was pretty sure she hated me from the second I set foot on that island."

"She did." He runs his fingers through my hair, brushing a wild strand from my forehead. "But don't take it personally. She hates everyone. And she's used to being the only girl around . . . except for Augustine, of course."

"I'm sure she feels protective of her brothers."

"That's maybe being a little too kind." He rolls his eyes. "Protective of the family fortune's probably more like it."

"Money makes people do crazy things." I drag in a long, deep breath and press my cheek against his bare chest. Inhaling his scent, I close my eyes and commit all this to memory. I never want to forget what this moment feels like, smells like, sounds like, or tastes like. It's warmth. Sunlight after rain. Sheer contentedness. "Had I known then what I know now, I never would've agreed to help your brother. I was blinded by all those zeros. And if I'm being completely honest here, the idea of spending my summer at the ocean instead of in some cubicle was also a huge motivating factor."

He kisses the top of my head, and I open my eyes to glance up at his handsome face.

"I'm so sorry I broke our promise," I say.

"You didn't break it. You weren't dating him. Technically."

Exhaling, I study the same guarded turquoise stare that lured me in the night we first met.

"You sure?" I ask. "Because I can't stop thinking about—"

Cupping my face, he tilts my chin and silences me with a punishing kiss.

"You're talking too much," he says with a mocking glint. "Making up for all the talking we didn't do on the island . . ."

"Fair enough."

He runs his fingertips along my arm, leaving a trail of goose bumps. "I never want to feel like that again."

"Like what?"

"Like you're so close but so far away at the same time. Like I can talk to you, but I can't really talk to you. Like you're with someone else when you should be with me." Quietude settles between us. "It *killed* me seeing you with him."

"It killed me not being with you, not being able to be *real* with you." I breathe him in again. "That day when you took me to the lighthouse, all I kept thinking about was how magical that would've been if you knew the truth. In some parallel universe, I was there—as your girl—and we were listening to your records and dancing and laughing and kissing and forgetting about the real world."

"That would've been perfect."

"Think you'll ever go back there?" I ask. "Maybe we could have a do-over."

Dorian doesn't answer, not right away. For a moment, I kick myself for asking. His father has only recently passed away, and that island must hold a lifetime of bittersweet memories for him.

"I'm sorry." I sit up, my hand clasped over my chest. "I shouldn't have said that."

"Someday," he finally answers. "Someday we'll get a do-over."

I curl under his arm.

"Come with me," he says.

"To the island?"

"On tour."

"I can't tell if you're joking or being serious." Which is ironic because, despite our intense and undeniable connection, we're still barely more than strangers, still getting to know one another.

"I don't want to be apart from you. I don't want to risk losing you again. And more than that, I don't want to wait any longer."

I rest my chin on his bare chest, gazing up at him through sleepy eyes. It's late afternoon, but it's been a long week. Hell, it's been a long month.

One could even argue it's been a long year.

I'm exhausted.

Blissful.

But exhausted.

"You never lost me," I tell him.

If anything, I'm the one who lost him.

"You know what I mean." He runs his fingers through my hair. "We still have one more year of touring. I don't want to wait another year to be with you."

My bedsheets are tangled around our legs, and I'm almost positive this is what heaven feels like, but we can't stay locked up in my apartment until the end of time.

"My entire life, I've never had anywhere that felt like home," he says, "until I met you. You felt like home to me."

"What does home feel like to you?"

He exhales. "God, I don't know how to describe it without sounding like a complete sap."

"This is a judgment-free zone."

"Well, in that case . . ."

We chuckle, and I reposition myself so that he has my full attention.

"Warm," he says. "Familiar. Nostalgic. Special."

"No one's ever described me in those terms."

"Is that a good thing or a bad thing?" Dorian traces his finger lightly along the back of my arm.

"Very good." I lean in to steal a kiss, tasting myself on his tongue. "And for the record, your answer was the antithesis of sappy."

"That's a relief," he teases.

"Can we make a new rule?" I propose. "Complete honesty. Always. No matter what."

"I fucking love that rule."

"Can I amend it to add no judgment, ever?"

"Sure thing."

"Okay, so in the vein of brutal honesty . . ." I bite my lip. "I adore this side of you. But also, it really turned me on at Driftway every time you got mad." I wince, eyes squeezed tightly shut. A moment later, I peek out of one of them, searching in the dim space we share for his reaction.

"Really?" he asks, his mouth half-open like he's contemplating something he's never considered before.

"Yes," I say. "And I don't claim to understand it. I just feel like you should know because if we go forward with this—"

"What do you mean *if?*"

"Sorry. *As* we go forward . . . as a couple . . . one of these days, we might have a quarrel of some kind. And if you get . . . I don't know . . . heated or something . . . it might turn me on . . . and then we might have to stop fighting and focus on . . . other matters."

"Fair," he says. "And I appreciate your honesty. Since we're opening up here, I think it's only right that I tell you something as well."

"Okay."

"Shortly after we went our separate ways, I looked you up online. Your social media was private, and I don't do social media anyway, but I found your LinkedIn profile," he says, pausing. "God, I can't believe I'm about to admit this."

"What? What?"

"I screenshotted your headshot photo so I could look at it anytime I missed you."

"Stop." I sit up.

"Does that creep you out? Honestly, it creeped me out sometimes too."

"No," I say. "Earlier this week, I screenshotted an old picture of you I found on Phantom Symphony's Instagram account."

"Holy shit." He pulls me against him, flashing a mischievous grin. "We truly are perfect for each other. We're both a couple of weirdos."

"So it's settled. We're doing this. You're coming on the tour with me. It's the two of us from here on out."

"Yeah," I say. "We're doing this."

EPILOGUE

BRIAR

Five Years Later

The Greek sun dips below the horizon, casting a warm, golden glow over the quaint streets of Mykonos as Dorian and I sit at an intimate table for two on a rooftop terrace that feels like it was made just for us.

Murmurs of soft conversations and laughter surround us, mingling with the hum of gentle waves in the distance, and I bask in a moment I wish I could bottle up and keep forever.

"Six years, can you believe it?" He reaches across the table to take my hand. "Six years ago tonight, we met."

While we both pride ourselves on not being the cheesy kind of romantics, we'd be doing ourselves a disservice by ignoring the significance of that night and the strange and crooked road that brought us back together.

We had a plan.

But fate had other plans.

"It still feels like yesterday," I say.

"In a good way or a bad way?"

"In the best way." I give him a wink before reaching for my wine. His mother's engagement ring glints on my right-hand ring finger.

We're never getting married—that much we settled on from the moment we met.

But we're committed.

It's he and I from here on out, come what may.

Wearing the ring on my right hand was his father's idea, actually—one he proposed in the thumb drive video Dorian received that day at the law firm. I've never seen it, nor do I want to, as it's a private father-son thing, but when Dorian gave me the dazzling pear-shaped stunner and explained what it meant to him, I couldn't say no.

"What do you want to do next?" he asks.

"I don't know . . . I was thinking maybe one of those boat tours. But it's getting kind of late. By the time we get out of here, they might not be open."

His lips turn up at one side as he sniffs a laugh. "No. I mean, what do you want to do after this? After Greece?"

Five years ago, after I quit my job, I boarded the next flight to Nashville with Dorian, tagged along for the remainder of Phantom Symphony's worldwide tour (a definite bucket list experience), and then stood by Dorian's side as he quit managing the band once and for all . . . nearly two years to the day he first said he would.

The day that should have marked the start of our relationship became our one-year anniversary, and we celebrated by taking a first-class flight to Italy for the sole reason that we could.

We were finally free.

"You ever feel like putting down roots?" he asks.

I lean back, cocking my head as I study a man whose dashing good looks make all the Greek statues pale in comparison.

"Why plant roots when you have wings?" I take another sip of wine.

By some miracle of God, Burke ended up paying me my million dollars all those years ago. I imagine Dorian had a little something to do with that, though he refuses to confirm or deny it. And it happened just in time. Turns out, Burke was underwater at his financial firm, hence why he needed his inheritance so desperately. As talk of his financial ineptitudes made waves in the Manhattan finance industry, his employees quit on him left and right until there was no one left, and he was forced to shutter his company.

Burke and Dorian no longer keep in touch, but last we knew, Burke was engaged to some East Coast steel heiress and working for her father. From what we've heard, the woman seems just as self-serving as he was—no doubt a perfect match.

Nicola and Dashiell divorced less than a year after she received her third of the Rothwell estate, though the actual divorce took two and a half years to finalize. Apparently, each of them had assets hidden from one another—as well as affairs. The instant Nicola filed, their divorce became Page Six fodder, and all their dirty laundry was aired for the entire world to see.

They say money amplifies what's already there.

If one's greedy or selfish, it'll only make them greedier and more selfish.

I can truly say that money has made Dorian more generous with his time and energy, which are, after all, the only truly priceless things any of us have in this world.

"Nothing makes me happier than giving you the world," he always tells me. "Nothing except being with the woman I love."

"I think we just keep doing what we do best," I say.

"We do a lot of things well together." My sexy-as-sin, forever non-husband winks. "You're going to have to be more specific than that."

"All right. I guess I'll spell it out for you, then." I roll my eyes, pretending to be annoyed, though I love when he gives me a hard time.

"Which is . . . ?"

"We take things one day at a time." My heart swells as I gaze upon the man who has brought me more love, contentment, adventure, and philosophical, late-night conversations than I knew a person could experience in one lifetime, let alone five years. "We don't plan anything anymore, remember?"

We learned the first time that life tends to go according to its plan—not ours—and we've yet to be proved wrong.

"You're quiet. What are you thinking?" I ask. A handful of times over the years, we've talked about what it would be like to put down roots. Together, we dreamed up different variations of the lives we might have. Lighthouse caretakers in Maine for one. Hobby farmers in Kansas in another. Once we contemplated finding a place in Malibu and taking up surfing. But in the end, the ideas were always just as fulfilling as the realities, and the thought of having to pick one broke our adventurous little hearts.

"I'm thinking the only thing I love more than that idea," he finally answers, "is you."

As the last rays of sunlight disappear into the deep-blue waters and the sky overhead fills with glittering stars, we toast to our future—the one we'll continue to take a single day at a time for the rest of our married-ish lives.

THE END

EXCERPT FROM
LOVE AND KEROSENE

CHAPTER ONE

ANNELIESE

solivagant (*adj.*) wandering alone

They say everyone has a doppelgänger. Statistically speaking, there could be seven people sharing the same face at any given moment. But the odds of meeting someone's double are in the neighborhood of one in a trillion.

Highly unlikely.

Impossible, even.

"Anneliese?" Florence, the owner of Arcadia Used Books, waves her hand in my face. "Did you hear me?"

I peel my attention from the brooding man on the sidewalk outside the shop—one who shares the same messy auburn mane, hooded gaze, and chiseled jawline as my late fiancé.

"You look like you've just seen a ghost," she says with a hesitant chuckle as she places her palm over my hand. "Sweetheart, you're trembling and pale as a sheet. Is everything all right?"

Cool sweat blankets my forehead as I focus on the small stack of used books on the counter. The words on their spines fade in and out, growing blurry before turning clear again.

"Um, I'm sorry. What was the total again?" I steal another glimpse outside. He's still there—standing the way Donovan used to: one hand in his pocket, the other tapping out a text message with his thumb. Same build. Similar height.

It's uncanny.

"Fifteen dollars and twenty-eight cents," Florence says, her stare weighing on me. "You sure you're okay?"

No. I'm not sure.

"I just . . ." I shake my head, a feeble attempt to pull myself out of this daze, and then I slide my debit card her way. "I thought I saw someone I knew."

Her crinkled gray gaze drifts to the man on the sidewalk. She squints, but her efforts are in vain. Florence wouldn't know him from Adam. We'd only lived in Arcadia Grove for two months before his untimely passing. Granted, this was Donovan's childhood hometown, but Florence isn't a local—she's as fresh off the boat around here as I am.

"That guy right there?" She swipes my card and hands it back. "In the brown jacket?"

"Yeah." I draw in a steady breath. My heart has yet to calm down, but it's not for lack of trying. "But it's not him."

It couldn't be.

Even if it were, Donovan would never dress in a leather bomber jacket, ripped jeans, and dusty boots. And he certainly wouldn't leave the house without running a comb through his hair. This guy looks like he's been riding on the back of a motorcycle for days.

"Well, he *is* a looker . . ." She slides me a pen and the receipt to sign before placing my haul in a thin canvas bag with *have a great day* in faded red print. "If I were your age, he'd make me break out into a sweat too."

Florence winks. Maybe she thinks I was checking him out. Or maybe she's trying to make me smile.

"I'll call you when the next shipment comes in," she says, referring to the vintage and international baby-name books and rare dictionaries she sources for me. As a part-time naming consultant, I'm always looking for new and unusual terms and monikers to add to my arsenal. Florence never fails to deliver.

I wait by the exit, feet frozen on the wooden floor, and watch as the man who isn't Donovan scans his surroundings, shoves his phone into his back pocket, and exchanges it for a set of keys. A second later, he climbs into an olive-green vintage Ford pickup, proving me wrong about the motorcycle. Cranking the window down, he fires up the engine and backs out of the slanted parking spot.

I emerge from Flo's shop as soon as he disappears over the hill, and I continue my Saturday-morning shopping with that stranger's image burned into my mind's eye.

Wandering the flower-lined merchant district of Arcadia Grove, I mostly shop the windows. It's all I can afford these days, though it's not like I'm in dire need of a new outfit for a hot date. I'm half-tempted to mosey into a home-accessories boutique to grab something pretty for the house, but then I remind myself I'm putting the cart before the horse per usual. There's no sense in buying kitchen accessories when my current one consists of a folding table, microwave, dorm fridge, electric teakettle, and single-burner hot plate.

I spot an empty park bench, take a seat, and flick through one of my books. While my eyes scan the words on the pages, nothing registers. It might as well be a jumble of nonsensical letters. I close it and return it to my canvas bag, opting to close my eyes and take a second to simply exist in this moment.

The late-morning sun is warm on my skin, trickling through the treetops and wrapping me in a much-needed hug—something I haven't had in three months, three days, five hours, and thirty-two minutes.

Not that I'm counting.

Before I met Donovan, I was content to wander alone. I wasn't trying to land a significant other, tangle myself up in some fairy-tale whirlwind romance, or wind up in some quaint town in the middle of Vermont. I also wasn't trying to uproot my entire life and pour every last cent of my savings into renovating a dilapidated Queen Anne.

But love—real or imagined—changes a person.

Some days, I hardly know who I am anymore.

Most days, I struggle to remember a time before he came into my life.

When I glance down at my left hand, there's a void where my engagement ring once glimmered.

After Donovan passed, it took me thirty days to take it off. I kept thinking *one more day*, and then that turned into *one more week*, which inevitably turned into *one whole month*.

I couldn't rip the thing off my finger fast enough when I found out he'd lied about the money I'd given him for the renovations. I'll never forget showing up at the Arcadia Grove Savings and Loan to find out if there was enough in our joint account to cover his funeral costs . . . only to be told there *was* no joint account.

The bastard stole my heart, and then he stole my life savings.

And now he's six feet under—a world away from having to atone for the mess he left.

My stomach rumbles when I notice a little pop-up coffee shop ahead. I collect my things, head that way, order a small latte and petite blueberry scone, and call it brunch. The sooner I get home, the sooner I can finish sanding the floor in the dining room.

Eyeing the sidewalk on my way back to my Prius, I look for the auburn-haired stranger in the brown leather coat, but all I spot is the usual cocktail of tourists and locals. Young couples holding hands. Families pushing strollers. Grinning teens taking selfies. Retired couples dining alfresco.

All around me, life moves on.

Yet here I am, wandering alone.

I make it back to my car and load my books onto the passenger seat. A white sedan pulls into the spot beside me, and a lovely-looking couple exits a minute later. They meet at the sidewalk. She picks something from his dark-chocolate hair, and he kisses her blissful strawberry-red smile. Before they vanish into the crowd, he wraps his arm around her shoulder as if to show the world she is his and he is hers. That was us once. I can only pray that what they have is real and not some get-rich-quick scheme.

I start my car, shift into reverse, and glance into the rearview. It's in that exact moment that the olive-green Ford passes by.

I pull out of my parking space and end up behind him at the light on the corner. A sticker in his back window says IN TRANSIT, and the spot that should hold a rear license plate is vacant. With my knuckles white against the steering wheel, I catch a glimpse of his eyes in his side mirror as he peers my way . . . and my stomach drops.

I'd know that copper-hued gaze anywhere.

I tap my fingers against the wheel, focusing on the beat of the tinny pop music playing low from my speakers, and try not to make eye contact.

The light flicks to green, and the truck turns right.

Without giving it a second thought, I do too.

"Oh my God, oh my God," I mutter under my breath. "What the hell am I doing?"

This is crazy.

I am crazy.

I stay a few car lengths back, as if that could possibly make any of this less obvious given we're the only two vehicles on this side street.

Five blocks later, he takes a left, pulling into the parking lot of the Pine Grove Motel.

My chase—if that's what I want to call it—comes to an abrupt end. It's all for the best, though, because I didn't have an end goal. I don't even know why I was tagging him. My fiancé is long gone, and he's never coming back. And it doesn't matter who this look-alike stranger is or how much he resembles Donovan—because he'll never be *him*.

And thank God for that.

Snapping out of it, I continue home to my empty house on the other side of town: past the main drag with the charming shops, beyond the cozy park with the shiny blue slide, miles from Arcadia Grove K–12 and all the places that remind me of the life that was never meant to be.

Once home, I slip into a pair of coveralls, crank my favorite Madison Cunningham playlist to drown out the echo of my lone footsteps, and sandblast the hell out of the dining room floor.

By three o'clock, I'm chugging a glass of ice water in front of an open window to cool off, debating whether I want to continue to the point of collapsing in exhaustion—or call it a night with a five-dollar bottle of twist-cap wine and a few episodes of *Curb Your Enthusiasm* . . . a show Donovan would never watch with me because he didn't get Larry David's offbeat humor.

It's then that I see him again . . . the striking look-alike in the vintage truck.

He slows down in front of my house, his piercing stare homing in on my front door.

But before I can do anything insane—like chase after him on foot this time—he's gone.

ABOUT THE AUTHOR

Wall Street Journal and #1 Amazon bestselling author Winter Renshaw is a bona fide daydream believer. She lives somewhere in the middle of the USA and can rarely be seen without her notebook and laptop. When she's not writing, she's thinking about writing. And when she's not thinking about writing, she's living the American dream with her husband, three kids, and two spoiled rotten pups. Renshaw also writes psychological and domestic suspense under her Minka Kent pseudonym. Her first book, *The Memory Watcher*, hit #9 in the Kindle store, and her follow-up, *The Thinnest Air*, hit #1 in the Kindle store and spent five weeks as a *Washington Post* bestseller.

Renshaw is represented by Jill Marsal at Marsal Lyon Literary Agency.

Connect at www.facebook.com/authorwinterrenshaw or winterrenshaw .com, or follow her @winterrenshaw on Instagram.

To make sure you never miss a new release, sign up for her newsletter here: winterrenshaw.com/subscribe/.